SOME TIME AWAY

Lovers In Time Series
Book Three

Marilyn Campbell

Book and cover design by eBook Prep
www.ebookprep.com

August, 2018
ISBN: 978-1-947833-77-7

ePublishing Works!
www.epublishingworks.com

PROLOGUE

In the beginning, *The First* personally conducted simple, random tests to determine if Earth's humans were developing within the parameters of *The Human Experiment* and whether or not it should continue or be terminated. As humans procreated, however, it became necessary to involve other observers.

The First could never forget how, without strict guidelines, some of the observers used the human subjects for their own experiments, or worse, personal amusement. Earth was thrown into chaos with humans being given every benefit and challenge simultaneously. Without rules or consequences, it was impossible to fairly judge humanity. That era was followed by a period of humans being constantly controlled and manipulated like marionettes. Again, without freedom of choice, it was impossible to properly judge The Human Experiment.

As a solution, a cosmic barrier was created to prevent undesirable entities from inter-dimensional passage into the Earthly realm. Then The First established *The Council of Abstracts*, consisting of the least self-centered beings of the initial group of observers, and placed them in control of The Human Experiment. They were instructed to set out basic behavioral guidelines for humans and the Abstracts observing them. Humans were to do no harm to one another or their host planet. Abstracts could occasionally whisper suggestions to humans but could not force them to act in any specific way. In special circumstances, as unanimously approved by The Council and The First, they were permitted to directly interact with certain humans for their mutual benefit.

Robert Davenport had been such a human.

Once the guidelines were agreed upon, The Council created a test through which humanity's development could be judged without disrupting the entire human population.

Time would select a time and place for the test to occur. *Justice* would present a relevant case where a good person's life was ended prior to *Fate*'s plan for that individual. *Love* would select a pair of humans who had proven themselves worthy of representing all humanity. *Curiosity* and *Reason* would present those humans with vague hints regarding the problem they were to address and resolve. *Mother Nature*, *The Muses*, *Synchronicity* and others were permitted to offer a limited number of small assists, and so on.

Then the pair of humans would have to work together, using their combined skills and experience, to deduce precisely what their task was, determine how to survive in an unfamiliar situation and save the doomed human from his or her untimely termination, all while facing a deadline.

Finally, a portal, controlled by The First, was established to enable the transport of the chosen pair to and from the relevant Earth time periods.

Crystal Island was that portal.

CHAPTER 1

Have I been kidnapped?

Maggie Harrison's thought was not completely unfounded. She had boarded The Davenport Spirit at two-thirty, exactly as instructed. The captain of the small yacht had handed her a mimosa and suggested she remain on deck in order to "catch the show," so she did.

But now they'd been leisurely cruising away from Florida's Treasure Coast for at least fifteen minutes and, not only had she seen nothing show-worthy, she still couldn't see any sign of land. Instead, it looked like they were heading directly out into the Atlantic Ocean.

She did her best not to panic but she'd heard enough weird rumors about Crystal Island and the Davenport Resort to make staying calm difficult. The entire island was said to be haunted by the ghosts of pirates, gangsters, murderers and their victims. Of course it was also famous for historical reasons, but knowing more than one U.S. President had stayed there in the last century didn't console her at the moment.

If there had been another hotel guest or two on board, she might have been less concerned. But she was alone, completely at the mercy of a stranger who might have hijacked the vessel for criminal purposes. If that was the case, the joke would be on him, for she wasn't one of the rich and famous who frequented the exclusive island hotel. She owned nothing of value and had no family member who could afford to pay a ransom.

She could only imagine one other scenario. The captain could be a human trafficker and she could soon be a commodity to be traded—She slammed a mental door on her runaway imagination.

Why in the world did I accept such an unusual assignment?

There were other temp jobs available with a lot fewer unknown factors. She sighed because she knew the answer to her question. She could never resist an opportunity to take some time away from her very ordinary life, especially to a place she'd never seen before, and for once, someone else would be paying her expenses.

Plus, there was the matter of who the client was.

Just as she began considering the odds of surviving a swim back to the pier if she jumped overboard, it happened. One second there was nothing ahead but ocean and sky. The next second a tropical paradise appeared on the horizon. She couldn't help but wonder if the vision were real or a mirage.

As soon as she had learned where she was going, she'd bought a book about the resort island's intriguing history but barely had time to skim it. A sentence on the back cover noted that Crystal Island was considered the gem of the Davenport holdings, but from her spot on the yacht's deck, the hotel buildings were nearly hidden from view by lush vegetation. Seconds later, Maggie could see glass-domed roofs of three towers that glittered in the sunlight as though covered with crystal shards.

As they drew closer, she caught sight of a long wooden dock leading from the deep water, across an expanse of beach and into the jungle. On one side of the dock was a yacht at least three times the size of the one she was on. Not surprisingly, it was named The Davenport King. On the other side was a mid-sized yacht named The Davenport Queen.

For the first time since leaving the pier, the captain spoke to her. "Beautiful, aren't they? The Davenport King is mainly used for large groups arriving from the mainland, but sometimes it's rented for social events or longer cruises. If you'd be interested in doing something like that, just talk to the concierge."

She could have explained that her visit was for work rather than play but the captain was already occupied with securing his modest craft to a post. On the dock was a golf cart with a lime green canopy and a little trailer hooked onto its rear. Standing beside the cart was an elderly man wearing an orange and yellow Hawaiian-style shirt. It made for a very colorful greeting against the tropical background.

"Welcome to the Davenport Resort," the man said with a happy smile. "My name is Aaron and it is my privilege to drive you to the hotel."

Not knowing exactly what she would be needing or for how long, her luggage consisted of a three-piece set covered in an identifiable black and white paisley print. The large suitcase and tote bag contained a little of everything from her wardrobe and bathroom. The medium-sized case held her computer and various supplies needed to set up a mobile office. As soon as the captain put her belongings into the cart's trailer, she and her driver headed away from the yachts.

"Are you vacationing or here on business?" Aaron asked as the dock changed to a wide, paved pathway with flowering tropical plants each side.

"Business," she replied. "I'm a…stenographer." She wasn't sure how confidential her assignment was supposed to be so she changed the subject. "How big is the island?"

"About two miles square." He slowed the cart. "Over here to the right is a very pretty spot for a picnic. Just ask someone to direct you to the nature trails. And on the left, close to the sunset beach, are the individual beach bungalows. The resort is pretty spread out but at least you can't get lost." He laughed at his own joke and she made herself chuckle with him.

Maggie thought she could hear a waterfall but she couldn't see past the giant elephant ear plants. A few seconds later they were passing through a small parking lot, half-filled with golf carts and multi-passenger trams. A sign stated that the golf course, tennis courts and clubhouse were straight ahead but they turned left before they reached any of those amenities.

"Electric vehicles are the only kind permitted on the island," Aaron explained. "Just let the front desk know if you would like one for regular use. And here we are. On your left are Towers One and Two; Three is on the other side of the lobby."

The instant they reached the main entrance to the hotel, an exceptionally striking young man greeted her by name, took charge of her luggage and directed her through two huge bamboo-covered doors. He was wearing a burgundy and green floral shirt that complemented his caramel-toned skin and dark red hair. A name tag identified him as Reynard, from Jamaica.

Maggie felt like one of the hotel's wealthy guests instead of someone reporting for a temp job. Was this typical? Or was it because of the very special position she had been selected for?

As Reynard led her through the lobby to the registration desk she looked up to see the enormous, glass-domed ceiling she'd seen pictured on the front cover of the book she'd bought. Between the sunlight streaming down and the continuation of the tropical theme in every direction, it seemed as though she were still outside…except for the air-conditioning. The front desk clerks were decked out in blue and cream flowered shirts and shifts but had the same welcoming expressions as the driver and bellman.

"Maggie Harrison," she told the smiling female clerk. "I was told—"

"Oh yes, Ms. Harrison. We've been expecting you. The Diamond Penthouse has been prepared for you and Mr. Nash according to his specifications." She asked to see

Maggie's identification then handed an access card to Reynard.

As Maggie followed her luggage away from the counter, she ordered the butterflies in her stomach to calm down. She'd had a lot of different jobs since signing on with the "It's Only Temporary" staffing agency. The owner, Tanya Sevrell, had always been very good about filling her in on important details, even more so after they became personal friends.

Maggie knew she would be assisting bestselling horror novelist, Noah Nash, while he was staying at the Davenport to work on his new novel. Because his long-time assistant was having a baby, he had asked the hotel to find him a temp, for an undetermined number of weeks. She was to handle a variety of administrative tasks but also act as a personal concierge to do whatever he required and be flexible about the hours. Given the off-shore location, it made sense for her to stay at the hotel throughout the assignment. At no time, however, had Tanya mentioned she and Mr. Nash would be sharing accommodations. Only now did Maggie consider what a personal concierge might be asked to do for a celebrity.

At the far edges of the vast lobby were a number of archways leading to different areas of the resort. Her escort pointed out the ones that would take her to the hotel's restaurants, the cocktail lounge, shops and fitness center, but she knew when the time came she would have to rely on the discreet directional signs provided.

The archway they passed under led into a very long hallway. To the left were doors to the Emerald Dome and Sapphire restaurants, while on the right was the elevator to the Tower 3 guest rooms and a door to the administrative offices. A sign at the far end of the hall pointed toward the Royal Spa and Fitness Center, but rather than continue that way, Reynard stopped and pressed the up button for an elevator made to look like a tree house.

"Dis be de only elevator dat accesses de Diamond Suites," Reynard explained in a distinctly Jamaican accent.

"When de hotel construction began in 1922, dis was a separate building, purposefully set apart as housing for de Davenport family and deir personal guests." Once inside, he slipped the access card into a slot labeled "P", which appeared to be the fifth and final floor. A few seconds later the rear doors of the elevator opened into a small garden with a glass ceiling. Beyond that was another bamboo door which also required the access card.

"Welcome to de Diamond Penthouse," Reynard announced as he motioned her forward.

The melodic sound of his speech pattern made Maggie smile as she walked past her escort. However, a glint of interest in his gold-brown eyes had her quickly straightening her expression. But the sight of the high, glass-domed ceiling over a spacious great room brought the smile right back.

"Dis be de Davenport's most requested accommodation," the bellman advised with obvious pride. "De founder, Robert Davenport, or his descendants resided in dis suite until 2012. If ya be interested in de history, dere be some more background in de hotel's information notebook on de desk."

Maggie's gaze darted from one part of the great room to another, taking in the corner workstation, the floor-to-ceiling bookshelves with a variety of books broken up by an assortment of knickknacks, the comfortable sitting area with its Tommy Bahama-style sectional sofa and a very large, curved-screen television. On the opposite side of the room was a dining table with eight chairs and a fully-equipped kitchen. Compared to the lobby, the tropical décor was considerably subdued through the abundant use of whites and beiges.

Reynard pointed at the closed double doors on the left. "Mr. Nash will be in de master, but I am sure ya will find your room most comfortable." He opened the single door on the right and again motioned for her to go before him.

Her concerns about their sharing accommodations were immediately alleviated. The secondary bedroom and bath were larger than her entire apartment in West Palm Beach, and there was a lock on the door if she felt the need for it. "This is perfect. Thank you."

Reynard placed her large suitcase on the padded bench at the foot of the bed and set the medium case and tote next to the bathroom door. "May I call housekeeping to assist ya with unpacking?"

"Oh, no, thank you," she replied with an appreciative smile.

"Den dere is only one more t'ing I need to show ya." He led her back into the main room, walked over to a framed oil painting of white cockatoos and orange bird-of-paradise blooms and opened it like a door. "Dis be de control panel for de lights, air-conditioning and window shades." He demonstrated what each button and switch operated, saving the best for last.

"De glass ceilings in here and de master each operate separately." With no small amount of dramatic flair, he made the glass change from letting in full sunlight to total blackout. "And if ya happen to be here during hurricane season, ya can be comfortable knowing dat de glass is shatterproof and de special construction of de domes allows dem to withstand winds up to several hundred miles per hour." He adjusted the glass to moderate shading and closed the hidden door. "I am sure ya can imagine how beautiful dis could be on a clear, starry night."

Maggie thought she saw another twinkle in Reynard's golden eyes but her brain leapt right over suggestive to how much such a system must have cost.

After assuring the bellman his assistance was not needed for anything further, Maggie tried to hand him a tip but he refused it.

"Much appreciated," he said with a sincere expression, "but all of your expenses, *including* gratuities are to be put on Mr. Nash's bill. Whatever ya require while ya be a guest here, ya need simply sign for it."

"Seriously? Whatever I need?"

"Dat is what de guest notes say." He winked then handed her the access card. "De spa and shops are part of dat arrangement, so do be sure to visit dem when ya have a chance."

As Reynard was walking out the door she asked, "Do those notes mention when Mr. Nash is arriving?"

He glanced at his watch. "He is due to arrive by helicopter at four, so ya should expect him shortly. Remember, just call de concierge desk if ya be needing *anyt'ing,* day or night."

Of course, she thought, someone as famous as her temporary employer would be coming in by helicopter.

Being told to expect him shortly had Maggie rushing to unpack so she would be ready to offer her assistance instantly. She couldn't get over being given carte blanche in a hotel like this. It was easy to imagine what another sort of person might do with such an opportunity. Mr. Nash was either insanely generous or far too trusting…or he was expecting more from her than she was aware of.

Not for the first time, she found herself wondering about the vague "additional requests" Tanya said might come from hotel management.

Along with the book she'd picked up about the Davenport Resort, she'd bought a copy of Mr. Nash's latest bestselling novel. As she placed both on the nightstand, she took another glance at the author's photo on the back cover. She intended to familiarize herself with his writing style, but she had yet to read the first page. His bio simply stated that he enjoyed being a storyteller and living a solitary life outside of Portland, Maine. Not much to go on.

In the black and white photo of him, he was casually leaning against a tree trunk, wearing jeans and a bomber jacket. In the background was a snowcapped mountain. He was looking at something or someone not in the picture. His face bore just a hint of a grin and a five-o'clock shadow, and it looked as though a gust of wind had mussed his wavy hair. If he was half as sexy as the photo, she imagined every woman in the hotel would be stalking him or even slipping him their room access cards. Perhaps one of her duties was to be his shield...or his beard. She could handle that and most other responsibilities...as long as she wasn't asked to do anything immoral or illegal.

Tanya had let her know there were a number of local women and one man who were equally qualified for the job and several of those would have taken the job for free just because they were fans of Nash's books. Maggie had never read a single one, being a diehard romance fan herself, but that turned out to be one of the reasons she was chosen. What set her apart from the others, however, was another fact entirely.

Shortly after Maggie had gone to work for "It's Only Temporary", she saw Tanya reading one of Nash's novels and mentioned she had briefly attended high school with him. When this assignment came up, Tanya suggested Maggie apply for it because he might be more at ease with someone he knew, even if it was only for a short time many years ago. Maggie had warned Tanya that she doubted he'd remember her; they barely knew each other; she only remembered him because he became famous.

Those responses were far from the truth but it kept her from sounding like a foolish girl.

About eighteen years ago, when she was in tenth grade, a painfully shy boy named Noah Nash transferred to her school. He might have come and gone without her ever meeting him except for their ending up as biology lab partners. He was an army brat who had already attended four schools before enrolling at hers. Not only was he continuously the new kid, he had a small, lean frame, shoulder-length, somewhat curly, brown hair and deep blue eyes with thick lashes, which made him pretty enough to be a girl and that made him an easy target for bullies. He had only been at her high school a week when some dumb jock called him a fag within Maggie's hearing.

She had thought Noah seemed too effeminate and gentle to be totally straight but she detested the macho mentality and thought of a way to flick the guy's nose. Though

Maggie was attractive, had noticeable curves and a lot of friends, she wasn't interested in a steady relationship with any of the boys she knew. The problem was, as long as she didn't hook up with anyone, she was always being approached and even pressured to do something she wasn't ready for.

Because she had been at the right place at the right time, Noah had accidentally become the answer to her teenage dilemma.

As the time for Noah's arrival neared she checked her reflection in the bathroom mirror. She kept her straight, dark brown hair chin-length with a thick layer of bangs, more for ease of care than style. For the same reason, she rarely wore makeup other than a hint of lip gloss, but today she had gone to the extent of framing her hazel eyes by enhancing her lashes with a few swipes of mascara. Not knowing what she'd be doing the first day, she had chosen a pair of black dress slacks and a loose, lavender jersey top which fit the guidelines of business casual. She wanted to look at ease but strictly professional.

As she made one final critique of her appearance, she wondered if he would remember her at all. It was so very long ago.

Suddenly the mirror clouded over and, thinking it was steam, she swiped her hand over it. A second later, the glass cleared and she was watching a remembered scene from high school. Stranger yet, the next instant it felt as though she were *there*, back in Clarksville, Tennessee, reliving the moment…

Maggie waited for the three bullies to tire of calling Noah names and tossing his backpack back and forth in a mean game of keep-away. As soon as they strutted off, so proud of putting the new kid in his place, she walked over to where Noah was sitting on a concrete wall with his head bent over a book.

"Hi."

He didn't reply or raise his head so she set down her books and hopped onto the wall next to him. "Those guys are buttheads." He let out a sound that was part snort and part sniff. "Wanna get back at them?" He raised his head and narrowed his eyes at her. She noticed they looked a little watery as though he was on the verge of tears. "I need a favor." She finally had his whole attention.

"From me?"

"Yes. I think you'd be the perfect person. You don't like biology much, do you?"

He snorted again. "Really don't like any of the sciences, or math for that matter. I get by but the thought of having to dissect a frog—" He made a gagging face.

"I could help you with it. Make sure you passed at least."

"Shoot. How big of a favor do you need? Just because I lived overseas for a while doesn't mean I have any drug connections or fake ID or anything."

"Wow, you think I'm a stoner or party girl?" She was rethinking her plan to save him from the bullies after all.

"What? No, no. That's not what I meant. It's…it's just that you're, you know, one of the cool girls at this school, which usually means—I'm making it worse. Just like I always do. Sorry."

She patted his knee. "No need to be sorry. I get it. But here's the thing. I need you to pretend to be my boyfriend. Go to a few dances and parties with me. Plus, it would really help if you'd sit with me and my friends at lunch. You know, that kind of thing."

His frown deepened. "Now I'm really confused. You're popular and really pretty. You could have any guy you wanted."

"But I don't *want* any guy. Not at the moment anyway. I want to have fun without…the other stuff. I was hoping you'd understand but if I'm asking too much…"

His whole expression lightened. "Let me get this straight. I hang with you and your friends. You tell everyone I'm your boyfriend. And you help me get through biology. Is there something you haven't told me?"

She shrugged. "Well, you'll probably have to hold my hand or put your arm around me when we're in public. Would that be okay?"

Noah threw his head back with a loud laugh. "I think you just might be the craziest girl I've ever met but you've got a deal." He squinted at her for a moment as though trying to visualize how this was going to work. "I'll need a good girlfriend's nickname for you. What do you like?"

She was pleased he wasn't questioning her explanation. "Oh, I don't care. Just so it's not Magpie. I got called that all through grade school."

"Okay, Punkinhead it is."

She lightly punched his arm. "Try again." His gaze shot to a spot beyond her and she turned to see the jocks had rounded up a few more of their pals and were heading back toward them. "Better yet, kiss me. Quick." Despite her command she hadn't really expected him to slam his mouth against hers. She tasted blood and knew her tooth had cut her lip. She pressed her palms to his shoulders and whispered, "Easy, boy. Like this." She tilted her head and gently touched her closed mouth to his, retreated and came back again.

His fingers trembled as he stroked her cheek and neck and when his hand moved down her back a tiny murmur of appreciation rose in her throat and vibrated against his lips. A heartbeat later he was kissing her in earnest and certainly didn't need any more instructions. His lips were soft and felt really nice against hers but it was his hands that had her melting. No longer tentative, his touch was light and feathery, then firm then light again, roaming over her back, into her hair, up and down her arm. And everywhere he touched she felt nerves tingling…*awakening*. It was a new feeling and she liked it a lot.

"Hey, Magpie, your boy's startin' to turn blue. Better let him get some air!"

Breathlessly Maggie and Noah parted in time to see the jocks walking away, howling over their unexpected discovery.

What the heck had just happened?

She had gotten carried away, was what happened. For the first time ever. With a *pretend* boyfriend. Who may not even be interested in girls. What the heck was wrong with her?

"Well," she said as cheerily as possible, "that should take care of letting the entire school know I have a boyfriend by tomorrow."

He picked up the book he had dropped at some point and held it on his lap. He cleared his throat. "Uh, yeah. I think you're right. But, I, uh, I'm not sure we should do a lot of that sort of, I mean, if it's just pretend…"

"Right," she agreed too quickly. "No kissing." It *was* pretend. He was just doing what she'd told him to do. Even though, for a moment, it sure had felt like something very real.

"But now I know what I'm going to call you." He ran his index finger across her lower lip then licked the tip of his finger. "Sugarlips. Pretend or not, it sure was sweet."

Her breath caught in her chest. How could something so corny make her want to throw her arms around him and start kissing again? Instead, she gave his arm another playful punch. "Just remember I hold the fate of your biology grade in my head." She hopped off the wall and gathered her books. "Gotta go. I'm already late."

That five-minute interlude set the stage for the next nine months. As far as anyone knew, Maggie had a boyfriend and was off the market. Noah had to be straight because he was with Maggie. And he got all B's in biology.

They held hands in public, slow-danced at social events as though they were the only two people on the gymnasium floor and exchanged whispers over the biology microscope. But they never made physical contact when they were alone, and they absolutely never *ever* kissed again.

Despite the pretense or because of it, they became best friends that year.

When the year ended, Noah announced his family had to move again. Maggie cried and Noah consoled her without saying how he felt about leaving. In an instant he had hidden himself behind a wall she couldn't penetrate. She promised to write once a week and call every day but Noah had been on this road before and warned her things change when two people live in different places, no matter how close the friendship had been.

The last thing he said to her was, "If we're meant to get together sometime in the future, it will happen. If not…" He shrugged, smiled and gave her a kiss on the top of her head—something he could now do after growing five inches in one year. "If not, I hope you have a great life and find someone you don't have to pretend with."

She leaned into him for a long hug.

"But you'll always be my little Sugarlips."

Maggie blinked her eyes at the mirror several times before she was certain the only image being reflected was her own. Still, she had the eeriest feeling something extraordinary had just occurred. It felt as though she had drifted off into a deep dream, but that wasn't possible. She was wide awake, still standing upright in the bathroom and—she glanced at the digital clock embedded in the corner of the mirror—it was exactly the same minute it had been when she last checked the time.

If this were one of the paranormal romances she enjoyed reading, the mirror could be a portal to another time or place but she hadn't actually gone anywhere and, besides, she knew very well that the magical sort of things found in romance novels could never actually happen in real life. Her history of unsatisfying to disastrous relationships was clear evidence of that.

Her self-analysis came to an abrupt halt as she heard a recognizable voice in the great room. It was Reynard, giving the exact same speech she'd already heard. Rather than being caught in the bathroom, she hurried out into the living room to greet her new boss and find out immediately if he remembered her or if she had embellished a minor encounter from their mutual past.

Reynard saw her and nodded but Nash had his back to her. He was even taller than when she'd last seen him but she remembered the thick, wavy hair. Her fingers curled into her palm as she recalled what it felt like to play with it when they slow-danced or when she was teasing him.

She swallowed hard and her lips parted as her gaze took in the breadth of his mature shoulders and the evidence of a firmly toned back through a light-blue t-shirt. Inching downward she noticed how his worn jeans were snug enough to show off—

Just then he turned around, glanced quickly at her face then at a spot behind her.

Maggie stepped forward quickly, holding her hand out. "Hello, I'm—"

He cut her off by holding up an index finger between them and turning back to the bellman.

The gesture was as rude as having a glass of icy water thrown at her face. She had her answer. The Noah she remembered, whether he recognized her or not, would never have cut her off like that. It was enough to yank her back to her normally poised demeanor.

She waited patiently in the spot where he had suspended her, hands gracefully folded at her center, happy-to-assist smile in place, as Reynard completed his guided tour and left the suite. She waited several more seconds while Noah stood facing the closed door.

Just when she began to wonder if he was okay, he turned around…and smiled.

"Hello, Sugarlips."

CHAPTER 2

"Sorry to interrupt, Boss, but you wanted to know when Mr. Nash arrived."

Lillian Davenport, owner and general manager of the Crystal Island Davenport Resort, motioned for her executive assistant to come in. It took her a few seconds to finish the email she'd been composing. She clicked send and gave Mercy her full attention. "Did Reynard check in with you yet?"

Mercy grinned. "Just now.

"And?"

"He called him…*sexy*." She chuckled at the surprised expression on her boss's face. "I don't think he meant it *that* way…although you never know with Reynard. When I asked him to elaborate, he said Mr. Nash is charismatic, confident and well-mannered, unlike some of the celebs we've had here." Mercy narrowed her eyes. "So why do you look worried?"

"I'm not—" After five years working side by side, she couldn't hide anything from Mercy. "I'm *concerned*. It's one thing to have a few so-called ghost hunters looking under rocks from time to time. They enjoy minimal credibility while their suppositions have added to the island's mysterious quality. However, someone of Noah Nash's fame, added to the sort of things he writes about…well, there's no telling what he might take into his head to investigate or what he might write."

"Your marketing people are convinced there's no downside to having him here," Mercy reminded her.

Lilli grimaced. "Life has taught me there's a downside to everything. Did Reynard feel we could trust him not to damage our reputation?"

"He said if Nash makes a promise, he won't break it, but what you consider damage, he could consider enhancement."

"You're right, of course. I'll just have to figure out a way to keep tabs on the direction his story is taking. Did he have anything to say about the temp?"

"He said Ms. Harrison seemed nervous but competent. I would be very surprised if the agency sent anyone who wasn't highly—"

"Did Reynard see them greet each other?"

Mercy made a face as though trying to remember exactly what was said. "It sounded out of character from the other traits Reynard listed. He said she tried to introduce herself but Nash cut her off with a hand gesture, which seemed rude on the surface, but Reynard felt sure it was something else…like he didn't want to greet her in front of the bellman."

Lilli filed that impression away for the moment. "Anything else?"

"Just that I can't wait to meet the man Reynard calls *sexy*!" She wiggled her eyebrows and got a slight smile out of her boss.

As Mercy updated her on a number of more routine issues, Lilli's mind wandered to something else that *concerned* her despite any evidence of there being a *downside*. Reynard's employment record was exceptional. Not a single complaint had ever been lodged against him. He clearly enjoyed his position and often received commendations for going above and beyond his job description, which is why he was promoted to bell captain and had the ear of the owner's executive assistant.

And yet, something kept Lilli from being completely comfortable around him, even though he had always treated her in a respectful manner. It had occurred to her that it was simply a matter of him being extremely attractive, even *sexy* in an exotic way, but there wasn't even a rumor of his behaving inappropriately with coworkers or guests.

More likely it was his eerily accurate intuition about people. Mercy had recognized it early on and occasionally, and *unofficially*, asked him for his opinion, as she had in the case of Mr. Nash and the temp. Lilli had too many secrets to be comfortable around an employee who might see through her façade…besides Mercy. Whatever Mercy knew, she kept to herself.

But there was also something curious about Mercy's relationship with Reynard. They both started work at the hotel on the same day, a fact which Mercy insisted was mere coincidence. But that very day, Lilli had accidentally seen Mercy and Reynard exchanging a few words with serious expressions. When asked, Mercy had brushed it off as a silly flirtation and yet, Lilli hadn't thought it looked silly or intimate. It looked like Mercy was chastising him and he was trying to defend himself. Not exactly a typical scenario between two people who'd just met. The strangeness of it stayed with Lilli all these years since, even though Mercy had become her most valued and trusted associate.

Born Esmeralda Mercedes Martinez, Mercy had inherited her physical characteristics from her Cuban-American parents. Nearly her opposite, Lilli was tall, lean, ivory-complexioned with gray eyes and light ash blonde hair that she usually wore in a conservative twist. Where Mercy was outgoing and friendly, Lilli was aloof and smiled only when the situation required it. When it came to their work ethic however, they were equally matched.

They had one other thing in common—on Valentine's Day six months ago, they had both turned forty. Because their positions required a close relationship and their being the same age, she had suggested Mercy call her Lilli rather than Ms. Davenport, as the rest of the staff was required to do. But Mercy refused, saying use of her first name was unprofessional, which was how she ended up calling her "Boss" more often than not.

What seemed strange about their relationship, however, was even more personal than their birthdays. Having lost her mother when she was only eight, Lilli couldn't be absolutely certain, but she often had the feeling Mercy was watching over her in a motherly fashion. She wasn't really worried about it, but she was concerned that Mercy might have become too attached to her.

Considering all the secrets Lilli knew about Crystal Island, it was impossible for her not to be *concerned* about anything she couldn't quite put her finger on.

CHAPTER 3

The sight of his Maggie instantly resurrected the gawky, scared, totally miserable fifteen-year-old and the memory of the teen angel who had swooped down from heaven and changed his life forever.

As he waited for her response, his heart pounded in his chest. Could she have forgotten him? He could barely breathe. She appeared to be confused so he took a step toward her and hesitantly held out his hands.

A moment later she closed the distance between them and threw her arms around his neck. He whirled her around twice before setting her on her feet, but rather than let her go completely, he clasped both her hands. "I gather you remember me?"

"Good grief, Noah, I thought you might not remember *me*. I mean, that would make sense. I'm nobody. But you…well, *everyone* knows your name. Who would have ever thought shy little Noah Nash would wind up being a world famous celebrity?"

He threw his head back and laughed the way he used to when she teased him out of one of his sad moments. "I'm hardly a celebrity."

"Really?" she questioned with a distinct smirk. "How many times have you appeared on TV talk shows?"

Rather than answer, he squeezed her hands then twirled her around in front of him like a ballerina. "You look exactly the same. Except for the short hair. I still had a picture in my head of you with the long ponytail." He stepped back and slowly scanned her from head to toe, lingering just a bit on her breasts. "*Hmmm*, your boobs look bigger than I remember. Don't tell me you—"

She punched his arm. "I think my not hearing from you in eighteen years revokes your privilege to comment on the size of my boobs. However, I am willing to admit they're all me. Just like the rest of the twenty pounds you're pretending not to notice. But *you*, geez, Noah, you look amazing. You must have women…and men throwing themselves at you all the time."

She gave him the same once-over he'd given her and the fine hairs on his arms stood up as though static electricity flowed between them. He remembered that happening the first time she touched him, so very, *very* long ago. "I got lucky. But I've never really enjoyed that part of being a *celebrity*. Being an author suits the hermit in me. And when I need to be in public, the fame's brought me enough money to buy…security."

"Like this suite?" she asked lightly, looking around.

He grinned and led her over to the sofa. It gave him a reason to keep holding her hand even after they were seated. After all, they used to hold hands all the time. He hadn't planned to be so touchy-feely with her, at least not right away, it just felt so normal, as though only a few weeks had passed since they'd parted. The fact that she didn't try to reclaim her hand made him think she might feel the same way. "You know what I've been doing the last decade. Tell me about yourself."

She shrugged. "There's not much to tell. High school was a lot less fun after you left. I did manage to get an associate's degree in business before I got sick of school. Worked a lot of different kinds of office jobs over the years. Nothing impressive. I tend to stick with temp assignments because I get bored so easily. Plus I love to travel and doing temp work allows me to take a week or so off whenever I get the itch to escape the nine-to-five world…which is pretty often."

When she didn't continue, he urged, "What was your favorite trip?"

She didn't even hesitate. "Exploring the South Dakota-Wyoming area. Mount Rushmore was impressive but my favorite part of that trip was that I got to climb Devil's Tower."

His eyes widened. "You climb?"

Chuckling, she gave him a light punch on his arm. "Don't be so surprised. I've done lots of daring things, especially after finishing a couple really boring temp assignments."

He wasn't sure he wanted to know, but he asked anyway. "Like?"

"Oh. Let's see. I jumped out of an airplane once, bungee-jumped off a bridge, raced around the Indy 500 track, did white water rafting through the Grand Canyon…things like that. The scariest for me was spelunking and scuba diving. Definitely didn't care for being underground or underwater, but I think it's important to do things I'm afraid of."

As she gave a few specific examples of temp jobs followed by mini-adventures, disappointment wormed its way into his mind. He had been imagining all sorts of scenarios for this reunion but none of them involved her being an adrenalin junkie—one of the few character traits he could never adapt to or ignore. He stopped himself from pulling his hand away from hers and focused on the rest of her update.

"Mom and Dad retired to Arizona and my kid brother became a plumber. He, his wife and two kids live in Utah. I spent last Christmas with all of them. Um, what else? Well, I've never married, though I did get close once. No kids. Plenty of friends are willing to share theirs. All in all, I have a good life."

"*Hmmm*, I seem to remember telling you to have a *great* life, not just a good one."

"I can't believe you remember that too." She smiled warmly and gave another little shrug. "Some of us are destined for great—like you—and some of us are fortunate enough to get good. But now it's your turn. I remember you hated science and math and liked English. And I sort of remember reading some of your short stories, but I don't remember any of them being scary. What made you decide to become a horror author?"

He grinned. "It wasn't so much a decision on my part as what one publisher was willing to buy. To be honest, luck played a big part in how quickly I sold my first book. One of my professors in college had a sister who was a literary agent in New York and he convinced her to take a chance on me. That was twelve years ago."

"And you've been on bestseller lists ever since. I doubt that would have happened unless you were really, really talented. My friend, Tanya, the one who owns the temp agency I'm with, she has every book you've ever written. She says you scare the hell out of her every time."

Tilting his head, he ventured a guess. "But you've never read any of them, right?"

"Sorry. It's not you. It's the genre."

He shook his head. "Not a problem. I actually requested an assistant who wasn't a huge fan."

"Which brings me to my next question. I was told the hotel hired me for you, but you obviously knew I would be here. How?"

He wiggled his eyebrows at her. "Maybe I've developed psychic powers." He got another smirk for that. The familiarity of it made his insides weak in spite of the major character flaw she had revealed. As much as he had been looking forward to seeing her, he hadn't actually expected the physical attraction to still be so strong. "Do you remember what else I said that last day?"

She furrowed her brow. "Goodbye?"

It had probably been foolish of him to think his last words had been as important to her as they had been to him. "I told you if we were meant to see each other again, it would happen."

"I remember being annoyed with your indifference. I was really hurt that you could walk away from such a good friendship without even trying to stay in touch. But eventually I realized you were probably right to make a clean break. We had different paths to follow."

He sighed and decided to tell her some of the truth. "Actually, ours was the one friendship I wish I hadn't cut off like I did with all the others before and after you. I've often thought about that over the years. At least I could have told you how angry I was about having to move again. Or how I—" He took a deep breath. "Sorry. None of that's important now. You asked me how I knew you would be here and my answer is, it was meant to be. The older I got, the more I realized life is much more interesting when I let go of the reins."

Narrowing her eyes at him, she asked, "Are you saying my being here today, with you, was somehow planned all along by some superpower?"

His mouth curved up on one side."I believe in fate. It's the only explanation that makes sense. And here's the proof. I had an idea for a new book called *Hotel Hellgate*—one of those 'you can check in but can't check out' stories." He noted how she wrinkled her nose and chuckled. "Anyway, after doing a lot of research about haunted hotels, I decided the Davenport had everything I was looking for. But I had to wait five months to get a long-term reservation in this suite."

"Yeah, I've heard they stay pretty booked up. Wait. What do you mean *long-term*? And why *this* suite?"

He grinned. "I won't know exactly how long I need to stay until I begin working on the story, but the reservation is for two months. As to this suite, it's where my story begins." He paused to gauge her interest level before continuing.

Her eyebrows raised, she leaned toward him and, in a hushed voice, asked, "Did something really horrible happen here?"

He couldn't have been more pleased. "Yes, though probably not as horrible as I'll make it. You see, in 1930, the founder, Robert Davenport, put a bullet through his brain right here, in this penthouse. At least that was the official ruling. The family always insisted foul play was involved."

She gasped. "Are you writing a murder mystery this time?"

"No," he said with a grin. "Well, not as a main thread. Anyway, there were a number of other unsolved deaths and disappearances in and around this hotel. So I figured, if ghosts really do hang around, it seems probable this could be a good place to find them."

She scrunched up her face. "I've heard stories about this island being haunted, but I don't really believe in such things, which is probably good because I don't think I could sleep here if I thought an old ghost was hovering over my bed."

Noah squeezed her hand. "Supposedly, Davenport killed himself in the master bedroom, so your room should be ghost-free. At any rate, I have no interest in proving or disproving those stories. I just figured it would make the perfect backdrop for mine."

She gave his words a moment of thought. "I guess that would work. But that still doesn't explain how I came to be here with you."

His satisfied grin broadened into a full smile. "When it got close to time for me to come here and get started, my assistant was too far along in her pregnancy to be away from her husband and home. I asked the hotel to send me five resumés to review. When I saw your name..." He remembered feeling his heart leap in his chest and excitement race through his bloodstream. "Well, I checked it out, confirmed you were the same Maggie Harrison who helped me pass tenth grade biology, and I told the concierge to give you the job, but under no circumstances were you to be told I selected you. The fact is, if any one of those elements happened differently, you and I would not be here right now. If that's not fate stepping in, I don't know what else you could call it."

"Synchronicity?"

He shrugged. "Same difference. Point is, we were meant to get together again and I'm really looking forward to working with you. It'll be like old times." He was actually hoping it would be nothing like those days.

"Okay, I'm convinced. Only, can I ask one favor?"

His eyes narrowed. "Uh-oh. I seem to remember the last favor was pretty huge." *And kept me physically uncomfortable for an entire school year.* "I've never been sure we came out even on that one."

She gave him another little punch to his shoulder. "Smartass. This is a little request. Please don't call me Sugarlips again."

He grabbed her hand. "Only if you'll stop punching me."

"Deal," she said with a giggle and gave him a quick peck on his cheek. Instantly she jerked away, looking more shocked than he felt. "I'm sorry. I wasn't…it just seemed…"

He leaned toward her, stopping an inch from her mouth and waited for her to retreat again but she didn't move. He could feel her breath exiting in tiny puffs from her parted lips. He lightly touched his lips to hers, giving her a chance to object but instead she exhaled with a soft moan. It was all the encouragement he needed after waiting for so long.

His mouth slanted over hers, deepening the kiss. Her arms snaked around his neck and he pulled her into a full embrace, the way he had only once before but thought of countless times since. His fingers traced the line of her neck and down her arm. She was all silk and heat, melting in his hands. She was no longer the pretty high school girl. She was one-hundred percent woman now. But she was still *Maggie.*

And *this* Maggie was an adrenalin junkie. A warning alarm sounded in his mind.

Abruptly breaking the kiss, he leaned back. "I can't...*we* can't do this."

She blinked several times before speaking. "Of course not. You hired me to do a job for you, not..." She didn't bother to finish.

"Do I need to apologize?" he asked quietly.

She closed her eyes and shook her head. "Absolutely not. That was all my fault. I broke our rule." As gracefully as she could, she inched back to create more space between them.

He gave her chin a gentle nudge with his bent index finger. "Hey. I didn't nickname you Sugarlips for nothing. But I completely agree. It's never a good idea to mix business with pleasure. So, what do you say we reinstate the 'no kissing' rule?"

She slowly raised her eyelids. "Maybe we need to extend the rule to no touching."

His eyes narrowed and his mouth shifted from left to right as he gave her suggestion some thought. He had thought the memory of how she'd hurt him would be enough to stave off any lingering desire, but apparently neither memories nor time could keep him from banging his head against the same old brick wall.

Besides, he now knew her lifestyle would never match with his, which translated to just another unhappy ending.

Despite all the logical reasons for not doing so, he reached out and held her hand. "I think that's going too far. We touched all the time back then, without leaving the friend zone. Besides, once again, you started it. So I think we'll be fine if you just control your baser impulses." She let out a gasp and raised her fist, but a wink and a grin from him made her smile and lower her hand.

"Seriously though," he added without sounding completely serious. "We just have to remember we both have jobs to do, like when we used to do homework together." Her quick nod of agreement confirmed that she never knew how difficult those hours had been for him. "I was thinking we could go over what I expect from you and some of my work habits first."

Her demeanor changed from friend to professional in an instant. "Perfect. I'll just get my notepad."

As she headed to her room he said, "Would you mind if we did this over dinner? Lunch seems like it was ages ago. Would you prefer the restaurant or room service?"

She arched one brow at him. "I think leaving this room for a few hours would be the wiser option. Then we can come back here and pretend the last five minutes never happened."

"Swell," he mumbled to himself. "We're already back to pretending."

Maggie took advantage of the break to compose herself. Even though she had come to her senses, she still felt the desire to go back out there and finish what they'd started. She only remembered having that feeling once before. It was nearly two decades ago. And it was with him.

There had been plenty of times since then when she really wanted to be aroused by a man and her body simply didn't cooperate. Why was it different with Noah? The only answer that came to her was that she was the instigator of the encounter, both back then and just now. Perhaps it was even because there was a chance that women were not his sexual preference. Perhaps, subconsciously, she saw him as a challenge. Yes, that made some sense.

Except, for just a moment, he had seemed as anxious as she was to do more than kiss. It was really very confusing.

She was reapplying lip gloss when she thought she heard Noah call her name. Hurriedly she grabbed her purse and notepad and went out to the living room, but he wasn't there. "Noah?"

"Come in here. *Quick.*"

His voice sounded strained and was coming from the master bedroom. She dropped her things and rushed through the open door. Noah was standing perfectly still in front of a freestanding, full-length mirror. It was framed by a beautiful piece of whitewashed furniture, just like the rest of the pieces in the room.

"Come here," he whispered without moving.

Maggie walked to his side.

"What do you see?" He was still whispering and staring at the mirror.

"Uh, you…in a really large bedroom, acting a little weird."

He stepped aside and pulled her into his former position in front of the mirror. "In the mirror. What do you see in the mirror?"

She stared at her image, scanned the entire glass for flaws and noted what objects behind her were being reflected. "I'm not sure what I'm looking for." She watched him move behind her and stare into the mirror over her head. He held her still by placing his hands on her shoulders. The effect such a simple touch had on her breathing was enough to make her forget why she was standing there.

"He's gone," he said, clearly disappointed.

Without moving, she raised her gaze to his face in the mirror. "He, who?"

"I don't know. But I definitely saw him. I was walking by the mirror and noticed it seemed a little foggy so I touched it to see if it was dirty or just really old and it cleared up but I didn't see myself in the glass." His words all ran together and his eyes were wide as he stared into the mirror. "I saw a man in the mirror, like maybe he was behind me, only when I turned around there was no one here. It was more like the mirror was a window and I was looking through it."

"Do you want me to call someone? Security?"

"No, no. Not yet anyway. I think I know what they'd say and I really don't want to hear about what anyone else has seen in this room until I'm ready to do my research."

"So, you're not…scared?" She tried not to sound as uncertain as she felt.

He gave her shoulders a squeeze. "Not at all. This kind of thing is exactly what I came here for." He gently moved her aside then ran his fingers over the mirror and its wood frame then inspected the back of the piece. Shaking his head in bewilderment, he added, "The weirdest part is it looked like he was in *this* room, buttoning his shirt in front of *this* mirror, but the bedspread and drapes were different. And…" He scanned the bedroom. "…there was wallpaper with big yellow flowers. And now that I think about it, there were suspenders hanging off the waist of his pants and there was something outdated about the shirt collar and cuffs. Like I was watching a scene from an old-time movie." He scratched his head and gave her a crooked grin. "I sound crazy."

"It sounds like you had a really vivid hallucination."

"I don't think so. It was something else." He made another pass over the entire mirror and stand. "You know, there are a lot of different beliefs and myths attached to mirrors, most having to do with the dead and undead."

"Undead? Like vampires not having a reflection? *Puhleeze.*"

"Hey, don't make fun of the undead. I've made a very good living off them. But I'm thinking of ghosts, the spirits of dead people who didn't move on. One theory is that they can use mirrors to pass from place to place or even possess the living in order to resolve some issue. The possession of an average person by the ghost of a serial killer was one of the angles I was playing with for this next book. I must have been on the right track. Maybe the man I saw is one of those ghosts looking for resolution. *Wow.* That would sure confirm my picking the right hotel." He grasped her upper arms. "Oh my gawd. It could have been Robert Davenport himself!"

Maggie was a little concerned over how thrilled he seemed over the possibility of encountering a ghost. But his description of what he had seen and his comments about mirrors made her recall the strange daydream she'd had in the bathroom before he arrived. Before she could stop it, a shiver overtook her.

He noticed. "Are you okay?"

She forced a smile. "Sure. Just got a chill. Probably the AC kicked on."

He made a face at her. "You were never a good liar. You'd better tell me now if talking about the supernatural scares you because—"

"It was just a chill. Or maybe I'm hungry. You did offer me dinner before your little spook show started."

CHAPTER 4

Maggie wasn't completely surprised when they were immediately ushered into The Emerald Dome, Davenport's award-winning restaurant. Apparently the sign recommending advance reservations was not meant for the likes of Noah Nash. Being with someone important was almost like being someone special herself.

The second thing she noticed was the twenty-foot-high cascading waterfall in the middle of the room. Beneath the water was an enormous rock formation speckled with crystal shards and reflective silvery streaks. Around the base and along three of the walls were large prehistoric-looking ferns, flowering bird-of-paradise plants and orchids of every type and color. The fourth wall was all glass, allowing for a view of the beach. Tables of graduating sizes were arranged in rings around the base of the mountain.

Though the sun had not yet set, the glass dome panels were darkened to make it look like night had already fallen. Candles and twinkling overhead lights dangling like stars from invisible strings illuminated the overall interior. She assumed the panels would be cleared later for a view of the real night sky.

She had been penny-conscious for so long, it took a few minutes for him to convince her to ignore the prices on the menu and just order whatever sounded good. Unfortunately she didn't even know what half the items were and the prices were too inflated to ignore. "Umm, which of these would you suggest for a meat-and-potatoes gal?" she finally asked.

"Seriously? I thought you were all about adventure and trying things you were afraid of."

Giving a little shrug, she admitted, "I've never had enough money to throw it away on food I might not like."

"Understood," he said with a thoughtful nod. "I, on the other hand, consider food one of the extreme pleasures life has to offer. And in a restaurant of this caliber, I like to go with the chef's selection for the evening. I've rarely been disappointed that way and sometimes I'm surprised by something I've never tried."

"I like your reasoning. I'll have the same." According to the menu she had just selected chilled gazpacho with a dollop of lemony sour cream, the house salad spelled with an "e" on the end, lobster thermidor and wild rice with white truffles. She wasn't sure what a truffle was but it was clearly one of those foods she could never afford to find out if she liked.

Noah also ordered an additional bottle of wine that was *not* part of the chef's recommendation. There wasn't even a price shown for that.

As soon as the waiter left them, Maggie got the pad and pen out of her purse. "I'm ready whenever you are."

His brows raised. "You do know you're not on a time clock with me, right?"

"I was told to expect irregular hours, which is fine. I'm just anxious to find out what I'll be doing."

"That's fine, but there's no need to write anything down." He waited for her to put away her writing tools. "The first thing I want to do is explore. Get the feel of the whole place."

"I brought a book about the island's history and the bellman mentioned an informational notebook—"

"Did you read any of it?" he cut in with a concerned look.

"Not the notebook. But I did skim a little of the book."

"Okay. The walk-around is more effective when you use your senses rather than someone else's accounting of facts. A good story is more than just a plot and I'm expecting this place to trigger all sorts of ideas. At this point I don't want to know any more than I remember from my initial research."

"How can I help?"

"You'll walk with me, monitor my recorder and generally be there for me to bounce thoughts off of. And I'll want to hear anything you think of also. Hopefully we'll have a few more experiences like I just had in the room. That would be very cool."

"Cool?" she asked incredulously. "Are you sure you don't mean creepy?"

He chuckled. "Honey, when you're in my head, creepy *is* cool."

His casual endearment stirred a flutter in her tummy but the rest of his statement made her smile. He had always had a peculiar sense of humor. "Speaking of creepy-cool, there's something—"

Just then the sommelier came with Noah's requested wine and two dainty glasses. Conversation stopped for the tasting and pouring ritual. She knew very little about wine but it seemed to her this bottle was much smaller than the norm.

Noah held up his glass for a toast. "To fate."

"And synchronicity," she added and clinked her glass to his. She took a sip then a larger swallow. "Oh my, this is delicious. I'm not much of a wine drinker but this could change my mind."

He grinned. "It's a limited ice wine from Germany. I thought you'd like it. The sweetness makes it more of a dessert wine and I'm sure the chef was horrified over my asking for it to be brought out first but I remember what a sweet tooth you had." He waited for her to have another taste. "You were about to tell me about something creepy…"

She took one more sip and carefully set down her glass. "I wasn't going to say anything. I mean, I really thought it was just my imagination but after what you think you saw, I'm not so sure."

He refilled her glass. "Even if it was your imagination, I want to hear it. Remember, I'm in the idea-gathering phase of this book. Anything could trigger the perfect plot twist. And I'm counting on you, as a non-author, non-horror fan, to come up with things that might never occur to me."

Her taste buds demanded another drink of the surprisingly quenching wine before she began. "Before you arrived, I was looking in the bathroom mirror and it got all cloudy."

He leaned forward, elbows on the table, fisted hands beneath his chin. "Did it seem to be moving or swirling?"

She blinked. "Now that you mention it, yes. But when I touched it, the glass cleared so I thought I was mistaken."

"Then what?"

"Then I saw, well, I'd call it a memory. Afterward I just figured I'd been daydreaming. I mean, I'd been thinking about a time in high school…and then it felt like I was *actually* there again." She didn't think it was necessary to tell him about the particular moment she'd been remembering or how it had affected her even before he'd arrived.

Their cold soups were served and she drained her glass. Since Noah had only refilled her little glass once, the down-turned bottle in the ice bucket confirmed that it was smaller than usual.

She watched the way Noah gently blended the thick white cream into the red vegetable concoction without clinking the spoon against the side of the small bowl and imitated his action. There was a confidence evident in his every move, so unlike the boy who had been her adolescent best friend. Again the first awkward kiss came to mind and her thoughts leapt to the experienced way his mouth had moved over hers in the suite, the way his fingers had trailed down her neck and—

"You're killing me here," Noah said with a chuckle. "Either taste the soup or finish what you were going to say."

She felt her cheeks flush and was glad for the dim lighting. "That was it. Cloudy then a clear vision of a memory but like I was actually there."

"Was I in it?" he asked quietly.

She delayed by tasting the soup and tried to focus on the spicy combination of flavors passing over her tongue. But his stare was insistent. "Yes. But that would make sense. You were arriving any minute and I was remembering…how we met."

He covered her hand with his and waited for her to look into his eyes. "When we met…or when we kissed?" His thumb moved back and forth over her wrist. When she didn't answer, he said, "Would it help if I confessed I've been remembering that kiss for the last eighteen years?"

She eased her hand back and sat up straight. "No. It wouldn't help at all." She exhaled heavily. "Okay, I need to say something. I don't understand. And I really need to understand if we're going to spend more than a few hours together. You make a living with words. I need you to explain to me, in very simple terms, what happened when you kissed me that first time. And what happened upstairs just now. And why, in all the years in between those two kisses, no other boy or man ever made me feel this way?"

"What way?" He cautiously reached for her hand and after a little flinch she allowed him to intertwine his fingers with hers. But when she didn't answer, he did it for her. "Satisfied and hungry at the same time? Feeling both vulnerable *and* powerful? Bewildered *and* certain? If you want it really simple, I'd say we have incredible chemistry together. What's so confusing about that?"

She squinted at him. "Are you kidding me? What good is incredible chemistry if one of the two people is…" She waved her free hand and shook her head.

"Is…what?"

He really didn't know what she was talking about. She tried to retrieve her hand but he held tight. She took a breath in and out before she whispered it. *"Gay."*

His jaw dropped and he stared at her as though she'd just grown another head. "Oh. I see. Then I guess I really do owe you an apology for that kiss upstairs. I remember you saying you didn't want a relationship with any of the boys in school, but it never occurred to me that you preferred being with your own gender."

She was momentarily silenced as the waiter brought their *salades* and fresh, warm rolls and took away their soup bowls. The aroma wafting off the bread made her mouth water but she had to make herself wait to taste because the sommelier had arrived with the bottle of white wine that had been recommended to complement the course.

As soon as they were alone again, Maggie leaned forward and said, "I wasn't referring to *me*."

"Well, it's not me, so who are we talking about?"

She narrowed her eyes at him. "Excuse me? Do you really think I didn't notice? We were practically inseparable back then."

He gave his head a quick shake. "Hold on. You think *I'm* gay? How in the world did you come to *that* conclusion?"

She squinted harder as though it would help her see the truth. "You never denied what those boys said about you. Not even to me. You certainly weren't anything like them or others I knew. You were sweet and thoughtful and we talked about feelings and philosophy and you even enjoyed shopping with me. You never once tried to kiss me let alone...*you know*. I figured it's why we got along so well. Plus, you never once got goofy over any of my girlfriends and some of them were really pretty. And your bio makes no mention of your marital status."

She watched a whole gamut of emotions pass over his face—curiosity, disbelief, comprehension, consideration and finally sincerity. He delayed his response by having some salad and a sip of the wine, so she did the same, then had one of the warm rolls while he spoke.

"First of all, my author bio is purposefully brief. There was no reason to mention that I *was* married…for one year, to a very nice woman named Alison. We met in college and got along well enough. She was exactly what I thought I wanted in a wife—someone who wanted to permanently settle down in one place, get involved in the community and be satisfied taking care of her home, husband and children."

She arched an eyebrow but took another bite of roll instead of questioning his thinking.

"I know. Old-fashioned concept. But after how I grew up, that's what I wanted. Unfortunately, as well as we got along and met each other's expectations of marriage, there was absolutely no passion and we weren't good enough friends to keep up a sham. Before our first anniversary, we both agreed our getting married had been a mistake and we amicably divorced. After that, there were a lot of women in my life, but none of them made me consider a second marriage."

He paused to have more salad and try a roll and, since she had no marriage of her own to mention, she sipped her wine as he continued.

"Secondly, I have a very close friend who is openly gay and he does have a few of the stereotypical traits you described. But I swear, I have never lusted after a member of my own sex. The only reason I never got 'goofy' over your friends was none of them were as pretty or smart or fun as you. It never occurred to me to declare myself to be more manly than I appeared."

He ran his hand through his hair and frowned as though he were searching for the words that would convince her to believe him. "Look, the deal we had gave me the opportunity to spend time with the prettiest girl in class and hold her close once in a while, even if it was just pretend. I was a scrawny, little sixteen-year-old with too many insecurities to mention. Of course I wanted more, but you held the pretend flag between us like it was a chastity belt.

It never occurred to me to trespass and risk the good thing I had with you."

She gave herself a minute to decide what to say by finishing her salad. "I made an assumption based on appearances. I am sorry about that. I guess it just made everything easier for me to believe you were fine with our arrangement. And I can see why you wouldn't have pushed for more while we were in school, but after you left, you never answered my calls or letters. I figured you'd found new friends and forgot all about me that fast. I really was terribly hurt."

He snorted. "And you think I *wasn't*? I intended to write and tell you how I felt once we were settled again, but in the first long letter you wrote, you went on and on about some guy you'd met and, well, in those days, that was all it took to convince me to forget about you."

"Geez. Usually it's the boy who takes longer to mature. But I wasn't anywhere close to where you were back then. I was completely honest about not wanting a relationship. It was another couple years before I was even ready to try. Just so you know, I'm pretty sure I made up the guy I was talking about in that letter. I just wanted you to think I was having some fun without you."

The urge to confess everything he'd ever felt about her was almost uncontrollable, but before Noah could share *all* his secrets, the waiter arrived with the main course, the sommelier brought the accompanying wine, and Noah had a chance to come to his senses.

"Enough about what was or wasn't. Fate separated us for eighteen years. I believe there's got to be a good reason she brought us back together now. I'm glad we've cleared up the past and acknowledged that we have plenty of man-woman chemistry between us. But as long as we have work to do, I still think the old 'no kissing' rule should stand and, when we're not working, we should focus on getting reacquainted as adults."

She smiled with her whole face and he visibly relaxed. "I think that would be wonderful."

The meal truly was an unexpected treat, even the mysterious truffles. That, and a lot more wine than she normally consumed, had Maggie feeling delightfully relaxed.

In between bites, they kept the conversation extra light by comparing movies and television shows they were currently enjoying. After finishing half of the second bottle of wine and all of the third, they both turned down the offer of an after-dinner cordial.

By the time they'd shared a piece of mango-key lime pie and sipped frothy cappuccinos, they were almost back to being comfortable with each other.

"Are you up for a walk on the beach?" he asked after he'd signed the check.

"Absolutely. But I think I'd have to walk all the way back to the mainland to burn off all the calories I just devoured."

"We'll make up for it tomorrow," he promised.

As soon as they were beyond the maze of tropical plants, Noah took her hand and she had no real reason to object. He seemed to know where he was going and it was easy to let him lead. She reminded herself this was an assignment, even if it felt more like a fairy tale. The job, and probably their reunion, was only temporary, but for as long as it lasted, she decided it would be crazy not to enjoy the perks.

The moment they stepped outside, a gust of chilly wind blew stinging sand in their faces and they stopped in their tracks.

"Maybe this wasn't such a great idea after all," Noah said, shielding his eyes.

"Darn. It didn't look windy a minute ago. And the moon is just about to rise. I thought it could be quite inspiring to start your walk-around."

He drew her back into the lobby. "Tomorrow night the moon will be completely full. The energy will be even better."

"Another superstition to aid your search for all things spooky?"

He made a face at her. "It's not all superstition. The moon has a very real gravitational effect on Earth and its inhabitants, even the ones who don't believe in all things spooky." He ended the sentence by running his fingers up and down her spine.

It made her shiver and giggle at the same time. "Don't tell me, one of my tasks will be to chain you to your bed tomorrow night and make sure you can't get loose to wreak havoc on the poor townspeople."

He drew her close with one arm around her waist and leaned down to whisper in her ear. "If you chain me to the bed I can guarantee I won't be thinking about the poor townspeople."

She gasped as though shocked by his insinuation and he nipped her earlobe. "Behave yourself," she ordered and gave him a playful shove.

"I couldn't resist. Sorry." He didn't look the least bit sorry.

"We agreed—"

"We agreed to no kissing," he murmured. "*That* was a bite. And *you* asked for it by suggesting I was a werewolf."

She felt her face flush and decided the only way to respond was to quickly change the subject. "Hey, did you know the glass domes were designed to withstand hurricanes?"

That made him chuckle, but he went along with her redirection. "Yes, I heard the bellman's speech. But did *you* know this little island was never shown on any maps until Robert Davenport *accidentally* discovered it when he was out sailing and got blown off-course?"

"I thought you didn't want to know a lot of facts in advance."

"I read it before I'd made a decision about this hotel. How could an island nine miles off the coast never be charted until the twentieth century? Even though the southern part of Florida wasn't well-populated before the twenties, fishermen and pirates were all over the Caribbean.

Someone should have made a note of this place at some point."

"Aha, so it wasn't just the ghost stories that made you choose this particular hotel. You're also looking for pirate-buried treasure."

He winked at her. "It was a lot of things, but I'd bet my next royalty check that the story about an *accidental* discovery isn't even close to the truth." He tucked her arm through the crook of his elbow. "Since Mother Nature doesn't want us outside tonight, let's go check out the Amethyst Cave."

"Isn't that the lounge? I'm not much of a drinker…despite recent evidence to the contrary."

He smiled and patted her hand. "You don't need to have anything alcoholic. I just figured we should check it out…rather than go back to the room just yet."

"Oh. Good idea."

They weren't disappointed. Enormous blocks of what appeared to be dry ice served as a bar and shelving for an extensive display of vodka and martini mixes. The tables and chairs also looked like carved ice sculptures, though Maggie quickly discovered those and most of the blocks of ice were actually made of Lucite. What was most amazing, however, was the collection of giant quartz crystal formations and huge rock geodes split in half to reveal rich amethyst cores. They appeared to be placed randomly throughout the room.

She watched a woman walk up to one of the taller crystal spikes and hold her hands up, palms toward the stone. "What's she doing?" she murmured to Noah.

"Feeling its energy. Maybe sharing it. Or trying to draw some of it into herself. Try it. Then tell me what you feel."

Maggie glanced around. No one seemed to be paying attention to the woman so she decided to do as Noah suggested. One of the rocks seemed to house a darker purple cluster than the rest and she walked over to it. She stopped a few feet away and held her hands out in front of her. She felt nothing unusual. Not wanting to judge the experience too quickly, she moved closer, an inch at a time. When her hands were about six inches away from the stone she thought she felt a resistance of some sort. She stepped back then forward again and decided she wasn't making it up. It had to be the energy Noah mentioned. She was about to try it from the other side of the geode when a whoosh of chilly air swept by her and with it came the muffled sound of someone sobbing.

Help me. Ple-e-ease.

Maggie's hands jerked back to her chest. She glanced from right to left then behind her. She was certain she had heard a woman crying for help but no one appeared to be in need, nor did anyone else look as though they'd heard the desperate plea. And it was definitely desperate. She approached the woman standing by the quartz.

"Excuse me. Did you hear someone cry for help just now?"

The woman turned her head without moving her hands. "Must have been The Weeping Woman."

Maggie frowned. "Shouldn't we do something? Report it?"

The woman huffed. "Oh, it's been reported. A lot. But unless you know how to calm down a ghost, there's nothing you can do to help her. It's that rock. I can't go near it without having an anxiety attack." She turned her head back toward the crystal and closed her eyes.

Maggie went back to where Noah had taken a seat and joined him. "That was…different."

"What did you feel?" he asked quietly. "I'm really interested."

"I, um, felt a little resistance about six inches away."

"Ah, the energy field is there but probably drained by people touching it or sucking the life force out of it."

She cocked her head at him. "How do you know about all this stuff?"

He grinned. "Research. Lots of research. If it's paranormal, supernatural or metaphysical, I've probably looked into it. I never know what I'm going to need in what book so I think of it as a buffet and make sure I try a taste of everything. The end result is that I know things exist that I can't see."

She smiled. "In other words, you're a true believer in the *anything's possible* theory of life."

"Without a doubt. Besides having witnessed the impossible firsthand more than once, it also helps me accept the things I cannot change. Are you familiar with the serenity prayer?"

She shook her head. "Should I be?"

"Not necessarily. I'll find it for you later. But something else happened while you were over there. I saw you react and go over to that woman."

"It's going to sound a little…" She waved away what she was about to say. "I know. You think creepy is cool. I felt a cold breeze then heard sobbing and a woman's voice begging for help. I thought maybe it came through an air vent but no one else seems to have heard it. The woman I spoke to said it was The Weeping Woman, like it's common knowledge."

"Probably one of the Davenport ghosts," he said with a nod. "If so, there will probably be a mention of her somewhere. We can look that up after we do the walk."

Maggie liked the way his eyes lit up with interest even if the cause was beyond her appreciation.

Noah rose, walked over to the amethyst geode and held his hands out. A few minutes later he returned. "I felt a little resistance too. I've felt much stronger than that, by the way. But no voices. Have you ever had anything like that happen before?"

She shook her head. "If I did, I'm sure I thought it was my overactive imagination. It does run off the deep end now and then. On the way over here this afternoon I couldn't see the island so I started imagining that I'd been kidnapped by a modern-day pirate or human trafficker."

He laughed out loud at that. "That's one thing we always had in common." His expression turned thoughtful. "You said you thought it was your imagination when you saw the scene from our past in your mirror. But when I said I saw a man in my mirror, you believed me."

"Of course. You never lied to me."

He arched one brow. "You're sure about that?"

"Without a doubt," she replied emphatically, using words he'd used earlier. "I've almost always been able to tell when somebody says something that isn't completely true."

"Really? You never told me that."

She shrugged. "It's no big deal."

"Maybe not to you, but I'd sure like to have that talent."

"It's not a *talent*," she countered with a smirk. "Not like what you have anyway."

"Wrong. There are different kinds of talents and I'm thinking yours might be more along extrasensory lines." Her doubtful look made him continue. "It took me a very long time to distinguish an energy emission. You picked it up the first time you tried. You're probably more sensitive to alternate realities than most people. I study that sort of thing; it might come naturally to you."

She just rolled her eyes at that statement.

"Fine, but promise to tell me if you feel, see or hear anything that you might normally dismiss as your imagination. In fact, don't just tell me, make a note of it. Include every detail you can think of."

Maggie hurriedly got out her pad and scribbled down the date, time and location.

"I didn't mean this second," Noah said with a chuckle.

"If you want every detail, I need to write it down while it's fresh." She waited for him to nod then got the rest recorded in shorthand.

"That's cool," he said looking at her scribbles. "How fast can you do that?"

"As fast as you can talk. Consider me a backup to your recorder. You never know when the batteries could die out on you."

"There's a great innuendo in there but since you're insisting I behave myself, I will resist the temptation to say aloud what *you* made me think. Anyway, I'm impressed."

She rolled her eyes again. "It's just a skill. Anyone can learn it."

He combed his fingers through her hair then gave her earlobe a tug. "But hardly anyone bothers to learn it anymore. Maybe that's why we're together again—to make sure you realize how very special you are."

CHAPTER 5

*W*ell? What do you think of them?

The Council of Abstracts opened their thoughts to one another in response to Love's question.

They definitely called on us by name, replied Fate and Synchronicity.

Moi aussi, added Mother Nature.

Nice redirect with the wind gust, by the way, Curiosity said. *It was an excellent way to get the female to the crystals and find out quickly if she was ready to acknowledge her innate abilities.*

Justice was anxious for a determination on the mission it had submitted. *They are acceptable examples of the best of humanity in its current stage. Also, there is undoubtedly a bond between them and the male's comfort with alternate realities will help her adjust rapidly. But...is their union developed sufficiently to risk their own desires for the sake of a stranger? Are they willing to do battle in order to right a wrong? Since we are limited to one test per Earth decade, we must choose our pairs carefully.*

They had a very strong connection when they were young, Love offered. *And they have already cleared up the misunderstandings. Their mutual physical desire to mate is very strong but I believe they will not allow it to distract them from what they need to do.*

As usual, Reason countered. *If there is a chance such a human weakness might distract them, they may not be the best pair to choose.*

Love had its answer ready. *Quite the contrary. I am certain that once they give in to desire, their bond will be even stronger.*

We do not have time for an extended debate, Time reminded them. *As always, the most successful tests have been launched during an eclipse of a summer's full moon. Such energy will be present in twenty-four Earth hours and the portal will open. Also, as it has been since the beginning, it will close again on the subsequent new moon, whether or not a pair has been agreed upon.*

Justice had one more concern. *Unfortunately, the case I selected has extenuating circumstances that do not allow for the full fourteen days in between the opening and closing of the portal. The pair will have five days at most to complete their task. Because resolving this case would have positive repercussions that would greatly benefit Earth's future at this stage of its development, I prefer not to choose another, simpler case. Therefore, I again question Love about the suitability of this pair for this particular case.*

Love hesitated a moment before responding. *I do believe they are capable of success, even in the shortened time period.*

The collective consciousness turned to one who could veto an otherwise unanimous Council decision. Karma always weighed these matters very heavily before speaking. *I see no harm in using them. They did not resolve their karmic issues during their first fated encounter and a second meeting was destined to take place. I believe using them for this particular mission fits within the parameters of their personal trials.*

With Karma's approval, The Council voted favorably on both the mission and the couple.

As customary, The First had not intervened in the discussion, but had the final say as there was much more to be considered than simply choosing the case and the pair of humans.

Because changing the past was the most tempting and potentially catastrophic sort of interference, the guidelines regarding such had to be the strictest of all. Most importantly, the change could not alter fixed historical events affecting a mass of humanity.

If the test ended with a successful alteration of events, the next generation of humans would be born with an upgrade in the form of a mental, physical or spiritual enhancement that would ultimately ease or improve human life on Earth. If the pair failed the test, there would be neither a reward nor punishment...unless ten consecutive tests ended in failure. In that case, The Human Experiment would be terminated and the human population on Earth would be reduced to the minimum required for humans to begin again...but *without* celestial guidance or assistance of any kind.

Although there were more failures than successes throughout the millennia, there was only one instance of ten consecutive failures and, as decided by The Council, a great flood nearly decimated the planet. Because it was so early in The Human Experiment, however, The First overruled the guideline regarding ending the experiment. But here they were, an eon later, and the last nine tests had ended in failure.

The future of humanity was once again in jeopardy.

Sadly, humans had never needed an upgrade as desperately as they did now. Too many humans had forgotten the basic guidelines they had been given. They were regularly doing harm to others, themselves and their host planet.

Weighing all the circumstances and conditions, The First did not believe there would be a significantly better time or more appropriate pair of humans. Therefore, that conclusion was shared with The Council.

With The First's endorsement of the pair, it was agreed that Noah Nash and Maggie Harrison would be sent on an event-correction mission tomorrow night. What The First did not share was the hope that Noah and Maggie would correct more than one event while they were away. Robert Davenport and his descendants were due a favor and The First believed Maggie and Noah were possibly the pair to take care of that debt while simultaneously, yet unknowingly, saving their world.

CHAPTER 6

As they rode the tree house elevator up to their suite, Maggie said, "Thank you for a lovely evening, Noah. Part of my brain keeps saying I should feel guilty for having fun when I'm supposed to be working. But I'm feeling too good to listen to it."

"Good," he said, hugging her close to his side for emphasis.

She couldn't seem to stop smiling and, since dinner had been hours ago, neither the wine nor decadent food could be blamed. The rest of their time in the lounge had been spent people-watching. Noah had introduced her to one of his creative games—making up a background for someone based on something he or she was wearing or doing—and it kept them whispering and laughing for over an hour. Afterward, they had rambled through the rest of the hotel's sprawling interior, making mental notes of where the various amenities were and doing a little window-shopping along the row of elite shops.

They'd made one more attempt to go outside but it had started to rain. There was nothing left to do but return to the penthouse.

Maggie tried to hold on to the easy feeling as they entered the living room but one glance at the couch where they had shared their second kiss changed the energy between them.

"It's not a problem," Noah said in a very sincere tone. "I meant what I said about us getting to know each other as adults. We have separate bedrooms and you can trust me to stay in mine."

But I'm not sure I can trust myself to stay in mine. She smiled softly. "I know that. I'm curious. Did our tour this evening count for any of the walk-around?"

He angled his head at her. "Why do you ask?"

"I usually read before I go to sleep and now I'm anxious to learn more about the hotel. I thought I might be able to find something about The Weeping Woman."

He frowned a little and walked over to the bookshelves. "How about something here instead? Just until after tomorrow." He pulled a hardcover book off a shelf. "This looks like a good one."

She saw it was one of his novels and chuckled. "Actually I have one by that author in my room. But like I said, I'm not a fan…"

"Then I promise not to ask your opinion."

"Sounds fair." She started to walk toward him then stopped short and walked to her bedroom door instead. "Good night, Noah."

As she closed the door behind her, she heard him say, "Goodnight, Sugarlips."

A short time later, she had taken a shower and donned her favorite sleeping ensemble—a pair of old gym shorts and a large Miami Dolphins football jersey. When she caught a glimpse of herself in the mirror she shook her head. No one could ever accuse her of packing with a romantic rendezvous in mind.

She was about to shut off her cell phone when she noticed someone had left her a message. She didn't recognize the number but decided to check it anyway. The feminine voice was polite yet noticeably authoritative.

"Hello, Ms. Harrison. This is Lillian Davenport. I would appreciate it if you would stop by my office tomorrow, at

your convenience. Please do not mention this to Mr. Nash."

Tanya had told Maggie hotel management might have additional requests but she certainly wasn't expecting to hear from anyone named Davenport. She decided the unexpected summons qualified as an excuse to peruse the hotel's informational notebook and quietly fetched it from the desk in the great room.

Back in her own room, she pulled down the bedcovers and stacked several plump pillows against the headboard for a comfy reading position. She instantly discovered Lillian was Robert Davenport's granddaughter, the current resident-owner and general manager of the resort. What could that woman possibly need from her? And why would she be instructed not to tell Noah?

Both answers would have to wait until tomorrow but, since she'd already opened the notebook, she couldn't stop herself from reading a tiny bit more. Noah wouldn't need to know about that either. Maggie already knew a few basic facts about the hotel, however, the background story added some interesting information she'd never heard about.

Like many of the wealthy northern families in the early 1920s, Robert and Patricia Davenport boarded Henry Flagler's new railroad train to vacation at the sunny playgrounds of the southeast Florida coast. Although Prohibition had been enacted on a federal level, it was not strictly enforced in the tropics and casino gambling was a respectable pastime in the luxury hotels there.

One day when Robert went sailing with his wife, Patricia, and their young son, Chester, a sudden storm blew them a distance northeast of where they were staying. They came to ground on a small but beautiful island not shown on their map. They enjoyed their picnic lunch next to the waterfall that was now part of one of the Crystal Island nature trails.

Robert Davenport was so impressed with what other developers had accomplished in Florida, he decided to invest everything they had in a dream of his own. He made a deal with the State of Florida to purchase the island he'd discovered in exchange for planting a U.S. flag on it and supporting Florida's legal claim that it was as much a part of the State as Key West. The Davenport Resort had its grand opening March 1, 1924.

For several years it was a booming success, until the 1928 Okeechobee Hurricane caused massive devastation to the hotel and grounds. Then came the Wall Street crash and the abrupt end of the first Florida land boom.

There was a mention of Robert's untimely death in 1930 but not a word of explanation. The narrative jumped right to his widow's valiant struggle to maintain ownership of the island and the damaged hotel through the Depression years, how she took advantage of Roosevelt's New Deal to rebuild and expand, and how a portion of the hotel was converted into a rehab hospital for injured soldiers during World War II.

Maggie's attention was piqued again when she saw the words "Amethyst Cave", but the mention was only in connection with the naming of the island and its various amenities. The enormous crystals were present when Robert discovered the island and he had insisted every one remain exactly where they were. Thus the hotel was designed and constructed around the geodes. For that and many other reasons, they provide a constant source of fascination to visitors.

Much to Maggie's disappointment there was no mention of The Weeping Woman, ghostly or otherwise. In fact the entire topic of ghosts and mysterious events was covered in two vague sentences—

Although many guests have visited the Davenport because of reports of paranormal activity, there is no evidence to support such rumors. However, we welcome the curious to come for a stay, explore our grounds and judge for themselves.

She smiled at the creative wording. The "curious" were welcome as long as they made reservations and the lowest rates available would effectively lock out the average ghost hunter. She closed the notebook and got more comfortable under the covers. The history book beckoned but her promise to Noah replayed in her head and she reached for his novel instead. The prologue was enough to give her nightmares but she forced herself to read the first chapter before closing the book with a shudder. Noah was clearly a very talented writer but if she didn't know him personally she would have concerns about his state of mind and how safe it was to be alone with him.

The one thing she could appreciate about his book was the press photo of him on the back. It looked exactly like him—devilishly handsome. She couldn't help but wonder what had put that half-smile on his face. Her finger stroked the picture and for a moment she imagined *she* was the object of that appreciative look.

What was it about Noah that could get her feeling all gooey inside by just looking at his photo? She set the book on the nightstand and turned off the lights. It had sounded like they would be very busy tomorrow and she knew she should get some sleep. But thinking about spending the entire day with Noah had her imagination creating scenes that worked against her good intentions.

A woman's humming caused Maggie to freeze and listen intently for the source. She couldn't hear anything now but a chill ran through her. It was the same eerie feeling she'd had earlier while looking into the mirror in Noah's room and when she'd heard The Weeping Woman's plea in the Amethyst Cave. Afraid yet curious, she slowly sat up in bed and let her eyes adjust to the darkness.

When the humming started again Maggie was certain it came from her bathroom. She quietly rose and tiptoed toward the sound. The tune became clearer the closer she got.

To her utter shock Maggie saw exactly where the humming was coming from—*inside the mirror*. As if looking through a filmy window, she saw a woman in an old-fashioned maid's uniform. Maggie touched the mirror and it immediately cleared. The maid was turned away, cleaning the bathroom floor on her hands and knees and the room looked very much like an outdated version of the same room Maggie was standing in. The maid had a long, reddish-blonde braid hanging down her back and seemed very happy as she hummed her little ditty.

"Hello?" Maggie ventured.

The woman stopped her scrubbing and swiveled her head from side to side. Maggie realized she was quite young, perhaps a teenager, and very pretty. The girl rubbed the crucifix hanging from a chain around her neck then used it to make the sign of the cross. "Angels preserve and protect me and me babe," she prayed aloud in a strong Irish dialect then went back to humming considerably louder than she was before.

Completely unnerved, Maggie took a step back then rushed from her room to Noah's. Bursting through the master bedroom's double doors, she whispered, "In my room. *Hurry!*"

Noah bolted into a sitting position, yanking a sheet to his waist at the same time. "Maggie, what the—"

"No time. Just hurry."

As he bolted to his feet, she realized he was naked and quickly turned away. A second later he was at her side wearing a pair of boxers. Ordering herself not to think about what she'd just seen, she grabbed his hand and pulled him across the great room.

"I heard a woman humming," she whispered. "It was coming from the bathroom mirror. I think it's like what you saw with the man in your room. Just look." She waved for him to precede her so he did.

Noah stepped into the bathroom, but from the doorway she could see the mirror was back to being a mere reflection. She sighed. "She's gone. And you didn't see her, did you?"

He came out of the bathroom, shaking his head. "No, but I believe you." Without turning on any lights he walked around the room, stared into the mirror above the dresser and came back to her. "I'm intrigued by the fact that you've *heard* something twice now. Could it have been the same woman?"

"I only heard three words in the lounge and the woman was crying. I'm just not sure. More important, I don't think the sound was only one-way. Noah, I said 'hello' and she reacted."

"Holy shit. That's fantastic. Exactly how did she react?"

"She made the sign of the cross, like a Catholic, and then asked her angels for protection. *Oh!* She definitely had an Irish accent and I don't think The Weeping Woman did. But I can't say for sure."

He paced back and forth very quickly. "This is just too friggin' cool! Would you have any objection to our switching rooms tonight? Maybe—"

"No way," she stated, cutting him off. "I mean, I don't care about switching. I'll sleep in whichever room you say, just so I'm not alone." She took a deep breath. "I felt the chill again. Like the other two times."

"Two?"

Maggie made a face. "Yeah. Two. I didn't tell you but I put it in the notes about the Amethyst Cave."

Noah pulled her close and rubbed her arms. "Your skin is ice cold. Are you feeling okay?"

She relaxed her head against his bare chest and nodded. His hands slowed to a stroking pace then moved to her back. "Actually feeling better every second."

"You certainly are." He kissed the top of her head. "Maggie, you know I find this kind of thing really...exhilarating. But if it's too weird for you, I'll understand."

She stepped back, took his hands in hers and looked up at his beautiful face. "It is definitely very high on my weirdness scale. But remember, I believe in facing my fears, and besides, I'm not feeling terrified. I know part of that is because I'm convinced you know what you're doing. But the other part is, well, I'm more intrigued than scared. I want to know who that was in my bathroom and who I heard in the bar. I never would have imagined saying this but I want to know if it's the same ghost or different ones and whether *my* hearing her, or them, means something significant. Maybe I'm related to one or both of them in some way."

By the time she finished her little speech, he was grinning broadly. "Thank gawd. I really wouldn't have understood."

She laughed. "So you were just being polite?"

"Sort of. But what I'm going to say next is being really, *really* polite. You said you don't want to be alone but we agreed—"

She cut him off by pressing a finger to his lips. "Just pick the room. Yours or mine?"

Without another word he grasped her hand and led her into the larger room…with the bigger bed.

Maggie had no illusions about what she had just set in motion or how what happened next could ruin everything. At least she didn't worry about feeling indifferent with Noah. She already knew they only had to kiss and her body would be ready for his.

Instead of immediately taking her in his arms and kissing her, however, he held up his index finger for her to wait a minute. She watched him take two blankets from the closet and hang one on each of the mirrors in the bedroom. Then he went into the bathroom and draped towels over the mirrors in there. Within seconds the room felt warmer. "Do I want to know what you're doing?"

He came back to her with a look that made her think of the shy boy who had been her best friend. "Just making sure we get a good night's sleep." He was clearly uncertain about what to do next. "I could sleep on the floor…"

"Don't be ridiculous. The bed is huge."

"Um, do you have a preferred side?"

Maggie shook her head, but they both remained where they were standing, not moving closer to the bed or each other.

Noah finally broke the tension. "It might help if we actually got into bed."

Maggie walked to the side of the bed that hadn't been disturbed, lifted the covers, and got under them. Then Noah got under the covers where he had been when she'd barged into the room.

Maggie stifled a giggle.

Noah coughed to hide a chuckle.

And suddenly they were both laughing at themselves and each other.

Noah shifted to the middle of the bed and raised his upper body to look down at her. "I have a confession to make."

She rolled onto her side toward him, leaving only a few inches between them. "Go on."

"I've always hated the no-kissing rule. It was torturous when we were in high school and it's just plain stupid now."

"You don't say." She placed her hand on his firm chest and murmured, "How do you feel about touching?"

He ran his fingers through her hair, down her arm and back up, raising gooseflesh along the way. "I'm okay with touching..." His thumb brushed over her lips. "Except for how much harder it makes it to obey the no-kissing rule."

She lightly dragged her fingernails down to his navel then back up, appreciating how his abdomen tightened under her stroke. "It sounds like you've changed your mind about mixing business with pleasure."

"Well, since I can't stop thinking about kissing you, I'd say making a change is the only way we're going to get any business done."

She realized that, although he'd clearly told her what he wanted, he was still leaving the decision up to her. She moved her hand to the back of his neck and whispered, "I agree." Then slowly pressed her lips to his.

That was all the assurance he needed to deepen the kiss. She parted her lips but it was far from submission as her tongue snaked between his teeth. She teased his tongue into a game of give-and-take as his hands skimmed over her body from neck to thigh.

The words he had used before—hungry, satisfied, vulnerable, powerful, bewildered and certain—all came back to her in a rush. Of all her adventures, she never remembered feeling this exhilarated. Nor had she ever imagined Noah being the one to take her to a height she'd never experienced. The only thing she knew for sure was she wanted more.

As though he'd heard her thought, Noah swiveled them both so he was lying on his back and she was stretched out on top of him, making her physically aware of the effect she had on him as well. Hungry kisses accompanied frantic grasping and kneading as their bodies strived for a closeness their minimal clothing prohibited. Mere seconds passed as mindless tugging and pulling at the annoying barriers got them what they wanted—heated flesh against flesh.

With a moan of intense need that she barely understood, she urged him to hurry. And when Noah joined his body with hers, the desire for something more escalated to desperation. There was no room, no world beyond the two of them, riding a hurricane to shore. It seemed she could not survive such a cataclysm but she didn't care. She definitely could not survive if he stopped. The landing finally came with an explosive roar and wave after quaking wave of pleasure.

Maggie had no idea how much time passed from that moment until she was fully aware of Noah lying partially on top of her, breathing softly next to her ear.

All she knew was for the first time in her life, there was no travel itch that needed scratching, no place she wanted to see, no new thrill she thought she should try.

For the first time since Noah had moved away so long ago, she was perfectly content to stay right where she was…which worked out quite well since the second she moved, he roused and took her on a longer, but equally exciting journey of discovery.

CHAPTER 7

Maggie awoke to the sound of male voices beyond the closed bedroom door, but her first coherent thoughts were of Noah and how very, *very* good she felt this morning. Her second thought was that she had overslept on her first day of work. Noah's side of the bed was cool, as though he'd been up for a while, but the clock showed it was not quite 8:00 a.m. Uncertain as to whom he might be speaking with in the living room, she decided to use his bathroom rather than cross through to her own.

She hurriedly showered and used the toothbrush and paste provided in the hotel's big basket of toiletries. Although her hairstyle allowed her to simply finger-comb and air-dry, her clothing options were limited to her unflattering nightwear or the plush white robe hanging on the back of the bathroom door. The breast pocket bore an elegantly embroidered green and brown palm tree with the name of the hotel in gold script. She bet the identification increased the odds of it getting taken home by guests. She wrapped herself in the big robe and stepped back into the bedroom.

"Good morning," Noah said with a bright smile.

He also seemed to be fresh from a shower. His damp hair looked darker than she knew it was, several stray curls fell over his forehead and his face was clean shaven. Just looking at him made her stomach flutter. Dressed in worn, fitted blue jeans and a just-snug-enough green t-shirt, he was standing by a large room service cart draped with white linen and laden with covered plates, a coffee service, pitchers of juice and a vase holding a single, magnificent lavender and pink orchid. It all smelled fantastic but if she had to choose between Noah and the lavish breakfast offering, the food would lose.

He crossed the room and pulled her into his arms. His lips pressed softly to hers. "*Mmmm.* You smell good enough to eat." He kissed her more thoroughly as if to prove his statement.

She felt her cheeks warm as her mind registered his innuendo. This…familiar teasing between lovers…was new to her, but she was already hooked on it. Though the kiss ended, he continued to hold her in a loose embrace. She looked up at him and asked, "How long have you been awake?"

"A couple hours. I don't need a lot of sleep and I didn't want to wake you, so I went down to the fitness center, worked out and used the shower there."

"And ordered breakfast for a half-dozen people."

He shrugged. "I have a healthy appetite and guessed that you still do too."

"Aha. So you did notice how much weight I've put on."

He patted her bottom with both hands. "Not so much noticed as appreciated. In fact, last night I remember thinking you could afford to put on a few more pounds." He gave her another pat for emphasis.

"Liar." She pushed at his chest and he released her. "Anyway, it smells delicious and I'm starving."

"Good. Get back in bed—which is where I had hoped to find you—and I'll serve."

Minutes later he had set up a buffet across the bottom of the bed and set a glass of fresh-squeezed orange juice and a cup of coffee on the nightstand next to her. At his insistence she put a little of everything on her plate.

"Did you have any strange dreams last night?" Noah asked in between bites.

"I don't think so. Why? Did you?"

"I'm not sure. But I woke up with a jolt, like my heart was given a jump-start. It was racing like I'd been having a terrifying nightmare only I don't remember any of it."

"*You* have nightmares?" Maggie made a face at him. "I read the beginning of one your books last night. If I hadn't been so distracted afterward I probably would have had some scary dreams for sure."

He leaned over and gave her a quick kiss. "You're welcome."

She tapped him on the nose. "I was referring to the girl in the bathroom mirror. Your contribution was…something else."

"*Hmmm. Something else.* I don't think I've ever had such a rave review."

She tore off a bit of the cinnamon toast she was eating and threw it at him. He picked it off his shirt, swallowed it and gave her another kiss.

As expected, everything was delicious, but the shrimp Mornay omelet demanded a second helping.

As soon as Maggie had the last forkful in her mouth, Noah began clearing away the bed picnic. For a while she had forgotten she was supposed to be working. "Oh my," she said. "I didn't realize I was taking so long. I'll be dressed and ready to get to work in a minute." She started to rise but he pressed a hand to her shoulder.

"Wait. There's something I need to say." With a very serious expression, he sat down beside her. "I owe you an apology. Well, actually I owe you *two* apologies."

She squinted at him. "For what?"

He shifted to face her directly. "Last night…well, there's no excuse…I mean, I swear, it wasn't intentional, but no matter how much I wanted that to happen, I hadn't actually believed it would, well, at least not like that…"

"What are you babbling about?" Maggie truly had no idea what he could possibly be apologizing for.

"I was irresponsible."

He looked so ashamed, she didn't want to make it worse, but she had to ask. "In what way?"

He blinked at her. "I didn't have a condom. Didn't even *think* about it. But I swear, I never have unprotected sex. And I've never been a fan of getting naked with strangers. When I'm not in a relationship, I'm not having sex, and I haven't been in many relationships in recent years. What I'm trying to say is, I'm free of any sort of disease but we should have discussed that *before*. And what if I got you pregnant? Like I said, irresponsible."

She stroked his cheek. "That is very sweet, Noah. But I was just as irresponsible as you were. Yes, we should have had *the conversation* beforehand. And I would have told you that I'm perfectly healthy as well. But I should have also told you that I can't get pregnant...at least not right now. I get injections to help with painful periods, and the side benefit is birth control. And since we're being honest, it's been a long time since I took advantage of that particular benefit, mainly because I've never been a fan of getting naked with *anybody*, stranger or not. I thought it was just my fate to never know what great sex was like." She gently kissed his lips. "Thank you for showing me." She kissed him again. "And thank you for thinking you needed to apologize."

"I wasn't finished," he said sheepishly. "And you can't take any responsibility for the rest of it, so just accept my apology and my promise that I'll do much better next time."

She wrinkled her nose at him. "Exactly *what* are you going to do much better?"

He exhaled heavily. "For our first time, I wanted to make love to you for hours, not jump your bones for two minutes then nod off. I never gave a thought to whether you were...*ready*...or satisfied. And I don't have a good excuse for why I didn't. To put it bluntly, I lost control like I was some horny teenager."

"*Hmmm.* I'm pretty sure we *both* lost control, just like we *both* took a little nap, and I reject your apology on all counts. I may not have a lot of experience, but I think our first time was exactly as it should have been—like a mouth-watering appetizer, which you followed up with a scrumptious feast. And as to your last concern, I think I've been *ready* for you since our first kiss, even if I didn't know it myself."

His mouth curved into a crooked grin. "So, does that all mean it was okay for you?"

She rolled her eyes. "Are you fishing for another compliment? I already said I thought it was great. However, like I said, I haven't had a lot of experience, so it might not have been as great as—" His lips pressed to hers before she could finish that thought.

Without breaking the kiss, he leaned her backward and untied the cord holding her robe closed. When he raised his head, she was captivated by the raw desire in his eyes as he eased the plush fabric away from her body.

"I'm wondering if there's anything I might do to get you to use a better description than 'great' or 'something else.' So tell me, Maggie, what would you call this?" He angled his mouth over hers and made love to her with his lips and tongue as his fingers lightly grazed her hip. Then he kissed his way across her cheek and nipped her earlobe and neck and licked the hollow of her shoulder blade.

When more than a second passed without further attention, she opened her eyes to see him looking at her with a questioning expression.

"Descriptive word please," he said with mischief in his eyes.

"Oh, I, uh, I'd call it…*intoxicating*."

"Excellent choice. But my ego still needs a bit more massaging." He continued his trail of kisses down to her breasts and when he took one peak into his mouth, Maggie gasped.

He withdrew his mouth. "And that?"

She made a soft sound of pleasure and whispered, "*Bewitching.*"

He chuckled. "I think that's fair since I'm certain you cast a spell over me a long time ago."

"*Hmmm.* In that case, maybe I should say *abracadabra* and see what happens when I do this." Her hand slid from his cheek, down his chest to between his thighs and without any further effort, magic happened.

His intention had been to make this time all about her, to build her arousal slowly, show her more of what she'd been missing and not take anything for himself. But the only thing he accomplished was to make it last three minutes instead of two.

If he could, he would stay inside her for hours.

Somehow that thought didn't surprise him at all. Not with her. With his Maggie he always knew it would be like this. He had assumed his attraction to her would have dwindled over the years. But in case it hadn't and he still found himself captivated by her, he had run through dozens of scenarios aimed at their becoming lovers over several weeks. Fortunately for him, none of them had been necessary. It had all happened very naturally. Well, maybe not naturally, but it happened exactly as all magical things should.

The nagging voice of reason in his head reminded him of her need for adventure and avoidance of stability and he silenced it by assuring the nag that he wasn't imagining anything long-term with Maggie. He was simply enjoying the moment.

In his mind, he heard Reason laughing.

Despite his inability to go through with his noble intentions, the totally sated look in her eyes made him feel like a hero. Though thoroughly sated himself, that look was enough to get blood flowing to his lower regions all over again. Instead of giving into the temptation to remain in bed with her all day, he rose, helped her to her feet and swiftly wrapped her in the robe, making sure she was snugly covered from chin to ankles, then redressed himself.

"Believe me when I say it is taking all my exceptional work ethic to do this. But I need to get to work."

"Oh, of course," she replied as she stepped away. "I'll be ready to head out in a minute."

He had mixed feelings about how quickly her expression switched to work mode. "Wait." She stopped at the bedroom door and he closed the distance between them in three strides. He pulled her close and gave her a slow, seductive kiss as his hands ran down her back. "Okay, *now* I'm ready." She smiled and turned toward her room but he tugged her back again. "Maybe just one more." They were both smiling too much for their mouths to properly come together. "Hey, I don't call you Sugarlips for nothing."

She poked his chest with her index finger. "You *promised* not to call me that at all."

"Really? I don't remember making that promise."

She gave him a playful shove and scooted into her bedroom.

Maggie's body continued to tingle with pleasure as she dressed, brushed her hair and applied the speed version of makeup. Knowing they would be outside in the heat, she chose a lightweight white sundress and flat sandals. Not certain what all she would need on their walk-around, she removed the hotel property map from the informational notebook. She packed that, her pad, several pens and a few other items in a shoulder bag rather than carry a purse. When she returned to the main room, Noah was on the couch, skimming a glitzy travel magazine. Her breath caught as though it were the first time she'd ever seen such a devastatingly sexy creature.

He stood as soon as she approached. His gaze slid over her and his smile broadened. "You are temptation personified. I think I need to add something to your job description. From this moment until I order you otherwise, it is your responsibility to keep my mind on work and my hands off you. Okay?"

Relieved to have him set such a sensible rule, she fixed a stern expression on her face and saluted him. "Yes sir.

Until you give me a counter-order, you and I are strictly author and assistant." She patted her shoulder bag. "I think I have everything I need except for the recorder you mentioned."

He reached into the chest pocket of his t-shirt and extracted a flat, palm-sized, black device. "It's voice-activated so there's really nothing for you to do as far as recording. But maybe you could glance at my pocket once in a while to make sure a light comes on when I'm talking. The built-in battery is supposed to be good for years but just in case…"

"I'll have my pad and pen ready to leap to the rescue."

He nodded. "I knew I was bringing you along for something besides your sweet—"

She quickly hushed him with her fingers on his mouth. "Work-related only."

He pretended to pout before going on. "When we get back here you just need to connect the recorder to my laptop and the computer will convert everything to text. The program isn't perfect though so I will need you to skim it, make corrections if needed, then print it out for me."

"Got it."

They checked the map on the way to the lobby and confirmed they had toured every foot of the ground floor of the main building the evening before. Noah said he needed to repeat that walk and check out the three towers of rooms but decided to cover the outdoors before the temperature and humidity hit the daily high.

Even at midmorning it felt as though they walked out of the hotel directly into a steam room. But as Maggie took in the clear blue sky, gentle salt-air breeze and white-capped ocean waves breaking on the sand, the heat was easy to ignore. They meandered along the beach and paused at the outdoor swimming pool with the island bar in its center. Noah got virgin piña coladas from one of several freestanding tiki huts and they sipped them while strolling along the golf-cart path that led to the ten individual bungalows.

The exteriors were all painted differently and made to look like beach huts with thatched roofs. She knew from the informational notebook that these units were fully-equipped, one-bedroom cabins leased out on a seasonal basis and always had a considerable waiting list.

Noah stopped in front of one with bright green shutters and two yellow rocking chairs on its narrow wooden porch. "Something about this reminds me of those fairy-tale tents that seem small on the outside but are huge and elaborate inside. Might be something I can do with that."

It was the first story-related comment he'd made and Maggie glanced at his pocket as he spoke to make sure the recorder had lit up.

A little beyond the last bungalow was a sign indicating the beginnings of three nature trails. The entrances were barely visible between the thick foliage. She glanced to her right and realized that was the paved pathway she'd been brought in on. "The driver who met me at the dock mentioned a nature trail and a good picnic spot. I think it has a waterfall too. But it sounded like there was only one, not three."

Noah picked the one on the left and she followed closely behind. He was being totally polite and didn't seem to be having any problem keeping his mind focused on work. Considering how sensual their morning had been, she was glad it wasn't up to her to be the strict one.

He stopped so abruptly she bumped into him. He held up a finger to signal her to wait. She stepped back and watched him cautiously slide the device out of his pocket and hold it in front of him. Realizing he was taking a picture, she followed his line of sight and had a silent moment of panic. Directly in their path was a huge, incredibly intricate spider web and its builder was about to snack on a fly it had caught. The spider's hourglass body was black with blue stripes and at least two inches long. Its eight stick legs increased its size by several inches more.

Noah nudged her around and whispered, "The big guy had no problem with my taking pictures but he isn't going to let us pass without a fight. It'll make one hell of a cover."

"What does a giant spider have to do with *Hotel Hellgate*?" she asked as they returned to the trail entrance.

"Nothing. But you've heard the expression a picture is worth a thousand words. That one is worth at least fifty thousand. I'll write a story to fit it."

"Wow. I could never do something like that."

Noah lifted her chin with his bent index finger and frowned as she met his gaze. "Why do you do that?"

She tried to circumvent his question with a tease. "Do I need to remind you about the new no-hands-on-Maggie rule?"

"I hereby order a temporary pause of that rule." He brought her hand to his lips and kissed her knuckles. "Most people don't see a monster spider and think about writing a story around it. But most of those people can do a lot of things I can't. You may not think you have any special talent but I know you're wrong. We just haven't identified it yet. So I don't want to hear anything like that come out of your mouth again." He gave her a quick kiss. "Mind you that doesn't mean you can't compliment my brilliance anytime you recognize it."

She couldn't help but smile and rose on her toes for a longer kiss, but he held his hand up between them.

"Sorry, time's up. Back to work."

She rolled her eyes but followed him obediently onto the middle trail. They walked for quite a while in silence without any primitive beasties blocking their way. Then, quite unexpectedly, the hair on Maggie's arms stood straight up then the hair on her head lifted as well and she stopped in her tracks. "Noah?"

He turned and gaped at the sight of her electrified hair. "What is it?" he asked as he retraced his steps to her.

"I'm not sure. Something…weird."

"More words please."

Maggie took several steps back and the hair relaxed. She came forward again, stopping exactly where she had before and the hair raised again. Taking another step backward, she explained, "It almost feels as though there's a solid wall in front of me." She put up her palms and found where it seemed to start. With conscious effort she had no difficulty passing through but her whole body felt as though it were tingling.

Noah narrated what he was watching for the sake of the recording. "I am now walking back beyond the point where Maggie is standing and testing the field myself." He closed his eyes and took a deep breath before stretching out his arms and walking forward again. This time he stopped right beside her. "It's an energy field. Like the one you felt coming off the amethyst geode in the bar. Only this one is a whole lot more powerful. Even still, I didn't notice it until I focused on it." He scanned the area. "I don't see any rocks or geodes that could be creating the field, just plants and trees. Are you willing to see how far it goes?"

She smiled. "If I didn't run screaming from that spider, I think I can handle a little force field." Still, she accepted his hand when he offered it and let him lead her for about twenty feet before she abruptly halted again. Like she saw him do, she closed her eyes and took a breath. She wanted to give him a good description of what she was feeling. "Whatever it is just got much stronger right here. It's almost like an electrical current is running from the arches of my feet up my body...ooh, my fingers are really tingling..."

"I feel it now too," Noah said. "Only it came from your hand to mine and, oh my gawd, this is one of the coolest creepy things ever."

She laughed as she saw how his hair was sticking out. "It reminds me of static electricity only it's continuous. There's no specific spark or discomfort."

"It sort of tickles." He chuckled then laughed out loud as though the current had just reached an especially ticklish spot.

Maggie realized the feeling was not so different from how she felt when he kissed her. If she stood there much longer, she wasn't sure what the weird energy might make her—

Is someone there? Ple-e-ease. It's so dark. I don't know where I am.

"Maggie? What's wrong?" Noah searched her widened eyes for a clue to why she was squeezing his hand so tight.

"Did you hear that?" she whispered.

"I didn't hear anything."

Maggie pulled him forward until she felt the energy dissipate. "It was *her*. The Weeping Woman. I'm sure of it. And this time I'm positive it was *not* the Irish maid. I heard her clearly, as though she was standing right next to me. This woman was scared and lost...someplace dark...like she was trapped underground below us...and she may have heard us talking...like what happened with the maid." She told him the exact words she heard.

Noah looked back along the trail. "Did you notice how the trail was winding before the point where you sensed the field begin, then went perfectly straight for about forty feet before curving again from here? And it looks like that spot we were standing on, where you heard the voice, was halfway, like an epicenter."

"Meaning?"

"Beneath that spot could be the most powerful crystal deposit on the island."

She hesitated for a few seconds then said the words that popped into her head. "Like a main server for a network of computers."

He grinned and bobbed his head. "Exactly!"

"So, The Weeping Woman could be the ghost of someone who died anywhere on the island and the only reason I could hear her more clearly here was because I was standing on the main server."

"That, or she actually died in this area."

She made a face at him. "You just have to make it creepier than it already was, don't you?"

He shrugged. "It comes naturally."

She grinned to let him know she wasn't truly bothered by it. "But tell me this, with all the people who've walked along these trails over the years wouldn't someone else have noticed it?"

"Maybe someone did and I'll find a notation of it when I start my research. Or maybe no one has ever walked across it with your ability to sense the energy. Or maybe your personal electromagnetism is tuned into the same channel."

She narrowed her eyes at him. "Are you making fun of me?"

"Not at all. You saw me walk right through and I'm more alert to metaphysical phenomena than a lot of people. I didn't feel that electrical flow until it came through your hand to me. I hate to tell you, love, but I think you've got some powerful ESP."

The word *love* set off the butterflies in her tummy even more actively than when he'd called her *honey*. She knew it didn't mean anything but she couldn't help but smile. "So the only thing to do now is figure out what one might do with such a *useful* ability."

He squeezed her hand. "All things in good time. Now let's see what's behind door number three."

The final trail took them to a lagoon filled with big orange, white and gold carp. A waterfall splashed into the lagoon on one end and there was a small container of fish food available for those who wanted to witness a feeding frenzy. Obviously this was the spot her baggage cart driver, Aaron, had recommended for a picnic.

It was after noon when they got back to the hotel's pristine beach so they had a cold lunch on the Quartz Café's patio outside of Tower 1. From time to time before their meals were brought to the table, guests approached Noah for his autograph. One even had a copy of his latest book. For a short while, Maggie had actually forgotten he was a celebrity.

"What's next?" Maggie asked as they finished eating.

"We still have the three towers. I want to take a walk on each floor, past every room, mainly to see if you pick up

any specific energy emanations. Maybe the front desk
could tell you how many rooms—"

"Towers one and two each have fourteen Jade rooms—
that's their least expensive—on floors two through nine,
plus eight Rubies—those are the penthouses—on the tenth
floors. Floors two and three of Tower three are all meeting
and event rooms, including a grand ballroom, then there are
eight Topaz rooms—larger and more expensive—on floors
four through nine and six more Rubies on the tenth. That
brings the tower total to two hundred twenty-four Jade,
forty-eight Topaz and twenty-two Rubies. Then there are
the five Diamond Suites, where we are. Grand total—two
hundred ninety-nine." She ended the list with a deep breath.

Noah's jaw had dropped halfway through her monologue
and it took him a few seconds to react audibly. "That was
amazing. How did you memorize all that?"

She shrugged. "I may have *glanced* at the informational
notebook last night."

"Don't tell me, on top of all your other amazing talents,
you also have an eidetic memory."

Her cheeks flushed and she shrugged again. "I think
that's what it's called."

"*Aha!* I don't recall you mentioning that while you were
earning straight A's in all your classes and I was struggling
to pass."

"I was always afraid it would make you feel less
confident than you already were."

"I don't think that was possible. Are there any more
unimportant talents, skills or mental abilities you haven't
told me about?"

She tapped her index finger against her chin. "*Hmmm.* I
am getting close to mastering invisibility."

He pretended to give that some thought. "I can see how
that could come in handy…as long as you aren't planning
on disappearing from me any time soon."

His tone was light, so she replied in kind. "Never fear. I
agreed to put up with you and your *eccentric* demands as
long as you are willing to pay for my services."

"I beg your pardon?" he asked with dramatic indignation. "Exactly which of my demands are you calling eccentric?"

A dozen replies popped into her head, all of which were highly suggestive and none of which were proper to say aloud in public. She let her flushed cheeks express her thoughts instead.

"Then I guess the better question might be, what sort of adventure will you need after you finish this terrible assignment?"

His question was reasonable based on some of the experiences she'd told him about. But his tone had an edge of bitterness to it. "What was *that*?"

"What was what?" he asked as he looked around for their waiter.

"I was only teasing."

He returned his gaze to her and gave her a sexy grin. "I know that. And when we get back to the room, I want to hear all about my *eccentric* demands."

She angled her head at him. "I will…if you tell me what you were really thinking when you asked me that last question."

He shrugged. "Just curious."

"You're lying."

Rather than deny that, he just exhaled heavily and muttered, "It was nothing. Forget it, okay?"

She frowned at him for a moment then shrugged lightly. "Okay. Forgotten. So, what's next on the agenda?"

He looked a little surprised to be let off so easily, but replied to her question. "Between hearing just how many rooms there are, plus what happened on the trail, I'm rethinking my insistence on not reading any of the material ahead of time. So I thought maybe we could go back to the room and do a little…*research*." The last word was delivered with a distinct eyebrow wiggle.

Maggie returned the gesture along with a small smile. "I think a little *research* with you would be quite—" Her smile slipped away. "I just remembered something. I'm supposed to check in with Human Resources today.

Something about filling out forms. Would you mind getting started without me?" She felt herself blush. "I mean with the research, the *book* research."

He grinned. "You'd better go before you dig yourself a hole I won't let you out of." She rose but he caught her wrist before she could walk away. "See if they'll give you the forms to fill out back in the room."

"Okay." She turned but he held fast.

"You mentioned a history book…"

"It's on my nightstand." Again he prevented her from leaving.

"I need a kiss."

She bent down and kissed the top of his head. "That's the best you can have in public. And the longer you keep me here, the later it will be when I get back to the suite."

CHAPTER 8

Maggie was practicing her patience but it was getting thinner by the minute. She wanted to get back to the suite. *To Noah.* The research. *Noah.* The need to be near him, touching him, *making love with him,* was pushing everything else out of her mind. She had never before been preoccupied with thoughts like these. He said it was about chemistry, so perhaps she was addicted to whatever chemical his body produced naturally that other boys and men lacked.

She needed something else to think about but she was being kept waiting without anything to distract her. The only thing that came to mind was the awareness that she should have taken a shower after their outdoor explorations. But she had only been thinking of getting this appointment over with as quickly as possible. And now she couldn't stop thinking about her questionable hygiene.

Even though she had shown up without a specific appointment, that had been Lillian Davenport's request. And when she told Ms. Martinez, the general manager's executive assistant, that she would be glad to schedule another time when it might be more convenient, she had been politely but firmly directed to sit and wait just a few minutes for Ms. Davenport to get out of her meeting.

Perhaps to keep her from leaving, Ms. Martinez started a conversation in a more friendly tone. "I hope Mr. Nash will give you time to enjoy some of the hotel's amenities."

Maggie did her best to give an appropriate answer without blushing. "He seems to be a very considerate employer."

"I heard the two of you have already done some exploring." When she noted Maggie's slight frown, she smiled. "He's famous, staying in our finest suite. The staff and guests can't help but be interested in what he's doing."

Maggie forced a smile. "He said exploring a book's potential location is part of his process. And I must say, the hotel is certainly beautiful. I like the way the décor is a blend of tropical island and old world."

The assistant chuckled. "Funny you should say that. The meeting in there is about some major renovations that would bring some very contemporary advancements and styles into the mix. But don't worry. Even if you're still here when the physical work begins, you shouldn't be disturbed."

Ms. Martinez almost managed to distract Maggie with bits of trivia about the hotel until the executive office door opened. Four people exited with folders and rolled blueprints and very concerned expressions on their faces. Maggie's guess was that they'd all been given assignments or deadlines they were none too happy about.

An impeccably groomed, statuesque woman with very light ash-blonde hair stood in the doorway. Maggie was no *fashionista* but the woman's dress looked like an original somebody-or-other's design. Despite her powerful position, her smooth complexion suggested she was in her thirties. However, her confidence and air of authority were easy to identify. This had to be Lillian Davenport.

"Ms. Harrison," she said with a smile that revealed perfect, white teeth but didn't seem to reach her eyes. "Thank you for stopping by. Come in please."

Maggie hurried to follow her into the inner sanctum. Rather than a stuffy executive office or a Tommy Bahama interpretation of one, the room was efficiently furnished with glass and matte chrome pieces. It was also incredibly neat for the work area of such a busy executive...which could have been the reason Maggie's gaze was drawn to the hodge-podge collection of photographs on the side wall. They were mostly of Davenport properties and autographed pics of celebrity guests posing with Davenport family members or staff, but Maggie's vision caught on a small one that didn't seem to fit amidst the others.

The photograph appeared to be of a younger Ms. Davenport and a dark-haired man sharing an intimate moment. The large pink-carnation heart behind their heads along with his coat and tie and her bright red Chinese-style top hinted at a special occasion. But the look of sublime happiness on her face was unmistakable. They had to have been deeply in love when that picture was taken. Engraved across the bottom of the plain, silver frame was the phrase, *Lilli & Connor...2/14/05.*

As Ms. Davenport moved to her high-backed executive chair behind the desk, Maggie hurried to sit in one of the low-profile arm chairs on the opposite side. It immediately established each of their positions for this meeting.

"I'm sure you have a lot to do for Mr. Nash so I'll only take a minute. Our human resources department speaks very highly of the 'It's Only Temporary' agency and I trust that you are as responsible as all the other temps they have provided us in the past. I understand the agency's owner explained that your assignment here was different from the norm. Your services are being utilized by Mr. Nash and he will be charged the agency's usual rate but the Davenport is the official client."

Maggie furrowed her brow both to show attentiveness and lack of complete comprehension. Ms. Davenport either didn't notice or didn't care as she continued on with a speech that sounded somewhat rehearsed and left no pauses for questions.

"We welcome the potential publicity that Mr. Nash could bring to the Davenport if he lets it be known we were the inspiration for his next bestselling novel. I'm sure you're aware of the effect Stephen King had on The Stanley Hotel. This property has always been a source of conjecture when it comes to its past but with all the increased interest in the paranormal, we have seen a correlation in the number and types of guest reservations, especially in the summer. In other words, we have accepted the value of all the rumors of ghosts and portals to other dimensions, though we will continue to deny the validity of such nonsense."

So far Maggie still had no idea what she had been summoned for but she forced herself to remain still.

"There is really just one area that we would prefer remain, shall we say, off-limits. Our concern is, if we specifically demand Mr. Nash avoid that area, he might be tempted to focus on it when it wasn't what he had planned on writing about to begin with."

Despite the confusing statement Maggie noticed Ms. Davenport's repeated use of the plural pronoun and wondered if the "we" referred to the group she saw leaving a few minutes ago, or the actual Davenport family, or if this woman just used the word to deflect responsibility away from herself. As the formidable woman finally got to her point, Maggie eliminated the employee group.

"You see, among all the rumors and ghost stories, there is one we absolutely will not tolerate being exploited for the amusement of the masses. There is to be no mention of my grandfather's death, either using the name Robert Davenport precisely or by implication. This is an area of great sensitivity to my family and there is no amount of publicity that would make a mockery of his life acceptable."

"I understand," Maggie said sympathetically. "I'm sure I would feel the same way. However, I'm not sure why you're telling me this."

Ms. Davenport's expression took on a stern edge. "I am telling this to you because part of your assignment here is to report on Mr. Nash's progress and how his story seems to be developing. You will make these reports directly and *only* to me, at least once a week, and not alert Mr. Nash in any way."

Maggie felt a rush of acid flood her stomach. She was being ordered to spy on and lie to Noah. Even if she didn't care about him, subterfuge was not in her character range. Something made her glance at the photo again. It was hard to believe that happy young woman was now the cold-blooded executive sitting in the power chair.

"I understand you and Mr. Nash were previously acquainted."

An alarm sounded in Maggie's mind. "That's correct. It was back in high school. But he barely remembered me." The lie slid out more easily than she expected.

"Good. If I thought you were too close to him, I would have to ask for a replacement."

Maggie wasn't worried. Noah wouldn't accept a replacement. But Ms. Davenport wasn't finished.

"Also, I was told you and your agency's owner, Tanya Sevrell, are very good friends. So let me add this—if Mr. Nash's book includes even one sentence about my grandfather, in any context, and you fail to warn me of that possibility in time to take preventive action, I will see to it that all of our staffing needs are taken away from 'It's Only Temporary'…*permanently*."

Lilli waited for the temp to close the door behind her before rising. She had not intended to threaten the friend's business to ensure Ms. Harrison's cooperation, but her instincts told her it was absolutely necessary. Mercy had let her know that Mr. Nash and Ms. Harrison had been seen around the hotel by a number of staff and the general consensus was that they appeared to be very friendly. Whether or not the temp was being honest about Nash barely remembering her, that woman had deep feelings for him. And she knew from personal experience how those kind of feelings could overpower all common sense.

She walked over to the photo wall and removed the one that had caught Harrison's eye. That was the giveaway.

Despite all the artistic shots of Davenport properties and photo-ops with recognizable celebrities, people in love were automatically drawn to the simple little snapshot of her and Connor.

How many times had she tried to store it out of her sight? Countless.

It never stayed hidden for long though. The same photo that made her heart ache also made her strong. Every day for the last thirteen years, she looked at it and remembered two things—the happiest moment can turn to ashes in a blink, and Love can never, ever be trusted.

Even more times, she had thought of throwing the reminder away, but she hadn't been able to do that either. It wasn't logical, but getting rid of the photo completely would be the same as accepting that she would never see Connor again.

And the day she accepted that would be the day she took her last breath.

All the way back to the suite Maggie wondered how she was going to get out of the spider web she'd just gotten caught in. It would be different if she didn't know Noah was already thinking of using Robert Davenport, or at least the idea of him, in his new book. If she didn't tell Noah about her secret orders, she'd feel like she was betraying him. She couldn't be sure where their relationship was headed but starting off spying on him didn't seem to lay a good foundation for the future.

On the other hand, if she told him about it and he purposely avoided a particularly good plot idea to make things easier on her, she'd be guilty of interfering with his creative process. Also not a great beginning.

If that wasn't complicated enough, she and Tanya had been close for some time now and she loved working for her agency. Davenport made up most of Tanya's business. If they pulled out, the firm's reputation would be severely damaged and it could take her friend a very long time to recover, if at all.

During the short elevator ride, she made the decision not to do anything for a few days. After all, she had a week before having to report to Ms. Davenport again. Meanwhile she would not tell Noah about the warning. She would not tell Tanya about the threat. And finally she would not ruin the time she had with Noah by fretting over the day when she would have to say something to someone.

Before entering the suite, she brought back the memory of the last minutes she and Noah had spent behind those doors. Instantly, the strange chemistry pushed everything out of the way except the need to touch him.

"Hi—" That was all she got out before he gestured for her not to talk for a second but come closer. She walked over to the dining room table, which he had apparently chosen over working at the smaller, more formal desk. He was reading something on his laptop screen, papers were spewing out of the printer and books, magazines and printouts of articles covered every inch of the table. He clicked one more key on his laptop and turned to her with a delighted expression.

Without a word he shifted his chair, pulled her onto his lap and gave her a full-mouth, tongue-twisting kiss that silenced the worries Lillian Davenport had put in her head.

"I take it you've had a good time while I was out taking care of annoying paperwork," she said teasingly.

Rather than respond, he nuzzled her neck while dragging one of her sundress straps off her shoulder.

Ribbons of pleasure unfurled from each spot he touched. "Uh, I'm a little confused. Am I still under orders to keep you focused on work or—"

"I missed you," he stated then engaged her in another deep kiss. However, a few heartbeats later he leaned back and took a deep breath. "But you're right. We have a lot of work to do." He slowly removed his hands from her. "So, are you all mine for the rest of the day?"

How about for the rest of my life? "Yep. And I can't wait to find out what you learned while I was gone." She made herself rise and move to the chair across the wide table from him. "Do you want to fill me in or give me a task?"

"Task first. I found something interesting on-line before you *distracted* me," he admitted with a grin. "I'd like to see if I can find anything about it in your hotel's history book before catching you up." He showed her how to download the morning's recording and perform edits, then turned his attention to the book.

The next several hours passed in relative silence, other than Maggie's typing and Noah's scribbling on Post-It notes and sticking them to various pages.

When Noah noticed that Maggie had stopped typing, he set aside the book and asked, "Hungry yet?"

"Surprisingly, yes. But if you want to keep working I'd be good with room service."

"Actually, I already made other arrangements. Don't ask. It's a surprise. But there is a dress code—a bathing suit, flip-flops and that robe you had on this morning."

"Do I have time for a shower?" she asked hopefully.

His expression went from lustful to pained. "Only if I don't join you. Go on. We have a little time to spare before our reservation."

A half-hour later she felt refreshed but somewhat self-conscious in the long robe. Until she saw he was attired the same way. She couldn't resist taking a peek to make sure he was also in a bathing suit. "Very nice," she said, noting the fitted black swim shorts.

With feigned modesty, Noah reclosed his robe. "If you knew what was waiting for us, you wouldn't risk waking the beast."

"Then tell me," she said, dancing her fingers up his lapel.

He grasped her hand and interlocked their fingers. "I'm pretty sure this is one of those cases where showing is definitely better than telling."

From the elevator he guided her to a side exit door that allowed them to avoid the lobby. A few minutes later they were walking toward the ocean on the opposite end of the beach they had explored that morning. She knew when they were nearing their destination by Noah's big smile and expectant look. Just ahead she could see ten colorfully striped tents. They were set up in two staggered rows a little ways back from the high tide line and separated by just enough space to give an impression of privacy.

As he led her to one on the far end, Noah explained, "I read about these cabanas today and, as luck would have it, there was a cancellation. Robert Davenport had the first tent put up when his hotel was overbooked and made it so unique and luxurious it became a very exclusive opportunity. There's a section in your book about it because a lot of famous people have had affairs in these over the years."

When he walked her around to the front of the tent, Maggie gasped. The flaps were pulled back to reveal a lavishly decorated interior befitting a sultan. A thick furry carpet cushioned the base. Brightly colored scarves lined the pointed top and back wall and large pillows were scattered around a low table. Interior lighting was provided by a lantern with an adjustable flame and as she took a breath, the seductive scent of freshly cut jasmine filled her nostrils.

Maggie rushed inside and reclined dramatically on the double-wide lounge. But she was too excited to stay still and was instantly back on her feet with him outside. "Geez, Noah. This might just be the most incredible dining room I've ever seen. Just look at this view." She waved at the ocean as though he might not be seeing everything she was. "And we'll be able to see the full moon rising over the water!" An involuntary shiver made her vigorously rubbed her arms.

In an instant he was behind her and wrapped his arms protectively around her. "Cold? Or is there another ghost around?"

She sighed and shook her head. "Neither. I'm just…excited."

He kissed the side of her neck. "Good. I like you excited." His hands moved up the front of her robe but before he could continue, a bell tinkled behind their tent. Noah drew Maggie inside and said, "Come in." Two young women in purple, flower-patterned saris entered the tent carrying large picnic baskets. Once Noah assured them they would serve themselves, they exited and a man wearing only a loose, short skirt of the same print as the saris entered with a tray holding two crystal glasses and a bottle of the delicious German wine in an ice bucket. Noah nodded for him to uncork the wine but then excused him as well.

Maggie would have been thrilled with a baloney sandwich in those surroundings, but of course such a travesty would never occur at the Davenport. Their feast began with a cold appetizer stack of crab, avocado and mango and ended with orange crème brûlée and chocolate-dipped raspberries. Neither felt the need to talk as they fully gave themselves over to the sights, smells and tastes of the moment. And with every sip of the wine Maggie pushed Lillian Davenport and her warnings further and further out of her mind.

Lilli waited for Mercy to say good night before she allowed herself to give into the roiling emotions simmering beneath her rigidly controlled image. It was one thing for her assistant to note her *concern* over a business matter. But she could not let anyone, not even Mercy, know there was a personal matter that could turn her into a simpering girl with the least provocation.

She pushed that thought aside by focusing on the oldest photographs on the wall—her grandfather breaking ground on the hotel in 1922, him posing with grandmother Patricia and their son Chester, in front of the enormous geode that the Emerald Dome restaurant would later be built around, sitting at a table of guests, that included silent film heartthrob Rudolph Valentino, at the Grand Opening celebration in 1924.

Robert Davenport always looked so happy. He loved Crystal Island, the hotel and, most especially, his family.

There was no reason for him to have taken his own life. And yet that is what the coroner's report had said—self-inflicted bullet to his brain. The newspapers speculated that he was distraught over the Wall Street crash. But that made no sense. From what her father had told her, the hotel was never in serious financial trouble, not even through the depression years when he and Grandma Patricia took over the operation. But without any evidence of foul play, the suicide verdict held and, as far as the family was concerned, it stained the otherwise marvelous history of the Davenport.

She had been given a chance to clear the stain once, but only succeeded in messing up her own life.

"Grandpa? Robert? What really happened to you?" She stood very still for a moment, just in case he felt like answering or making an appearance, but nothing supernatural occurred.

Before closing up for the night, she allowed herself one more look at the little photo that had sent her down memory lane. Had she been paying more attention to the world outside of her office, she may have realized there was a full moon tonight and guarded her emotions more carefully. Ever since that fateful night in 2005, a full moon was something to be wary of.

But she hadn't been aware of the moon's phase before Ms. Harrison arrived for their meeting, and now she couldn't stop the flood of need taking over her body and mind. For long spans of time she was able to put memories of Connor to sleep. But when they were awakened, as had happened today, the need to see her love, hear his voice and be touched by him was nearly unbearable.

From her office she headed for the main kitchen. She and Chef Gerard carried on a long-standing arrangement started by her father thirty-two years ago, after her mother died. Every evening, around the time the organized chaos of preparing dinner for a thousand guests was in full swing, she stopped in to wish the staff a good evening, just to make sure they knew they were appreciated by the owner.

The rest of the time, she, like her father, left the management of the kitchen up to Chef and, in turn, he made sure she rarely had a major problem with that area of the business.

As she did on most days, she gave him her dinner request and assured him there was no rush.

Also following family tradition, Lilli lived in a suite in the Diamond section of the hotel. Robert's original apartment had been turned into the Diamond Penthouse after her father's death and was rented out for an exorbitant amount of money, but Lilli maintained possession of the less valuable suite on the second floor.

It was the same apartment she'd moved into after graduating from college, ready to take her place as the Davenport heiress. Like her office, it was free of anything tropical or brightly colored and was minimally furnished. It served her basic needs.

And provided one secret indulgence.

She barely had time to shower and get into comfortable clothes before her dinner arrived. She turned on the television and chose something to distract her while she ate. However, despite the entertainment, the excellent meal and a second glass of wine, her thoughts kept wandering back to Connor and what awaited her in the bedroom.

If anyone really looked through Lilli's living space, they might notice the one uncommon decorating element—not a single mirror was visible. Actually, there were two in the apartment—one in the bathroom concealed in a cabinet over the sink and a full-length one hidden inside a wardrobe on the wall opposite her king-sized bed.

Even if someone did notice the absence, it might be chalked up to some quirk of Ms. Davenport's personality, like she didn't want to be reminded she was aging. Although there was some truth to that, Lilli took care of hiding her physical maturity by supplementing a good nutrition and fitness program with regular visits to the hotel salon's aesthetician. She wasn't a vain person, just conscious of how important image was. A beautiful, youthful appearance combined with money and power could get a woman *almost* anything she desired.

Just not what *she* desired most.

The real reason she kept the mirrors concealed was for her own sanity. She didn't know if it was because of the specific suite she inhabited, or whose granddaughter she was, or what had happened with Connor thirteen years ago, but she never knew when a mirror would show her a simple reflection of herself or a vision from the past. Usually it was nothing more than a replay of an insignificant moment that had occurred in that room. A few times, she even heard a snatch of a conversation.

Regardless, it was always disconcerting. Although she never acknowledged such reports as legitimate, she was aware of that sort of thing occasionally happening in other rooms because a number of guests had filed inquiries or complaints over the years. However, since no one seemed able to force such a vision on cue, those sightings remained with all the other unsolved mysteries of Crystal Island.

What she had *never* seen a guest report about was the other thing that happened to her when she looked into one of the mirrors in her suite and touched it while thinking of a person or event from her own past. If it had happened to anyone else, they may have chalked it up to imagination or daydreaming. Or they had kept it secret, just like she did.

It had been quite a while since Lilli had indulged herself with a trip into the mirror. The temptation to stay in that dimension was too powerful to do it too often. She understood that what she experienced through the mirror had to be all in her mind, but it felt completely real in that moment. And it was the only thing she had to ease the heartache when it overflowed, as it had today.

Her preparation ritual was simple but it helped her transition from hard-shelled, hotel magnate to the soft, sensual young woman Connor had known and loved. She slipped into the turquoise satin negligee with silver lace insets that she had worn the last night they were together in that room. Then she drew down the bed covers, lit the two candles set inside hurricane glasses on each nightstand and turned out all the lights. Once the stage was set for comfort and romance, she cleared her mind of everything except the face she missed so much it caused her chest to tighten, even after all these years.

She placed her right hand against the mirrored surface, called up a memory, then whispered, *"Connor."* A white mist slowly obscured her reflection. As the cloudiness rolled and thickened, she backed up and made herself comfortable on her bed without breaking eye contact with the mirror. She felt the journey begin and let the memory take over her conscious mind.

The space around her blurred, the room went black and she felt the drop in temperature before she saw when and where she'd been taken.

It wasn't even close to the sort of memory she had hoped for…

CHAPTER 9

It was autumn of 1998 and the trees on Harvard's campus were in glorious shades of reds and golds. Though this term marked the beginning of her third year in New England, Lilli was no less fascinated by seasonal changes. Growing up on a tropical island owned by her family had not prepared her for "the real world" but she was enjoying every minute of the experience and her education.

Initially she had vehemently disagreed with Chester about the necessity of going away to college to learn how to run a business. She would repeatedly ask, what could some stuffy old professor teach her that she didn't already know from hands-on experience? And he would answer that he didn't know, but the only way for her to find out if those professors had anything to offer her was to go to the best business school he knew of.

In desperation, she'd tossed out the argument that he hadn't made Bradley or Paul attend college. His answer always silenced her complaints; *she* was the one who would be running the family's flagship property, so *she* had to be better than both her older brothers put together.

And, as always, Daddy was right. What she was learning would take the Davenport profitably into the future. Her private tutors had given her a well-rounded education to supplement what living and working in a hotel had taught her. But she still had to spend every non-class, non-sleeping hour studying in order not to fall behind. She didn't really mind missing the parties or football games though. She knew exactly why she was at Harvard and it was *not* to have a good time…or catch a husband like her freshman roommate had instantly admitted to.

What she *did* mind, however, were the hours spent in classes she had absolutely no interest in, like the one she was on her way to now. Instead of the regular economics lecture, there was to be a guest speaker—a professor from Penn State who had written a controversial book comparing and contrasting the economic and moral elements that contributed to the financial disaster of 1929. *Yada, yada, yada.* The guest speaker sounded like a theorist and theorizing made her brain hurt.

She liked facts. Two plus two always equaled four in her world. She really didn't care about some genius economist's opinion of what may have happened in the 1920s. She knew the one fact that was most important to her—the Crystal Island Davenport Hotel had its Grand Opening March 1, 1924. Spending the next hour studying for her marketing exam would be far more worthwhile.

But as she considered skipping the class, she imagined how her father would scold her for not taking advantage of an opportunity to learn something she didn't know. Thus, she was on her way to yet another lecture on something she could not care less about.

To her surprise, rather than walking into the usual half-empty auditorium-style classroom, nearly every seat was already taken. Apparently, the guest speaker's lecture had been opened to other students. Lilli quickly scanned the entire room and opted for an empty seat near the aisle in the last row. That way she could easily escape if she chose.

"Excuse me," she said to the man sitting next to the aisle. "Is that seat taken?" Her expectation was that he would do the gentlemanly thing and move over one spot but he just shifted his legs so she could squeeze past him. She quickly settled in and extracted the appropriate notebook and a pen from her backpack.

"Are you enrolled in this class?" the ill-mannered fellow asked.

"Yes," she replied without giving him her attention. She hoped he wasn't one of those rude students who talked all through the lecture.

He didn't take the hint. "I was just wondering because I was told today's class was open to history and sociology students as well as business majors."

Since he hadn't asked her a question, she didn't feel obligated to respond. Instead, she opened the notebook to a blank page and printed the date and guest speaker's name at the top.

"Is there something in particular you're hoping to hear about?"

She sighed and turned toward him. "I'm sorry, but—" For the first time in her entire life she was awestruck by a good-looking man. No, not good-looking, *Gorgeous*, with a capital G...nearly jet black hair that fell over his forehead and hadn't been trimmed in a while, dark, soulful eyes and a shadow of beard along a strong jaw.

He smiled and she had to remind herself to breathe.

"I'm the one who should apologize. I should have introduced myself before asking such *personal* questions, but I guess I'm a little nervous. I wasn't expecting this large of an audience." He held out his hand. "Connor O'Malley."

Lilli blinked, swallowed, glanced at the name she'd just printed then back at his expressive eyes. She finally shook his proffered hand. "Lilli." She gathered her wits in time to withhold her last name, as she always did when meeting strangers, no matter how attractive they were. "I'm, uh, looking forward to your lecture."

His expression implied that he doubted that was true, but before she could think of some way to make up for her bad manners, he was already on his way down to the podium.

Based on the level of enthusiastic applause, Lilli guessed she was the only student in the room who didn't know who

Connor O'Malley was. And the surprises continued to mount with each passing minute.

Dr. O'Malley grabbed everyone's attention with his opening words. "Illegal hooch, primitive dancing, stable economy, flashy cars and loose women. Who can tell me which of those are rarely used to describe 1920s America?"

Lilli barely noticed that she was listening to a theorist. Of course, he shared his educated opinions and deductions, but those and his complex reasoning were cushioned between colorful anecdotes about the Roaring Twenties. Every person in the room seemed caught up in the professor's passion for his subject. Contrary to his claim of being nervous over the large audience, he exuded confidence.

And every female in the room devoured him with their eyes.

Lilli couldn't blame them. He didn't just have an attractive face; he was tall and lean and moved around the open space with a dancer's grace. It didn't hurt that he was a full-grown man with a boyish grin that he effectively used to punctuate the occasional innuendo.

She also noticed that, although he made a point of meeting the eyes of students seated throughout the auditorium, his glance touched on her often enough to have her wondering if he was making sure she didn't slip out.

At the end of the lecture, the teaching assistant announced the hours that evening when Dr. O'Malley would be signing copies of his new book at the Harvard Book Store. Lilli wanted to apologize to him for her unintentional rudeness but when he was immediately swarmed by students, she decided her apology would seem more sincere if she went to the book signing and had him autograph a copy.

Rather than make her way back to the library as planned, Lilli went off campus to her studio apartment. Her plan was to study until it was time to go but her mind kept drifting to the contents of her closet. What did it matter if she wore the jeans, sweatshirt and sneakers she'd had on all day? It wasn't like anyone would notice. Blending in was her choice, not an easy thing to do when you topped five feet eight in bare feet and your family name was Davenport.

Immediately she heard her father's lecture voice. *You must never forget, image is just as important as knowledge and accomplishments. Proper attire and grooming tells a client you respect him enough to dress your best when meeting him and it tells an employee that you are the boss, not a coworker.*

No amount of rationalizing could ever override the lessons Daddy had taught her. Professor O'Malley wasn't a client or an employee, but she did want to show him the respect he deserved. After a quick shower, she put on a pair of navy-blue dress slacks and a pink cashmere sweater. She even put on her heeled dress boots despite the added height. Usually, she kept her light blonde hair in a knot at the back of her head but she let it hang loose over her shoulders instead. Once she'd gone that far, she added a touch of tinted lipstick and mascara to her pale features.

As she inspected her image in the mirror, she barely recognized herself and was fairly sure none of her classmates or professors would either, which was fine with her.

Shoulders back. Chin up. You're a Davenport, girl. Make us proud. Daddy always knew she needed more of a push than her big brothers when it came to social interactions.

She had to remind herself to stand up straight at least a dozen times before she got to the bookstore. Because of the crowd the professor had attracted for his lecture, Lilli was prepared for a long line of admirers wanting to buy an autographed book...or get a closer look at the sexy author...so she had timed her arrival for the end of the signing session. As it turned out however, at least twenty people were still in line and she had no choice but to join it.

As one person after another glanced in her direction as though she looked familiar but they couldn't quite place her, she was tempted to kick off the boots to keep from being a head taller than most of the people in front of her.

Minutes later she *was* a head taller than everyone in front of her and Professor O'Malley looked up at her.

At first he just glanced in her direction and returned his attention to the person he was signing the book for. As the line inched forward, his gaze paused on her face long enough for his expression to go from polite notice to recognition. The pleased smile he sent her made everyone turn to see who had caused the reaction. If she could have crawled under a table until they'd all left, she would have.

Finally it was her turn and she started to deliver her planned apology but he interrupted her.

"Would you mind letting the two people behind you go first?" he asked quietly, then added, "They were here earlier but had stepped out of line."

That didn't sound like a valid excuse for making her wait but she stepped aside…and kept reminding herself to stand up straight when what she really wanted to do was magically transport back to Crystal Island where no one ever dared tell her to step aside.

"Thank you for coming," the professor said to the last person in line and then turned his infectious grin on Lilli. "I really didn't expect to see you here. I'm honored."

Did he know who she was? She narrowed her eyes at him. "Why would you feel honored?"

A twinkle in his eyes was added to his smile. "Because you really weren't interested in my lecture, but you stuck it out."

Rather than admit he was right or contradict him, she said, "I came here to apologize for being disrespectful. I should have known who you were and politely responded to your questions. My only excuse is that I was totally preoccupied with an upcoming exam. You were surrounded after class so I thought I would come here to apologize. And get one of your books."

He raised one brow. "That's really not necessary."

She picked up a book from the short stack remaining on the table and handed it to him. "Yes, it is. My father is an avid collector of anything about the twenties. This will be a perfect Christmas gift for him. Please make it out to Chester." Lilli couldn't read what the professor wrote in the book but it was several lines long.

"Please tell your father I'd be pleased to hear what he thinks of my theory," he said, handing the book back to Lilli.

"Thank you. I'll pass that on. And again, I apologize." She gave him a timid smile and turned away. She didn't expect a response from him, nor did she expect him to rise and follow her to the cashier.

"I've decided not to accept your apology," he said quietly behind her.

She looked over her shoulder at him. "Excuse me?" She couldn't help but notice that he was still an inch taller than she was. She also noticed that his grin suggested he was teasing, which made her stomach feel strange.

"Maybe, if you'd bought the book for yourself...but you didn't. So, if you want me to believe you're truly sorry, you'll have to buy me a cup of coffee. And give me an honest critique of what you thought of my lecture."

As she pulled out her credit card and handed it to the cashier, Lilli tried to think of a polite excuse to give him but the thought of having those dreamy eyes gazing into hers in such close proximity emptied her brain of coherent thought.

"I saw a place we could go just down the block. Unless you know of a better one."

She signed the receipt, put her card away and picked up her purchase.

"C'mon, take pity on the out-of-towner."

He actually sounded lonely. Considering how many of the female students would have leapt at the chance to keep him company, his being all alone seemed unlikely. But then, maybe he just wanted to talk to someone who wasn't drooling over him...at least not blatantly. "All right. Coffee, but I really do still have studying to do tonight."

As they walked to the nearby coffee house, Lilli remembered how to make small talk. The key was to not look directly at him and pretend he was just another guest at her hotel. "I know you're a professor at the University of Pennsylvania. Are you from Philadelphia originally?"

"No, but close enough. I grew up in Harrisburg, did my bachelor's and master's at Penn State and got my doctorate at UPenn. I was very fortunate to get hired right out of the program."

She nodded in appreciation. "But how did you do it so fast? Were you one of those wonder kids who skip high school and go straight to college?"

He gave her a curious look. "No. It took me the usual time, maybe even a little longer because I had to hold down a job the first couple years."

She frowned. "But you don't look that old—oh, I'm sorry, professor, not my business."

That made him grin again. "Since that almost sounded like a compliment, you needn't apologize. I turned thirty a few months ago but I think I still have some time before the gray hairs start showing. Also, I'm only an associate professor and you're not my student, so please call me Connor. Ah, here we are."

The coffee shop was clearly a popular gathering place but as they entered, a couple vacated two armchairs in a far corner. "Why don't you stake a claim on those chairs while I—"

"Absolutely not," she stated firmly. "The deal was I treat *you* to coffee. So tell me how you like it and *you* go squat." He obeyed and she headed for the "Place your order here" sign.

Now that she knew how old the professor was, she could blow away all the silly girl feelings he triggered and have an interesting conversation with a mature adult. In fact, she was now looking forward to that. Once she returned with two hot mugs, the professor excused himself and went to the rest room.

Lilli took the opportunity to read the inscription he'd written to her father:

To Chester, a fellow Roaring Twenties enthusiast, may you always find value in the past. By the way, you have a lovely daughter. Cheers, Connor O'Malley

She felt her cheeks flush over his compliment. It didn't seem appropriate but since she didn't want him to know she'd taken the first opportunity to read what he'd written, she put the book back in the bag.

When the professor returned, his first question to her was just the sort she felt comfortable with.

"So, how much longer have you got to go?"

"If I keep pushing like I have been, I could be done in a little over a year."

"Master's or are you going all the way?"

She rolled her eyes. "Heavens no. Four years is more than enough time in a classroom for me. Once I get my bachelor's, it's straight home and back to work for me."

"You're…a junior?" he asked a bit too carefully.

She watched him lean back in his chair, adding a few extra inches of space between them. "Yes."

"So that would make you…twenty-one?"

She wondered why his tone of voice had changed. "I will be, in February." She smiled and added, "On Valentine's Day."

"Well then, I'd say we're tied. You thought I was younger than I am and I thought you were older."

She shrugged. "My father always said people thought I was older because of my height. But I'm pretty sure it was because I spent all my childhood with adults." She watched him shift in his chair again, and when he spoke, he was no longer being overly careful but neither was he as relaxed as he was when they first walked in.

"You said you'll be going *back* to work after graduation. What sort of work?"

She chuckled. "I thought you wanted to hear my critique of your lecture."

He nodded. "It helps if I know the basis of your opinion before I hear it."

"That's fair," she said, continuing to smile even though he had turned serious. "But *I* would rather do it the other way round." She took a breath, straightened her spine and her expression. "I thought you were exceptional, both as a speaker and a scholar. You were passionate, animated and attentive to your audience. You had a great hook, your line was taut and the sinker closed the session with a memorable quote from your book. I walked into that room expecting to be bored and ended up surprised at how quickly the hour had passed. Plus, I learned quite a few new things I'd never considered before. If Michelin ranked academic lectures, they would give you all three of their stars."

He laughed and relaxed a little more. "Would you mind putting all that in writing? My editor could always use a little more convincing of how talented I am. Now let me guess your background based on some of the words you used. Hook, line and sinker is an old phrase; could be because of those adults who had you growing up too fast, or your family's in the fishing industry."

She giggled. "Fishing is a hobby of my father's and we spent a lot of time together. Try again."

"Your bold use of adjectives tells me you might be descended from fiction writers…or professional reviewers. English teachers?"

She made a different face at him for each wrong guess.

"All right. This one has to be the definitive clue—three stars from Michelin, which, by the way, pushed your critique into the sucking-up category, and tells me that you grew up working in the family restaurant."

"Very close. I grew up in a hotel owned by my family. And *that's* what I'll be going back to after graduation. I'm only here because my father refused to let me step into a management position until I earned a business degree."

He frowned and squinted at her. "Hotel business? The name on your credit card was Lillian…*Davenport*…and your father's name is Chester…"

"You looked at my credit card?"

"It was sitting on the counter right in front of me. Don't change the subject. Is it a strange coincidence or are you one of the Davenport Hotel heirs?"

That caused her to straighten her spine without needing a reminder. "I don't like the word *heir*. It suggests I'll be given something valuable that I haven't worked for. But let me tell you, my father not only insisted I get a business degree, but I have to graduate in the top ten percent of the class to *inherit* anything. All I've been doing for two years is studying to make sure that happens. Besides that, he insisted my brothers and I work in every department of the resort, including grounds maintenance and housekeeping, with no special concessions for who we were. At five years old, when the children of guests were splashing in the pool or playing in the arcade, I was helping the gardeners pick up fallen palm fronds and litter. And at—"

The worried look in his eyes stopped her rant. "Oh dear. I can't believe I just went off on you like that." She took a deep breath. "I don't suppose it will help to apologize again. Or swear I have no idea what made me tell you those things. I never tell *anyone* personal information. It's a Davenport family rule."

"Never?" he asked, still looking wary.

She shook her head.

"Not even to a girlfriend?" He paused a beat before adding, "Or boyfriend?"

She picked up her coffee mug and took a sip. "My circumstances have never made it easy to have friends, girls or boys, at least not ones I could confide in. Besides, my father always said 'complaining just makes a tough job harder and makes people around you uncomfortable', which is obviously what I did to you. I am sorry. Again."

He raised one brow. "I'm thinking you were lucky to have such a wise father. But what do you say we call a moratorium on you apologizing to me. You didn't make me uncomfortable, just really curious. My life circumstances are so far removed from yours that there's a thousand questions buzzing in my brain. But since my use of one word opened a locked door, I'll silence my curiosity about your personal life. However, if you wouldn't mind, I would like to ask a question about my lecture."

"Of course," she said, relieved to have the conversation back on an impersonal track.

"Because of my field of study, I'm familiar with the name Robert Davenport and his hotel's relevance to the era. Was there anything I mentioned that struck you as incorrect or even different from what you've been told about that time period?"

Lilli wrinkled her nose. "Not that I noticed. But I have to admit, I'm not much of a history buff. Not like my father."

His eyes noticeably brightened and he sat forward. "You said your father was an avid collector. Might he have any memoires or journals from either of his parents?"

She shrugged. "I really don't know. He never mentioned having anything like that…which is odd now that I think of it. I could ask." His excitement was palpable and she couldn't decide how that made her feel.

"At the risk of pushing another sensitive button, if he does have anything like that, would you also ask if he'd be willing to let me view them, strictly from a scholarly point of interest, of course."

Now she knew how she felt. *Disappointed.* Somewhere in her girly brain she had imagined this gorgeous man was interested in her. Before she could respond, he spoke again.

"If I were you, I might be wondering if I'd known who you were all along and just insisted we have coffee to give me an opportunity to take advantage of you."

"Well, it is a little—"

"Wrong," he interrupted, holding up a finger. "I swear I had no clue who you were, not even when I saw your credit card. The reason I wanted to spend some time with you is because from the moment you sat next to me in the lecture hall, I was ready to forget about everyone else in that room and what I was there to do. And then you made it clear you had no idea who I was and didn't care to find out, which, of course, only made you more attractive. To be perfectly blunt, you had an immediate *physical* effect on me, and the last time that happened to me, I was a teenager."

She felt her cheeks flushing and was about to admit that he had affected her as well when he continued.

"But now that I know how young you are, I realize how inappropriate my thoughts were, and I only admitted my reaction to make sure you understand my motives may have been selfish but had nothing to do with you being a Davenport."

Lilli's thoughts seesawed back and forth with each of his sentences. He was instantly attracted to her, but was only interested in her because she hadn't shown interest in him. He considered her a child, but thought her father sounded wise. He was excited about her being a Davenport, but for historical research reasons rather than her wealth or status. Instead of responding to his confession, she took one more sip of her coffee and set the mug down in a way she hoped would indicate an end to their chat.

"Like I said, I still have some studying to do for tomorrow's exam." She rose and held out her hand to him. "It was very nice to meet you Doctor O'Malley. This was…a welcome distraction."

He got to his feet and enclosed her hand in both of his. "Likewise, Miss Davenport."

She gave him a closed-mouth smile and tried to withdraw her hand but he held on.

"I parked my car at the bookstore. Let me give you a ride back to your dorm."

"Thank you, but I don't live on campus. I can easily catch the bus from here to my apartment building." She tried not to notice how firmly he was hanging on to her hand.

"Nonsense. It's late and I tricked you into keeping me company for an hour when you needed to be studying. At least let me save you from waiting for a bus."

He was just being logical, she thought, and she wasn't even sure when a bus was due. "That would be helpful." With that, he released her hand and they went outside. "Are you scheduled for any more speaking engagements?" It was the only impersonal question she could quickly think of to fill the short distance to his car.

"I'll be at six schools over the next ten days. My editor assured me it's the best way to get the book talked about quickly. Tomorrow afternoon I'll be at Brown."

Seconds later, he was opening the passenger door of his car and she stepped in. Giving him driving directions one piece at a time eliminated the need for more conversation until he came to a stop in front of her building's entrance.

"Thank you," she said, clutching the bookstore bag in one hand and her purse in the other. She was not taking any chance of his holding her hand again. "Good luck on the rest of your tour." She cracked open the door then remembered what he'd asked her to do for him. "Oh, I almost forgot. I promise to check with my father about his collection, but how would you like me to let you know what he says?"

He chuckled. "I really must be distracted." He turned toward the back seat then frowned. "My cards are in my briefcase and it's in the trunk. Any chance you have a piece of paper and pen?"

"Sure." She pulled a pen out of her purse and tore off a piece of the bookstore's paper bag.

He wrote down his office and cell numbers, and his email address, and finished by adding *Connor* at the end. As he handed back the paper and her pen, he said, "I'd like to be able to reach you also…just in case I don't hear from you, say in a year or so."

Since she felt certain he was far too busy to bother her needlessly, she tore off another piece of the bag and wrote down her name and phone number. But as she handed him the scrap of paper, he captured her hand again.

To her complete surprise, he placed a soft kiss on her knuckles. "Thank you for making this a memorable day."

She swallowed hard and stared at the spot he had just kissed. It felt funny.

He let go of her hand but touched her chin with his index finger. "Do I need to apologize for that?" he asked softly.

She raised her gaze and met his eyes. He seemed closer than necessary. And she couldn't seem to make herself move away. She managed to whisper, *"No."*

"What is it about you that makes me want to forget about everything else?" There was confusion in his voice and wonder in his eyes. When she didn't answer, he made another confession. "Your hand isn't what I wanted to kiss."

She took a breath and screwed up the nerve to say what she wanted from him. "I think...I think I'd like to know what it would feel like if you...kissed my mouth...if you wouldn't mind." She closed her eyes, tilted her head back, pursed her lips, and waited for her first real kiss.

Instead of feeling his mouth touching hers, his finger stroked her cheek. She opened her eyes and instantly saw that he was leaning back against the door, as far from her as possible without getting out of the car. She pushed the passenger door open to escape the humiliation but he grasped her arm.

"Lilli, wait. I wanted to, believe me. I mean I *really* wanted to. And normally I would have happily accepted such a sweet invitation and not given it another thought. I don't know, maybe I suddenly developed a conscience, but something told me kissing you the way I want to, well, it would be a mistake. At least for tonight. So, here's what I propose. If, on February fourteenth, you still think you'd like me to kiss you, call me, and I'll come back here to properly follow through. But if you change your mind between now and then, for any reason, you don't need to tell me anything."

Lilli blinked as she felt herself return to the present and frowned at the reflection in the mirror. Of all her memories involving Connor, why would that one have played out in minute-to-minute detail? She couldn't remember a single time when the mirror hadn't replayed a scene connected to what she had in mind and she had definitely been thinking about making love with Connor. Their first encounter was the least sexual of all their time together.

She reviewed that day with her conscious mind and, considering her innocence and the speed at which their relationship escalated afterward, she knew Connor's actions had been extremely chivalrous. And although there wasn't even one hot kiss, he had awakened a desire in her for something other than academic achievement.

Although it was almost unheard of among her classmates, Lilli was still a virgin when she'd met Connor, not because she was holding out for Mr. Perfect or a wedding ring, but she simply couldn't see the point in expending any of her energy on something she had no interest in. In the time it took to drink one cup of coffee, sex had gone from the bottom of her priority list all the way to the top.

By her twenty-first birthday, Lilli had no doubt about what she wanted from Connor O'Malley and wasted no time denying it.

So why not *that* scene? The birthday celebration that winter evening had begun a bit awkwardly but ended with a bang, several big bangs in fact.

Or why not the picnic by the waterfall the first time he came to the island? Or the night he put the engagement ring on her finger? Why replay how they met?

A tinkling sound, like wind chimes, grabbed her attention. It seemed to be coming from the balcony outside her bedroom. She rose and moved the drapery aside just enough to take a peak. There was nothing out there to explain the sound but what she saw gave her a chill. The full moon had just risen above the horizon and a brilliant beam of light was streaking across the ocean and onto a particular spot on the beach.

She remembered another night thirteen years ago when a full moon sent out a beam exactly like that. The mirror had allowed her to relive her and Connor's first hours together. The moonbeam was an eerie reminder of their last.

It meant *something*. Of that she was certain. But what?

"You need to remember."

Lilli whirled around to see who had dared to enter her bedroom. But no one was there. She had clearly heard a man's voice, however. "Grandpa? Is that you? I don't need a reminder. I could never forget how Connor and I met."

Several seconds went by before she heard the voice again, but this time it sounded as though it came from far away. *"Remember the girl you were. It's time…"*

The voice drifted off and a shiver was the only confirmation Lilli received. She had just been visited by a Davenport spirit, possibly her grandfather, Robert, but the admonishing tone made her think more of her father, Chester.

Why would one of them talk to her tonight, after all the times she had called out to them in the past? And, if it was Robert and he only had a momentary connection, why would he waste it like that, when all she ever wanted to hear from him was how he'd died?

It wasn't like she'd actually forgotten what she was like back then—young, naive, trusting her feelings and filled with the confidence that her future would be everything she dreamed it to be.

But then Connor didn't return when he was supposed to, which meant he was prevented or chose not to. Either way, she'd lost him and the girl she used to be ceased to exist.

Nothing good could come from remembering any of that.

CHAPTER 10

"I was so envious of you back in high school," Maggie admitted. After enjoying the delectable picnic, they'd stretched out on the lounge to watch the moon rise over the ocean.

Noah grazed her arm with his fingertips. "Because of my beautiful long hair or long eyelashes?"

She giggled. "Well, those were two of your most talked-about features. But, no, it was because of all the places you'd been to and things you'd seen. I remember you had moved to Clarksville from Germany, and before that it was, um, Hawaii?"

His chest automatically tightened but he forced his voice to sound casual. "Japan. Hawaii was before that and San Antonio before that. I was too young to appreciate the fact that I got to stay there long enough to get through all of grade school."

"And when you left Tennessee, you went to…"

"Fort Bragg, in North Carolina. Then there was another stint in Germany before I could get off the Army train by going to college."

She shook her head. "Wow. I have yet to leave the continental United States. Tell me, what was your favorite place of all?"

He closed his eyes for a moment and took a slow, calming breath. "Clarksville, Tennessee, because that's where I met the best friend I ever had. It was also my least favorite place because I had to leave so soon."

She gave him a soft kiss and a smile. "Thank you, but I meant favorite like—"

His expression tightened again. "Could we change the subject please?"

She finally noticed how tense he was. "What's the matter? Did I say something—"

He cut her off with a quick kiss on her mouth. "Of course not. I'm sorry. I make a point of *not* thinking about those years."

"Oh. I didn't realize—" She eased out of his arms and sat up to look at his face. "I just got the same feeling I had before…at lunch, when you asked me about what adventure I planned for after this assignment. You keep insisting I have a talent. Well, if I do, it's telling me you're hiding something. It must involve me or else I wouldn't feel it. But I don't see what I have to do with any of the places you lived."

He frowned and narrowed his eyes at her. "I'm starting to lose my fascination with your special talents." When she just kept staring at him without speaking, he groaned. "You're not going to let this go are you?"

She shook her head. "I could, but it would change how comfortable I am with you."

"If I tell you, it'll probably change anyway."

"Then you have nothing to lose."

It took him a few more seconds to give in. "Fine, but remember that I warned you." After another pause, he delivered the statement he thought explained everything. "I'm not like my father. I could never be happy with the life he had."

She tilted her head. "And I'm not like my mother."

"No, but I'm afraid you might be like mine."

Her eyes abruptly widened. "I only talked to her once, or maybe twice. She seemed nice enough but I don't remember thinking we had anything in common…besides liking you."

He snorted. "The reason you hardly talked to her was that she was hardly ever there. A good part of that year and the next, she was in Afghanistan, *unofficially*, of course. My parents had a relationship that not many couples would choose but somehow it worked for them. She was already on the officer track in the army when my dad met her and he understood from the start that he could support her goals or move on. He loved her enough to follow her to the corners of the Earth with no assurance that they would ever have a permanent home or that she would not come home to him in a box one day. The only thing he asked was that she have one child with him."

Maggie took advantage of his pause to comment. "I gather *you* were that child. But I remember you and your dad having a good relationship."

"We had a *great* relationship," Noah said sincerely. "He was a better father *and* mother than a lot of kids have. And I am absolutely certain he is still completely happy with the choices he made in his life."

"What are they doing now?"

"They finally own a home. Outside of D.C., in Virginia. Mother retired from active duty as a full colonel, but she's still bucking for General through some sort of national security consultant position. Dad is still the one who makes sure she never has to be bothered by the little things that are part of ordinary people's lives. It took me a really long time to accept the fact that he never resented her ambition the way I did."

He was quiet again for a bit before continuing. "As far as I could tell, he never questioned what she was doing or whether she loved him as much as he loved her. But I could see that neither of us would ever be exciting enough to compete with the adventures the army offered."

Maggie nodded slowly. "And that's why you wanted an old-fashioned wife. But it doesn't explain what I have to do with any of it. And don't lie or give me some half-truth."

He made a face. "I told you how crazy you made me as a kid and how it tore me up when I had to leave. Now we're together again as adults, and I'm having a really hard time not thinking about a future with you."

"That doesn't sound bad to me." She leaned forward to kiss him but he held her back.

"But it does to me. You admitted that you get bored easily and need risky adventures in between tedious assignments. Being with you, being able to hold you, and the way you respond to me…well, now I can barely imagine a life without you in it. And at the same time, I can't imagine having a life with someone who needs a fix of adrenalin on a regular basis in order to put up with an ordinary life."

As understanding set in, annoyance did as well. "What do you know about an ordinary life? Believe me, ordinary people do not stay in exclusive resort penthouses for months at a time, or *usually* go with the chef's recommendation in five-star restaurants. Ordinary people don't eat truffles. Or have assistants. Nor do they have the luxury of working when the mood hits them. Ordinary people have minimum wage jobs and live in apartments because they can't afford to buy a home."

He opened his mouth but she pressed her finger to his lips. "No. I'm not finished. You had a father who loved you and showed you how to make compromises to be happy. You had a mother who showed you how to go for whatever you want no matter the obstacles. You learned about the world and the people in it by real experience. You went to college and came out with an opportunity to have a dream job, while other graduates couldn't even get hired in a coffee shop because they were now over-qualified for minimum wage. If you had had an *ordinary* life, your imagination may never have developed enough to become a bestselling horror author.

"I admire what your mother has accomplished, but I am *nothing* like her. If I had a major career goal or even one ounce of ambition, do you think I'd be working temp jobs?

The only goal I've ever had is to live a good life, to see as much of the world as possible and to experience as much good, *safe* fun as I can afford. I told you about some of the boring jobs I've had, but I've also had some really interesting ones. In fact I just started one that is so fascinating, I'm having more fun than any adventure I ever had before."

She took a quick breath then finished her defense. "I have lived in the same apartment for five years. Yes, I like to travel, but I always want to have a home base to return to. And, by the way, if I was ever fortunate enough to have children, I would want to be as much a part of their upbringing as your father was in yours."

He watched her with a wary expression for a moment, in case she had more to say before he spoke. When her expression softened a bit, he took his chance.

"In other words, I've been a spoiled brat who's lucky to be sitting here with the most beautiful, brilliant, talented, sensitive, and *tolerant* woman on the planet." He sighed. "You're right…about everything. And I'm truly sorry for jumping to a conclusion based on very little. Forgive me?"

She leaned forward and kissed him softly. "Of course. It's only fair since I thought you were gay all these years."

He grinned. "And don't forget how you tortured me for a year. I think that alone is worth my being forgiven for a mistake or two."

She curled into his body. "All right. I'll give you that, but you're only allowed one more mistake before I get to lecture you again."

He hugged her firmly. "So are we good?"

"Not good. We're great."

"Let's take a walk," Noah suggested, drawing her to her feet. "We won't need these." He shed his robe and helped her out of hers.

Despite being totally exposed several times, she still felt self-conscious in her old, one-piece bathing suit. If this situation had ever crossed her mind, she would have bought a new one. But as his appreciative gaze slid over her body she guessed the faded fabric wouldn't be staying on for long anyway.

The moon had risen high in the sky while they'd been in the cabana, and between its brilliance and the clear, star-studded sky, they had no trouble seeing where they were going. They strolled along with their arms around each other's waists, but they were not alone on the beach and that awareness kept them from doing anything more intimate.

Maggie was perfectly content to remain quiet…for about two minutes. "Okay, I agreed not to talk about it while we ate, but I'm really anxious to hear what your research turned up today."

He gave her waist a little squeeze. "Quite a bit actually, and I'm feeling really good about all the ideas I got. I found dozens of real-life mysteries and reports of supernatural phenomena that I could work with. Of course Robert Davenport's supposed suicide still stands out for me."

Her stomach soured a bit as he went on with obvious excitement.

"The era of the 1920s generally makes a great backdrop for almost any story, but the family's insistence that Robert would never have killed himself opens the door to several possible plots. A straight murder mystery is obvious but too boring for my readers. Evil demon lurking in the hotel hallways is more my staple, but there's also the angle of him hanging around as a ghost, terrorizing anyone who stays in his suite. Or he could have possessed some innocent person to carry out his retribution on…well, I'm not sure who might have wanted him dead or why. I haven't developed that thought much."

"They all sound good. But, um, wouldn't you need the permission of the Davenport family to use their ancestor?"

He shrugged. "I wouldn't use his real name. I'm not even using the hotel name, although it will probably be obvious from other details I include. When my agent contacted the Davenport's marketing division, they were really stoked about the publicity potential so I don't think there'll be a problem."

You couldn't be more wrong, Maggie thought, then reminded herself not to dwell on problems tonight. She had plenty of time and a lot could happen before she had to do anything. Her mood lifted considerably with Noah's next words.

"I found several mentions of The Weeping Woman. One of the accounts suggested she might be a young hotel maid who was found dead on the beach in 1927. It was generally believed the girl had gotten pregnant illegitimately and just walked into the ocean to end her shame. But here's the interesting part. The examining doctor reported seeing bruises on her throat and stated she may have been strangled first. In those days though, her death wouldn't be important enough to investigate so the possibility of murder was buried along with her body."

"The maid I saw said something about her *babe* but she was turned away from me and on her knees so I couldn't say whether she had a pregnant belly."

"Sounds like the unsolved murder victim could have been your Irish maid but your noticing the lack of brogue in the voice you heard on the trail would seem to contradict her being The Weeping Woman. Besides, the earliest mention of her was in 1945."

"*But*," Maggie countered. "That could have just been when the spirit was given an identifying nickname."

"True." Noah added that possibility to his mental file. "The other specific incident that caught my attention was a mention of another suicide death in 1927. That one was a man."

"Not Robert Davenport?"

"No, his was three years later. Plus, this man's was by drowning, like the maid. But it did make me realize how often a questionable death on the island was labeled suicide."

Maggie made a face at him. "Let me guess. You're thinking Hotel Hellgate makes people want to kill themselves."

Noah laughed aloud. "I hadn't gone in that direction yet. But I probably would have eventually. Anyway, there are a lot of possibilities besides those. The 1928 hurricane alone accounted for at least a hundred dead on the island, mostly employees of the hotel who were outside or in the workers' barracks when it passed over. Back then they had no warning and may not have had any idea what a hurricane was. Bottom line is, there were a lot of people who died or disappeared from here over the years."

They had walked quite a distance before their way was blocked by a thick stand of sea grape plants. There, where the cleared beach ended and the broad-leafed vegetation began, was an egg-shaped geode, as tall as Maggie. It had a long crack down the side facing the ocean but it wasn't possible to tell what sort of crystal was inside.

Noah stroked the smooth rock face then turned to her with a broad grin. "But here's the best part of everything I read. A group of ghost hunters spent some time here a few years ago. They picked up so many different hot spots, they concluded this whole island is a doorway between dimensions. Would you believe that? A supernatural portal could be the perfect tool for *Hotel Hellgate*! What do you think?"

"I think…" She was distracted by the strong energy that seemed to be pulsating off the rock. It was different from what she'd felt in the Amethyst Cave, different from the energy field along the nature trail. Her gaze focused on how pointedly the moon's beam was illuminating the crack, as though awakening something inside. *"How strange,"* she mumbled as she ran her index finger along the crack.

"Maggie?"

She forced her attention back to him. "I think…you're right. It's perfect." *Now if you'll just steer away from Robert Davenport as a main character…*

"In which case, the person who built the resort would be like a gatekeeper for Hell." He gave her a firm hug. "Thank you."

Her eyes narrowed with alarm as she envisioned her name being mentioned in his book's acknowledgements. Her voice came out slightly pitchy as she asked, "Why thank me? I've hardly done anything yet."

He shrugged. "If not for you I wouldn't have done all that research so soon. I think you're my new muse." He slipped his hands around her waist and eased her closer. "Enough talking." He leaned back against the rock, drew her close and kissed her forehead. "It's a beautiful night." He kissed each cheekbone.

A strange tingling enveloped her bare feet.

"The moon is putting on a show just for us." He kissed her nose.

The tingling spread up her legs.

"And that ocean is really warm." He kissed her mouth then outlined her lips with his tongue.

Her body was being aroused yet her mind was sidetracked by the ticklish sensation now shimmering throughout her body. Something physical was happening to her that had nothing to do with Noah's seduction. The peculiar sensation strengthened, peaked with a strong wave of dizziness then completely went away.

"We're completely alone…and you did say you like trying new things…"

She gave herself over to his mesmerizing kisses, his voice, his touch, his suggestion that they continue their play in the water. There was nothing she would *not* do with him.

Until a wave splashed over her feet and deposited a clingy glob of seaweed. She kicked it off and watched a family of tiny crabs scramble back toward the sea. She was no longer entranced enough to follow him into that dark abyss. "Maybe another time, but I wouldn't mind returning to that cushy lounge for two in the caba—"

Noah grabbed her hand and pulled her into a light jog back down the beach. A minute later they came to an abrupt halt. Where there had been ten colorfully-striped tents, there was now only a single tan one. As they got closer they heard a woman's shrill giggle and the flaps of the tent were securely closed. It made no sense.

On the sand beside the tent were two neatly-folded, green-striped seersucker cover-ups with gold waist ties. Maggie picked them up and handed one to Noah. "Something's very wrong here," she whispered as she put on the wrap. "Maybe we got turned around somehow. Let's just go back inside the hotel and get our bearings. We can return these once we find the cabana you reserved."

Noah's confused expression elevated to worry when they couldn't find the side door they had used to exit. Anxious to figure out where they'd gone wrong, they walked the hotel's perimeter until they came to the lobby entrance, only to be brought to another sudden stop inside the doors. Everyone was in costume. Flapper dresses, feathered boas and sequined headbands. Old-fashioned tuxedos and white spats over shiny black shoes. Even the staff's Hawaiian-patterned uniforms had been changed to old safari-style outfits to match whatever party theme was going on.

"Mr. and Mrs. Nash?"

Maggie recognized the Jamaican accent immediately. It was the bellman, Reynard, wearing a crisp khaki ensemble complete with pith helmet.

"If ya will please follow me, I will take ya to your bungalow."

"Bungalow?" Noah asked in an edgy tone. "We have the Diamond Penthouse. Here, in the main building. And we also had a private cabana reserved for this whole night and something—"

"I assure ya I can explain everyt'ing but now ya *really* must come with me. Quickly, please."

Maggie nudged Noah to follow Reynard as he hurried outside to a horse-drawn carriage on a wooden boardwalk. "Am I crazy or did I completely miss seeing this before?"

He helped her into the back seat then joined her. "Not crazy. There was a paved path here this morning…for golf carts, not carriages."

Reynard lightly flicked the reins and the horse clopped forward.

It was all much too strange, so Maggie chose something simple to question. "Reynard, you know I'm not Mrs. Nash."

"It will be much easier if ya be introducing yourself as such while ya're here."

Noah leaned forward and tapped Reynard's shoulder. "What do you mean, *here*?" He didn't get an answer but the carriage came to a halt mere seconds later.

Maggie and Noah shared a bewildered look. They were in front of a row of bungalows, somewhat similar to the ones they'd seen that morning though not nearly as many. The architecture seemed different and none of them were painted the same colors as before. The only thing that hadn't changed were the two yellow rockers on the porch of the one Reynard had stopped in front of. They waited until they were all inside then spilled out their questions in a rush.

"What's going on?"

"Why can't we go back to our suite?"

"Why weren't we advised of any of this in advance?"

"Why do we need to pretend I'm Mrs. Nash?"

"Which brings me back to what you meant by *here*?"

Reynard held up a hand as he lit a kerosene lamp. "I only have a few minutes before being discovered so I must give ya de short version. Ya are still at de Davenport Resort. In fact, ya passed by dis exact bungalow earlier today. However, when de full moon reached its zenith while ya were at de portal, de two of ya were transported to de year 1927. Ya cannot go back to de suite ya were in because Mr. and Mrs. Robert Davenport are in residence dere at dis time."

"1927?" Maggie and Noah exclaimed simultaneously.

Reynard quickly continued before they could ask more questions. "Ya were unable to bring anyt'ing with ya but what you were wearing or holding at de time. Unfortunately dat was not much so I left the dressing gowns for ya to find. Because someone felt sorry for ya, I was given a rather unusual opportunity in exchange for making certain arrangements for ya, like dis bungalow.

"The closet and drawers have time-appropriate clothing and ya will have no problem signing for meals in de dining room or through room service. But in case you need cash, dere be a supply of currency in de jewelry cabinet. Matches for de oil lamps can be found dere as well. At dis time, only de main areas of de hotel have electric lighting."

He handed Noah the key to the bungalow then turned to Maggie. "Oh yes, about your name. De mid-nineteen-twenties were hardly an era of Victorian morals in dis place, but saying ya are his wife will avoid a lot of unnecessary explanations." He started toward the door then turned back. "Also, if asked who sent ya, say *Teddy Roosevelt*. And now I must be on my way. I hope you have a pleasant and successful stay."

"Hold on," Noah said, grasping Reynard's arm before he could get out the door. "Say we accept everything you said, what are we supposed to do now? How do we get back?"

Reynard's jaw tensed and his gaze darted upward, as though he were listening to someone above. "Dey know I am here."

"They *who*?" Noah demanded.

Reynard's speech picked up to auctioneer speed. "Dere is somet'ing ya have to fix or someone ya must save from catastrophe. I was not given dat information. Usually de pair has an idea about what dey must rectify…like a matter or person dey were discussing right before dey transported. Ya had better figure dat part out quickly because ya will not be able to get back unless ya complete whatever ya were sent here to accomplish.

"Even if ya do succeed, de reverse transport can only take place from de same spot on de beach—" His gaze shot upward again, then his expression was one of annoyance.

"Ya only have five days to complete your task, beginning today. Each night, when de moon is at its zenith, de portal will allow ya through *if* ya have completed your task. It is important ya stay together at dat time to make sure ya *both* return. De fifth night will be your final opportunity to go back."

"That's ridiculous!" Maggie exclaimed. "What if we don't succeed in five days?"

"Ya will live out your days here on Crystal Island, in *dis* time. I am quite sure ya would not care for de…restrictions. I must go."

Noah tried to stop him again but he was gone. Reynard had literally vanished in the blink of an eye.

CHAPTER 11

*W*ho did that? Karma roared. *Who gave the fox freedom to interact?*

None of the Abstracts spoke but one by one their thoughts shifted to Love.

I am sorry, Love replied. *But the test was unfairly difficult. They only have five days before all their fates are sealed forever. It was illogical to have them spend half that time figuring out when and where they were and how to manage.*

Justice rose to Love's defense. *Love has a valid point, one that I had been thinking of raising. Though I am not convinced releasing the fox was the best solution. Since I presented this mission I will take the responsibility of getting Deception back in his cage.*

Karma was far from satisfied. *See to it that you do without delay. Earth's humans are having a difficult enough time without the trickster running freely through the ages, stirring up all manners of mischief.*

Justice had not finished its thought on the matter. *What is done is done. As I brought up previously, this case is an important and time-sensitive one, but it is not an easy one to resolve. The unusually short time period created an additional challenge that others did not have. Therefore, the assistance this pair was given somewhat balances the scales. However, Love broke a rule and her method put humanity at risk. It is up to The First to determine Love's punishment, but I recommend leniency due to extenuating circumstances.*

The First refrained from offering an opinion. Although no previous pair had been given so much assistance at the outset, Justice was correct in the conclusion that the extra assistance balanced the shorter time. What had not been repeated was that if *this* pair failed all of Earth's humans would suffer.

At the moment, The First had to decide what to do about Love's transgression despite the rationale of it.

Deception was serving a sentence of restraint on Crystal Island due to his unapproved involvement in the development of American technology in the 1970s. It didn't matter that his interference turned out to be generally beneficial. It was against the rules to interact directly with Earth humans unless agreed upon by The Council. And they would never have granted such permission to Deception. The fox's desire to be free, even for an hour, would make a deal with him the quickest solution to Love's desire to help Maggie and Noah. The problem was that Love had not made proper arrangements to re-incarcerate the fox immediately afterward.

An official reprimand should be recorded in The Book. It definitely should. But that would not be done in this case. The First always tended to give Love more leeway than the others…perhaps because *Love* tended to only break the rules for *very* good reasons.

CHAPTER 12

Noah slowly carried the kerosene lamp throughout the room, opening drawers, checking behind curtains, the backs of pictures and the bottoms of lamps.

Maggie watched him get more agitated as the seconds ticked by. "What are you doing?"

"Looking for a hidden camera or recording device. This has got to be an elaborate practical joke of some kind."

"Noah, we just saw that man disappear into thin air. That would be awfully hard to create."

"Maybe not. A lot can be done with special effects. Maybe a magician is involved."

"Didn't you say you believed anything is possible?" She got a smirk for her reminder as he continued his search. Maggie bit her lip as he continued crawling along, looking under every piece of furniture. "Noah? You know that talent you insist I have?"

He looked up at her and his expression changed from annoyed to curious. "Are you picking up something?"

"Maybe. And maybe before too. Back on the beach. When we reached the end of the cleared sand. I didn't say anything because you were kissing me…"

He rose and grasped her hands. "What happened?"

"I felt tingling, or maybe it was more of a shimmering, different from what I felt on the trail this morning. It started at my feet and moved up my body."

"Do you think you experienced a temporal shift?"

She shrugged. "I don't even know what that means. It just felt...weird and then it went away. But there was something else very strange. The moonlight...it...was shining a beam directly into the crack in that rock and...and I swear I saw a glow deep inside."

He combed his fingers through her hair and quietly said, "Okay. That could have just been a reflection...but adding the feeling you described does push it into the weird category."

She made a face. "Well, as long as you're giving me the benefit of the doubt, there's one more thing. When Reynard was telling us where, or rather *when* we are, and about us having to accomplish something, I was filled with the certainty that he was telling the truth. Like I told you this morning, I've always been pretty good at telling if someone was lying. What he told us sounds crazy. I don't understand how someone could be transported through time, except in a novel or a movie. And yet, I don't have a doubt in my mind that we're now in a different time period than we were."

"He may have given us a hint about the how. He said 'they' knew he was here, and twice he looked up as though whoever *they* are, they're on a higher plane. Does that make sense?"

She raised one eyebrow. "I'm pretty sure none of this is going to make sense. But if we really did travel back in time, why not blame it on a supernatural power? We certainly didn't travel in a time machine. What makes even less sense is Reynard's explanation about us having to fix something or save someone in order to get back. Plus, it sounds like we'll be *punished* if we don't. At least he, or *they*, could have given us a clue."

"Well, maybe he did. He hinted that it was about something or someone we were discussing right before we got to that rock. That could be The Weeping Woman."

"Or the Irish maid," she added.

"Or the other suicide-by-drowning victim. Or Robert Davenport. Or the countless others who died here over the years. We were talking about a lot of people." Noah let out a frustrated sigh then added. "But we were definitely talking about people dying of causes other than illness or old age, not a *thing* that went wrong or an event that could be changed by someone going back in time. From that we could at least focus on saving rather than fixing."

"And, yes, we were talking about a lot of people, but I would think it would be about someone who died in this specific year, 1927. Plus, I think it's relevant that we personally only had something supernatural happen involving three of them...assuming the man you saw in your mirror was Davenport."

"Reynard did say the Davenports were in that suite at the moment."

It was her turn to sigh aloud. "How are we supposed to figure out which one we're supposed to save?"

"Maybe it's obvious. After all, we only know one of them by name and where to find him this week. We're both smart and have active imaginations. I have no doubt we'll figure this out...as long as we don't waste time trying to make sense of it." Noah finished his inspection with a shake of his head. "I don't see anything here that suggests we're being punked. But before we cross over the impossible line with both feet, let's get dressed and go back to the lobby. If we've been transported in time, we should be able to find some hard evidence there."

Noah lit a second oil lamp in the bedroom to help them review their clothing options. The female underwear alone was enough to keep them from dressing quickly. There were no bras or panties as Maggie was accustomed to but there were stiff, silk bodice pieces that laced up on the side and flattened the bosom, silk boxer-style drawers, chemises and a variety of slips. Garter belts and stockings with black seams were in abundance. It all made Maggie frown and Noah grin.

The array of dresses ranged from lightweight shifts made up of layers of pastel chiffon to brightly sequined and fringed flapper numbers. Her only other choice seemed to be a dowdy, navy-blue pleated skirt and long jacket with a selection of silk blouses and striped jerseys.

Noah had much less to choose from—brown, gray or white, wide-legged trousers with high waists and cuffs and a matching suit jacket for each. There were five starched white and pinstriped shirts and two tuxedos, one with long tails, and lots of ties and suspenders. Much to Maggie's amusement, there was also a pair of plaid knickers and a pullover sweater.

"I'm pretty sure that goes with my navy ensemble…maybe for when we go golfing."

Their moods rose another notch when they discovered the cache of hats, shoes, accessories and jewelry, all of which looked very expensive…and very old. Whether this all turned out to be a hoax or they had really been transported, it seemed to have a fairly substantial fun factor built in. They had noticed how dressed up everyone was and chose accordingly so as not to stand out in any way, at least until they figured out what was going on.

They both agreed Maggie looked adorable in the sleeveless gold fringe over black silk shift. She accessorized with a gold sequined headband, a long black pearl necklace and several bracelets. Noah especially liked the dark, seamed stockings but he wasn't crazy about the bright red lipstick or the kohl eye shadow even though Maggie insisted she was copying what she'd seen in the lobby.

Noah, on the other hand, was incredibly handsome in the black tuxedo with the shorter jacket and gold brocade cummerbund and bowtie. Taking Maggie's makeup lead, he used some goo from a Murray's Superior Pomade jar to slick back his hair. Before leaving the bedroom he grabbed some bills out of the jewelry cabinet and stuffed them in his pocket.

He started to close the cabinet but stopped to take one more accessory—a gold pocket watch with an ornate cover and a gold chain with a clip on the end. He flipped open the cover and his look of admiration turned to a frown. He squinted at the inside for several seconds. "It's showing ten-thirty. That seems about right. I think it was a little after nine-thirty when whatever happened, happened. But *this* is really strange." He handed her the watch. "Am I seeing things or do these two people look an awful lot like us?"

She held the watch closer to the light. Inserted opposite the timepiece was a small round wedding photo of a couple who looked just like them. "Funny but I don't remember posing for this."

He shrugged and gave her a wink. "Not remembering doesn't mean it didn't happen. Maybe it was taken in one of our past lives. Or maybe we've been here before. Remember, anything's possible."

Rather than get into a theoretical discussion that would only delay their getting to the truth, she stood back and gave him a head-to-toe inspection. "I didn't think you could get any more handsome." Maggie gave his tie one last straightening then gave him an air kiss so as not to smear her fire-engine red, greasy lipstick.

He flicked the loose fringe hanging over her nearly flattened chest. "You look pretty damn fabulous yourself. He leaned down to kiss her lips then pecked her nose instead. Putting his arm around her, he said, "Let's go see if our bellman buddy told the truth about the year. If so, I think we have to assume we have a task to complete and we're on a pretty tight deadline to figure out what we're here to do *and* do it."

In her mind, Maggie heard Reynard's warning. *Ya will live out your days here on Crystal Island, in* this *time.* The shiver that ran down her spine could have been one of confirmation...or a reaction to his mention of *restrictions* they would be forced to endure.

* * *

Noah leaned down and whispered in Maggie's ear. "Satisfied?"

His question and his breath both tickled her. It shouldn't have made her think of sex but it did. Apparently, the chemistry he blamed for her reaction to him hadn't been diminished by time travel. "We've seen today's newspaper, the calendar on the concierge desk and the registration book. The lobby furnishings aren't the same. People are smoking cigarettes and cigars. *Indoors.* A hoax of this magnitude would take more than a few hours to set up."

"And we really can't ignore one more major thing. Look up. The glass panels in the dome seem different, less clear. I remember reading about them being replaced in the nineties. That absolutely could not have been accomplished while we were outside. But how could there be electricity to those chandeliers?"

Noah shrugged. "There must be a pretty big generator somewhere nearby."

"Maybe this is all a dream or hallucination," Maggie ventured with no conviction in her voice or expression.

"A joint dream? I'm voting no on that guess. What's your gut feeling?"

She sighed. "It's not a dream or hallucination."

"Well, I'm convinced we've traveled through time. I can't explain it but I can't refute it either."

"Same here." Maggie shifted from one foot to the other. "These shoes are killing me."

"Ah, the high price of fashion." He placed his arm under hers to give her a little support.

Maggie scanned the lobby from one end to the other without seeing anything else helpful. "As fascinating as all this is, maybe we should go back to the bungalow and start focusing on what we need to do to get back. Reynard said the five days begins *today*, which is practically over already."

His expression indicated how little he liked the idea of going back to the bungalow. "I think we should approach this as a book I want to write, which means a walk-around comes first. We need to observe the natives. I don't know about you but I could sure use a drink. Let's go see what the Amethyst Cave looked like, er, *looks* like now. You can get off your feet there."

They walked directly to where the entrance to the lounge was but were faced with a bamboo-paneled wall camouflaged by tropical plants in huge clay pots.

"I hear music," Maggie said, turning an ear toward the wall and frowning. "Maybe the entrance is from outside."

Noah listened for a moment then laughed. "I can't believe I forgot something very important about this era. I think we're in for another treat."

He held her hand as he walked up to the only completely unobstructed spot on the wall and knocked. A moment later a very small door opened just above Maggie's eye level. A man's eyes and nose appeared and he gave them a quick once-over. "Who sent you?"

Noah squeezed her hand and replied, "Teddy Roosevelt."

The small door closed and a full section of paneling slowly opened inward. Instantly live jazz music reached their ears and Noah gave her a nudge forward.

"Oh my gawd," she said as quietly as she could over the music. "It's a speakeasy! It really is 1927."

Except for the large crystal formations looking exactly like they had last seen them, they never would have recognized the Amethyst Cave. It was at least three times the size, filling the space where they had seen retail stores and the Quartz Café. In this time it had a bandstand and dance floor and full-size dining tables as well as cocktail rounds.

An excited shout rose from a crowd of people gathered at the far end of the room but Maggie couldn't see the cause.

Noah's greater height gave him an advantage. "It's a casino," he told her with delight. "I've never been much of a gambler but—"

"Will you be dining this evening?" a tuxedoed man holding menus asked them.

Maggie looked to Noah. She was feeling totally off balance while he seemed to have slid right into this alien world.

"We may have a little something," Noah said to the maître d' and they were guided to the only available table for two near the dance floor.

"You look like you belong here," she murmured close to his ear.

He winked at her and muttered out of the side of his mouth. "I'm just pretending I'm on a movie set for *The Great Gatsby*."

As they perused the menu, another man brought them two champagne glasses and filled them from an open bottle with a French label. "Courtesy of Al Jolson and Warner Brothers Pictures. They're celebrating the opening of *The Jazz Singer* and hope you'll make a point of experiencing the miracle of Vitaphone."

"Is Mr. Jolson here tonight?" Noah asked without even trying to appear nonchalant.

The waiter nodded toward the crowded dance floor but Maggie's gaze was glued to the man with the champagne bottle. His straight black hair was slicked back from his face, making his dark eyes stand out. The features seemed very familiar, as though she had recently seen him somewhere else. Her gaze dropped to his name tag. *Connor.* That was familiar too. But before she could grasp the memory, Noah took her attention.

"Do you see him?"

"I wouldn't know if I did," she replied. "Was he the one who wore blackface makeup when he sang? I have a vague recollection of learning about that in a music appreciation class."

He nodded. "Sure couldn't get away with that in our time. Anyway that just sounded like a movie plug. But geez, wouldn't it be incredible if we actually got to meet someone famous from this time?"

He chuckled as he picked up his champagne glass and held it toward her. She raised hers and lightly clinked the rims. "Here's to anything being possible."

They each took a sip and Maggie held up her glass for a toast of her own. "And to mysterious bellmen without whom we'd be in real trouble right now."

After another sip, Noah had another toast ready. "Here's to Maggie Harrison, my best friend from the past, my adventure partner in the present, and always, my heart's desire."

She blinked at him in awe. Did he really mean those words or were the outrageous circumstances to blame for such an emotional declaration? Nothing she was thinking would equal his words so she just smiled and took another sip that drained her glass.

When another waiter came by, Noah ordered an assortment of appetizers and a bottle of the champagne being passed around.

She was overwhelmed by the glitz and glamour filling every square foot of the high-class speakeasy. Reading a novel or watching a movie set in the Roaring Twenties only slightly prepared her for the real thing. Everyone seemed to be *trying* to be wilder and more flamboyant than the next person. The only unpleasant thing for Maggie was the amount of smoke in the air. They had barely been there half an hour and her eyes were already burning.

"Shall we?"

Only when Noah spoke did she realize he was standing with his hand out, asking her to dance. The band had just begun a slow song and the lights were dimmed to a romantic level. Once she confirmed the couples on the floor weren't moving in any way she couldn't emulate, she placed her hand in his and rose as gracefully as possible with cramped toes and a head full of champagne bubbles.

The moment he drew her into a proper yet clearly possessive embrace, she forgot all about her feet. His touch was all it took to melt away all her concerns. It didn't have to be sexual. They didn't need to be kissing. They certainly didn't need a perfect place or time.

The room seemed to darken even more and the other couples faded from her vision. It was only the two of them swaying to the sinuous tendrils of a saxophone's tale of forbidden love. She felt her breasts straining against its compression garment and immediately wished it could be his hands instead. Her gaze lifted to his and she thought she saw her desire being mirrored there.

With the merest pressure on her lower back, he brought their bodies together and her thought was confirmed. "I can't stop thinking about what you're wearing under this dress," he murmured in her ear. "There's just something about a garter belt and silk stockings with seams up the back that makes me want to take them off with my teeth."

Maggie felt a sudden chill and shivered. She quickly glanced all around them but nothing she saw felt connected to the chill.

With Noah's words echoing in her mind, she gave him a small smile. "I'd rather you tear this straight-jacket off my chest. It almost makes me forget how bad my feet hurt."

He kissed her forehead. "Poor baby. I promise to massage whatever body parts are being tortured by your clothing…as long as you give me a minute to drool over you in the garter belt first."

The chilling sensation ran up her spine and, this time, Noah noticed.

"What is it?" he murmured into her ear.

"Something's wrong. But I'm not sure what yet."

Right then, the lights abruptly glared and the band lurched into a lively number. Noah led Maggie off the floor, along with a few other couples, and the polished wood floor was taken over by Charleston-dancing flappers and their partners.

It was amazing to watch but not quite enough for her to banish the image Noah had planted in her mind. Appetizers and champagne had been delivered in their absence and her stomach growled at the sight. It was the only part of her *not* focused on sex.

Noah squeezed her hand and leaned close. "I've heard waiting can be a kind of foreplay."

She gave him a half-smile. "And I see oysters on that platter. They're supposed to help too."

He laughed. "Yeah, like we need a lot of help. Okay, let's not skip any of this experience."

"Well, maybe we could skip one or two." She pointed to the energetic dancers as they took their seats.

The music was much too loud to have a discussion so they gave up the attempt. It turned out they were hungry enough to finish off every appetizer in a short time and the champagne was the perfect accompaniment. But the third time he tried to refill her glass she stopped him.

"I'm already way past my limit. We still have some brainstorming to do tonight."

"My brain does not storm after the sun goes down." His hand slipped under the hem of her dress and fingered a garter. "We have something more physical to take care of tonight."

And *bam*, she was ready for him to follow through right there, on the table. And a heartbeat later she felt another warning chill. This one made her fingers icy. She was now quite sure what it was connected to. She subtly moved his warm hand with her cold one and leaned close enough for him to hear her serious tone. "We need to go back to the bungalow. *Now.*"

A horse-drawn carriage was waiting outside the rear exit of the lobby, but Reynard was not the driver. All Maggie cared was that she wouldn't have to walk. As soon as they were settled in the passenger seat, Noah hugged her close and vigorously rubbed her bare arm. She felt her body begin to thaw in the short time it took for the carriage to reach their destination but the sense of warning remained strong. Noah quickly helped Maggie down and handed the man a dollar, which, based on the man's delighted reaction, was much more than necessary.

The moment they were inside the bungalow, Maggie took Noah's hand and led him into the bedroom. The look on his face was a strange combination of desire and concern. "I'll be right back," she promised, then hurried into the bathroom. As quickly as possible she removed the uncomfortable shoes and all the restrictive clothing, leaving on only the shorts and chemise. Over those she donned the seersucker wrap, tying it securely at the waist.

As soon as she exited the bathroom, she noticed he had undressed down to trousers and shirt but looked far from comfortable. When he took in how she was covered, his concerned expression turned to genuine worry.

"I can explain," she said quickly as she sat on the edge of the bed and patted the spot beside her. "First, I want you to keep in mind that you are the only man I've known who can turn me to mush with a touch and make my body ready for sex with a kiss. And that I am really, *really* happy that we've become lovers."

He grinned and leaned toward her for a kiss but she pressed her fingers to his lips just hard enough to make him ease back.

"That was really hard for me to do," she confessed.

"Then why—"

"The chills. It wasn't cold in the lounge and there wasn't anything spooky around. It was a warning."

"A warning? Like something horrible is about to happen?"

She made a face. "Sort of, but only if we don't do what we were sent here to do. I got the distinct feeling that we were being warned that we could get distracted by...how you make me feel. To the point of failing."

He slowly nodded. "Correct that to how *we* make *each other* feel. It's always been that way for me."

"Always?" she asked softly.

"Always," he assured her. "And now that we've finally given in to it, whoever sent us here wants us to put it aside."

"It's only for five, no, *four* more days."

He rolled his eyes. "Hardly a blink of time in comparison to eighteen years."

She smiled and consoled herself with the idea that, if they don't succeed in their mission, at least they'd be stranded there *together* and could have all the sex they wanted. Unless *that* was one of the restrictions they'd have to live with. She refused to consider such a severe punishment on top of not being able to return to their own time.

"I'd like to suggest a compromise," Noah said. "Let's see if it'll pass your chill test. What if we go back to how affectionate we were in high school, you know, hand-holding, hugging, slow dancing?"

She closed her eyes for a second and waited for any sort of sensation. "That seems okay."

"All right. So what if we add kissing, the closed-mouth kind?"

She felt a hint of a shiver. "Iffy. I think we'd both have to agree to keep it…*sweet*. No, that's not quite it. I think the warning isn't so much about *what* we do but about our lack of control once we pass go."

"And maybe how much brain power we're using by thinking about sex when we should be focusing on the task we've been assigned?"

"Like an addiction," she offered with a frown.

"I prefer obsession. It seems a little less harmful. Either way, Reynard told us we have to work together to solve the problem, so we can't just stay away from each other."

"No, but we can help each other keep our minds on the mission." She paused. "Yes. That feels right." An involuntary yawn caught her by surprise. "I'm suddenly really sleepy."

"I'll take that as a confirmation that you correctly interpreted your chills. But there's something I promised to do for you and it could be an easy test of our resolve." Noah grasped her hand and brought them both to their feet. A few seconds later he had the bed covers pulled back and motioned for her to lay down, which she did, though rather stiffly.

He snuffed out the lamp and said, "Now, close your eyes." As soon as she obeyed, he sat down at the bottom of the bed and wrapped his fingers around one of her bare feet.

Her instant reaction was an audible moan. "That feels so-o-o good. But I'm sure you're as tired as I—"

"*Shush.* This is not a completely unselfish act." He rubbed a spot at the base of her middle toe that made her sigh, so he gave it a bit more attention before doing the same for each of the other digits. "I've never given much thought to a woman's feet but there's something about yours that I find terribly sexy."

"Really?" she asked slyly and grazed his thigh with the toes of the foot he was not massaging. "That sounds like something we should look into."

He chuckled and placed the wandering foot back on the bed. "That move and my follow-up thoughts go into the no-no column. And if you can't be good, I'll have to stop."

"Fine," she murmured then moaned again when his thumb worked on the arch of her foot.

Noah tried to focus on the muscles and joints he was massaging. He was performing an act of kindness not seduction. And yet he felt as though he were the one being seduced. He tried to concentrate on the task they'd been assigned, the mysterious beings that had sent them back in time, the plot ideas for his next book. None of it worked.

No matter how he tried to distract himself, every thought led right back to Maggie…the first and only one friend he'd ever cried over when they'd parted. And because of the conversation they'd had earlier, he no longer had any reason to hold back from imagining a life with her.

He forced himself to spend the same amount of time on her other foot before releasing himself from the torture of touching her without doing everything he wanted to. When he realized she had fallen asleep, he was actually relieved. He covered her with the sheet, stripped down to his boxers and undershirt, then got beneath the sheet on the other side of the bed.

Unable to completely resist temptation, Noah leaned over and kissed Maggie's temple before turning his back to her. She was already so deeply asleep, she didn't even notice. So he told himself there would be no harm in a little asexual hugging. He shifted onto his side and put his arm around her waist. She still didn't wake, but a few seconds later, she also turned and nestled her body against his. Under the circumstances, he didn't expect to sleep at all, but Morpheus soon overtook him as well.

"Maid service."

The words broke into Maggie's dream first. Then she heard the light knocking. She opened her eyes a crack but the bright sunlight coming through the window made her squeeze them shut again. Her head felt like someone was playing tennis inside it...or as if she had drunk a bottle of champagne.

The next sound she recognized was running water. Noah was in the bathroom. He had told her he didn't need much sleep but she didn't feel like they'd been in bed that long. She made herself open one eye enough to see the clock on the nightstand and was truly shocked to see it was already eleven. No wonder there was so damn much sunlight.

"Oh! A thousand pardons, ma'am. When ye didn't answer, I thought ye and the mister be out. I'll come back later."

Maggie managed to get her eyes focused on the maid just before she whirled around with her stack of linens and disappeared from the bedroom doorway.

Two things wormed their way into Maggie's foggy consciousness. The maid was a very young woman with a long, reddish-blonde braid and an Irish brogue. And she was wearing a uniform exactly like the one Maggie had seen in her second bathroom mirror vision.

CHAPTER 13

The fearful look on the maid's face when she reappeared made Maggie soften her tone. "I was wondering if you might have some aspirin. My head is pounding."

Relief immediately replaced the girl's worry and she quickly took a small white packet out of her uniform pocket without setting down the stack of linens. "There be quite a need for such remedy this morn," she said, adding a smile to her pretty face as she approached the bedside. "I've heard some speak of the hair of the dog what bit ye."

Maggie noted how the girl kept her eyes averted. She pulled herself into a more upright position, holding the sheet up to her neck in an attempt at modesty. She forced a return smile. "I've heard about that dog but I prefer aspirin." She held out her hand and the girl placed the packet on her palm. By feeling it, she could tell it was a powder and had to trust that it was safe to take. "Thank you."

"I'll fetch some water."

She watched the girl walk out and return with a few ounces of cloudy tap water in a glass. She figured whatever was in the water couldn't make her feel any worse than she already did. Maggie poured the contents of the packet into the glass and drank the bitter mixture as quickly as possibly. She wondered about the way the maid continued to clutch the linens in front of her. Surely it would have been easier to set the pile down...*unless she was hiding something*.

Maggie heard the water turn off in the bathroom as she handed the empty glass to the maid. She wanted Noah to see this girl. "Thank you again." The girl smiled again, curtsied and hurried to the door. "Excuse me." The maid glanced at the opening bathroom door and back to Maggie. "I was just wondering if you would tell me your name. I'd like to let management know how helpful you were."

The girl's face lit up. "Me name's Moira, ma'am. Moira Flanagan. And that would be very kind of ye ta be sure."

Noah did not come out of the bathroom until the maid closed the front door of the bungalow.

"What took you so long?" Maggie asked in a slightly peeved tone. "I wanted you to see the maid."

He arched one dark eyebrow at her. "I heard you talking to someone and thought I might be underdressed for a formal introduction."

Only then did she realize his only cover was a rather small towel. Her head was killing her, she had a mystery clue to offer and yet her body instantly responded to the luscious sight in front of her. She rubbed her eyes. "Sorry. Bad headache." She allowed herself the tiny pleasure of ogling his well-toned upper body as he walked to the closet and found a man's robe to exchange for the towel. "Last night...did we...?

He gave her a wink and grinned as he walked toward her. "No, we did not. You conked out sometime during the second half of your foot massage."

She frowned. "Well, that was certainly rude of me. I'm sorry. I guess I was just dreaming about...something else."

"Well, there may have been a *little* 'something else' while you were sleeping."

Her widened eyes made him chuckle. "We just snuggled. Nothing we should punish ourselves over." He plopped down on the bed and gave her a light kiss before she could cover her mouth to shield morning breath. "And since it didn't take any thinking time away from our mission—"

"That was the maid."

"I gathered as much. There's no shower and the old bathtub is short but deep enough. The water gets warm enough to wash. It might help if you—"

"I meant, it was *my* maid," she cut in. "From the vision in the mirror. She was really young, maybe sixteen or seventeen at most, and had the same hair and Irish brogue."

"Pregnant?"

She shrugged. "I couldn't tell for sure. She held a pile of linens in front of her the whole time which could have been her way of hiding a swollen belly. I would assume an illegitimate pregnancy would be unacceptable here. Her name is Moira Flanagan. Do you remember the name from anything you read? Could she be the girl who was found dead on the beach?"

He shrugged. "I don't recall any name being given. And the only date I saw was the year, 1927." Noah nodded. "You know what, before we get deeper into speculation, let's order breakfast. I remember Reynard saying the words 'room service'." He found a menu in the nightstand drawer and read her a few suggestions.

"Just coffee. *Lots* of coffee. And maybe toast."

She watched him study the black candlestick phone on the nightstand. It had no dial or buttons. Finally Noah simply lifted the part hanging on a hook and held it to his ear. She could tell the instant an operator came on line by the broad grin on Noah's face.

"Oh yes. Room Service please," he said loudly into the part on the candlestick that looked like a speaker. As he was waiting to be connected, he whispered to Maggie, "This is too cool."

Maggie propped several pillows behind her head and closed her eyes while Noah ordered several items on the menu. The aspirin powder was kicking in. When he hung up, she said, "It's just not fair that I feel this bad and you're raring to go."

"Okay, c'mon." He got up then pulled her to her feet. "Put your head under the sink faucet. The water isn't icy but it's cool enough to shrink the blood vessels. Then brush your teeth. You'll feel better by the time the urn of coffee I just ordered gets here."

Before he closed the bathroom door on her, he added, "And just so you know, I felt like hell when I first woke up. Then I looked around the room, saw you next to me and realized last night wasn't just the craziest dream I ever had. I was about to wake you up in a very special way and then remembered what you figured out before we went to sleep. So I dunked myself in some cold water instead. It helped. You've got about a half hour."

Noah's directions and estimate of time were both accurate. By the time breakfast arrived she was ready for a little food with her coffee.

As soon as he downed his tall Virgin Mary, devoured a helping of each entrée and washed it all down with black coffee, he was ready to get the brainstorming started. Maggie was way behind on the breakfast but anxious to hear his thoughts while she savored her caffeine and carbs.

"I've been comparing what Reynard told us with some time-travel plots in books and movies. In most of the ones I know of, there was a personal connection to the one who gets transported."

She swallowed a bite of blueberry muffin. "There's nothing in my past I've ever thought about wanting to change."

He angled his head at her. "Not even how we parted?"

She smirked at him. "I think we've covered that ground and besides, we didn't need to go back to the Roaring Twenties to find each other."

"Point taken. And I would add the same conclusion. Other than the us factor, I've never felt the need to fix something in the past to improve my life circumstances."

"Not even how many times you had to move growing up?"

He narrowed his eyes. "To change that I'd have to have been born with different parents and that's not fixable by time travel." When he saw the sympathetic look in her eyes, he got back to analyzing. "So maybe it's not so much you or me specifically but whoever is staying in the Diamond Suite when the portal opens. Reynard said something about *the pair* knowing what they needed to do, right?"

"Yes," she replied, a bit surprised she could recall anything at the moment.

"I didn't pick it up until now but he made it sound like we're not the first pair who's had this happen to them."

She wrinkled her forehead in thought. "Which could go along with the idea of it being whatever couple is in the suite at the time when the portal opens. So maybe those other pairs also had to deal with a lack of information."

Noah got up from the bed and started pacing. "We could have guessed right about a supernatural power orchestrating all this. Or, it could be aliens from another universe playing a game and using us inferior humans as their pawns. We're thrown into an unfamiliar environment and given a puzzle to solve. There's even a ticking clock. Maybe they're taking bets on whether we'll succeed or fail. Unfortunately, if we fail, we can't get back to our own time."

"I know you enjoy making up stories, but you're starting to freak me out."

He was back at her side in a blink and gave her a quick hug and kiss on the head. "Sorry. I got carried away. Anyway, it really doesn't matter who's behind our being here or why, because we're going to figure it out." He was quiet for a moment then brought her hand to his lips for a kiss. "And if we don't figure it out? Would that really be so bad? This time and place could be a lot of fun. As long as we were together."

A swarm of butterflies took off in her stomach. He was right. It might not be so awful. She turned toward him and kissed his mouth. "That was really romantic. But Reynard said we would have to live out our days on this island and there would be restrictions. What if we couldn't stay in this nice little bungalow with a maid and room service? What if we had to get jobs to survive here? Would you really want to be a bellman or waiter? I know we could manage but I'd really miss things like air conditioning and a microwave oven and bras that don't squish my boobs. And then there's that major hurricane coming next year, then the Depression and—"

He silenced her with a quick kiss. "I get it. But to be fair we'd also be in the unique position of knowing what was about to happen in advance. Maybe we'd figure out a way to invest our earnings in one of the original Dow Jones companies like General Electric or U.S. Rubber, then we could afford this bungalow."

"And risk changing history? The smallest thing we do could cause all sorts of problems. Like throwing a little pebble into a pond and making big ripples. You're not the only one who's picked up a theory or two about time travel from books and movies."

He laughed and pulled her close for a good long hug. "We'll figure out the puzzle or we'll figure out how to manage if we don't. I promise."

She tried to give him a doubtful look but ended up smiling. "I believe you. So, setting aside the mystery of who's behind our challenge, have you come up with any thoughts that might actually help us get back to our own time?"

"Going back to what you said last night, there has to be a reason we came to this precise moment of 1927. If we're supposed to save someone and we only have a small window of opportunity, it has to be something happening right here, right now."

Maggie nodded slowly as she thought about how an amateur sleuth in a book might begin. "You only mentioned two people who died in 1927—the pregnant maid and an unidentified man. Since we have no information about him, we have no clue to follow, so unless one falls in our laps, I'd set him aside."

"I agree," Noah said firmly. And the same has to go for The Weeping Woman."

"Right. Which makes Moira Flanagan the only strong possibility. I don't think it's a coincidence that the Irish maid in my bathroom mirror is our maid in this bungalow at this time. And it shouldn't be too hard to confirm if she's pregnant and alone. I'll try to start a conversation with her when she comes back. Figuring out who might have strangled her would be the hard part. We can't just start walking up to strangers and ask questions without raising suspicions."

Noah took a minute to refresh both their cups with hot coffee, thanks to the little candle still burning beneath the pot. "I agree that the maid is a strong possibility if she's pregnant, but I don't think we can eliminate Robert Davenport. In fact, I still think he's our number one target based on his connection to this island."

"Even if we're three years early?"

"If Davenport's the one we're supposed to save and we go with the idea he was actually murdered, maybe this is the time he makes a bad decision, like taking on a greedy partner. Reynard said he's in residence at the moment. Maybe there's a way to bump into him somewhere."

"Or maybe we have those stylish golfing outfits because we'll have an opportunity to play a round with him."

"We can't dismiss anything but you'd better hope our figuring this thing out doesn't depend on my golf game. I really suck."

Her mind instantly focused on his last word and his chuckle let her know he could tell exactly where her thoughts had gone.

He tugged on her earlobe. "You just can't help yourself, can you?" She blushed and he added. "Don't feel bad. I had the same thought the instant I said it. It may only be for four days but they could be the longest four days I've ever known."

"We just need to stay aware of how easy it is for us to get sidetracked." She drew his head closer and pressed her lips to his for several seconds. "Maybe we could take turns being the strong one. This one was mine."

He gave her his best little-boy pout and stood. "Since the only reason for abstinence is to keep our minds on the mission, I think we need to get moving."

As they dressed, Maggie couldn't help but think about whether anything they did now could change Davenport's fate. Of course, if there were no suicide or murder, there would be no reason for Lillian Davenport to be so defensive about her family.

Thoughts of Lillian Davenport's warning and order to report to her caused Maggie's brain to leap to a different question. "With everything being so weird I didn't think about what is happening in our time. Isn't there someone expecting you to check in with them? I mean, a day or two might not cause a problem but what about after that?"

He shrugged. "Maybe there's a version of us continuing to do whatever we'd be doing there. Or maybe a week here is only a blip in time there and no one will notice our absence. I think that's one of those questions that won't get answered until we've played out our time here."

Maggie had found the first walk-around with Noah quite fascinating. What they'd been doing for the last two hours, however, was more of a sit-in. She had donned comfortable flats and a lightweight shift in readiness of whatever path they would be taking, but after a leisurely, arm-in-arm stroll halfway around the property, the oppressive afternoon heat had gotten to both of them and Noah changed the plan for the day. Choosing two, throne-like rattan chairs under a giant potted palm in the lobby, they had settled in. Huge fans blew a salty breeze through the open doors, making it relatively comfortable, which accounted for the number of guests doing the same thing they were.

But she sure missed air conditioning.

A wave at a bellman had gotten them copies of the hotel's weekly circular, the *New York Times* and the *Chicago Tribune*. The larger papers were three days old but current enough for what Noah had in mind. He had suggested they look for anything in the papers that might be relevant to their quest. He had also told her to let him know if she got a *feeling* about anything she read. The coverage of old news as if it were new was quite interesting but absolutely nothing raised a red flag for Maggie in the *Trib* or the *Times*.

Noah handed her the multi-page circular. "Okay, try this one. It's mainly a promo piece for the hotel's amenities, but it also has a society gossip column and a schedule of upcoming events. It gave me an idea of how we could meet the Davenports."

Maggie could tell Noah was still talking about his idea but an article on page two had her full attention. If he hadn't instructed her to use her intuition she probably would have ignored the way her gaze caught on a picture of a newly engaged couple. "We need to get an invitation to this party."

He stopped talking. "What? What party?"

She showed him the article. "It could be because of him or her or both of them. But I think they have something to do with why we're here. I can't explain—"

"There's no need. Remember, I'm completely on board the anything's-possible train with your *feelings* in the conductor's seat." He took the paper back to read the first line of the article she pointed to. "Okay, let's see what we've got. 'Florida Legislator George Hampshire and his wife will host a reception in the Davenport's Sapphire Ballroom to celebrate the engagement of their son, Broderick, to Amelia Gaviston of the Chicago Gavistons.' It's tomorrow night."

"We need to be there. Just thinking about it gives me the shivers. "I know we eliminated The Weeping Woman, but maybe she's the bride-to-be or one of the mothers."

"Or maybe Broderick is the one we need to warn Robert Davenport to stay away from. It says the Hampshire family leases a cottage on the island, so it would be logical for them to be acquaintances of the Davenports."

Maggie sat forward. "So they would probably be invited to the reception as guests."

Noah refolded the two larger newspapers, set them on the wicker table in front of them then scanned the article again. "I'm not sure about one of them being The Weeping Woman, but I don't think we can completely dismiss the parents of the happy couple for other reasons. Prohibition offered a lot of opportunity for a crooked politician. And this write-up makes the Gavistons sound like an old-money family. I can think of several different motivations for murder with this group of players."

Maggie smiled. "Just thinking of television crime dramas, I can come up with at least a half dozen."

"Well, unless something more obvious triggers your intuition, I'd say we get an invite to the party and see where it takes us."

"Sounds good to me. Any ideas on how we might manage that?"

Noah grinned slowly. "Yeah, I think I've got a good one." He removed the page with the reception announcement, folded it and put it in his pocket. "First rule for getting away with a lie is to stick as closely as possible to the truth. I'm a bestselling author wanting to set my new book here. As my assistant…and *wife*, it will be your job to brag about how popular I am and how good it would be for the hotel to have me mention it. Of course, if I'm going to use the hotel, I'll need to be able to get a good look around the whole place. If we act important enough and drop a few famous names, no one should question our story." They discussed a few different possibilities then walked over to the concierge.

Maggie hardly got their cover story out before the man escorted them directly to the manager's office and introduced them.

Mr. Eckhart was a slightly built man with a bald crown surrounded by a ring of thin, gray hair. He looked both nervous and exhausted but he rose instantly and greeted them as though he had nothing to do more important than talking to them.

Maggie put on her most serious, professional expression and rattled off some make-believe titles in hopes the man wouldn't know the difference. "I'm sure you're familiar with Mr. Nash's *very* popular novels—*Coming Home*, *Sophie's Journey* and, of course, the one they're making a movie of, *Saving Private Jones*."

The man's head bobbed vigorously. "Oh my, yes, of course. Naturally I was alerted that you were guests and was truly hoping I would have the opportunity to meet you both." His smile wavered. "Is there a problem? Was our hospitality fruit basket delivered?"

She pursed her lips. "There was no fruit basket but otherwise everything is satisfactory. In fact, Mr. Nash would like to have it noted that the maid assigned to our bungalow was exceptionally helpful this morning. He would like an extra dollar put in her pay envelope this week from him. She said her name is Moira Flanagan."

Mr. Eckhart frowned, clearly having no idea which maid she was, but he scribbled the name down on a piece of paper with a dollar sign. "That is very generous. I'm sure she will appreciate it. Is there anything else I can help you with?"

Maggie quickly delivered their almost-true cover story, which he bought just as quickly. "Besides a tour of the back offices, he would like to interview Robert Davenport."

"I don't see a problem with that. I will check with Mr. Davenport about his schedule and let you know."

"Mr. Nash would also like to attend one of the hotel's bigger social events. There's a high-society party scene in his new book and he would like to make it as realistic as possible. Is there something like that scheduled in the next day or two?" She forced herself to keep breathing as he looked at his calendar.

"As a matter of fact, there is a reception in the Sapphire Ballroom tomorrow evening that could be ideal for Mr. Nash's purpose. Of course I will have to speak to the client but under the circumstances, I would think he would be delighted to have Mr. Nash as a guest."

"And my wife," Noah added quietly, speaking for the first time since they'd entered the manager's office.

Mr. Eckhart smiled nervously. "Of course. Of course. I will have a message delivered to your bungalow as soon as I have all the arrangements made."

"Thank you," Maggie said, holding out her hand without thinking. The man looked at it with a bit of surprise but then touched her fingertips with his. "Is there anything else I might assist you with today? Perhaps dinner reservations?"

She turned to Noah. "What do you think, dear?"

Noah fought a grin. "I was thinking about something outdoors at sunset."

The manager's smile was confident this time. "I would suggest the Emerald Patio at seven thirty. Because of the heat, jackets and ties are optional for gentlemen." He gave Maggie a quizzical look.

"That will be perfect," she replied with an approving smile. Without another word, the famous novelist and his wife/assistant left the manager's office.

Maggie and Noah maintained their aloof expressions until they were back inside the bungalow, then he picked her up and swung her around. "You were fantastic!"

"I *know*," she exclaimed. "That was so much fun. Well, as long as you ignore the fact that we might be tracking down a killer."

"I don't know why I'm surprised but you just got even sexier for me.

She rose on tiptoes to give him an appreciative kiss and immediately felt his body's reaction. "Oh, my."

His mouth came back to hers with a hunger that stripped away her common sense.

Knock. Knock. "Bellhop."

Noah broke the kiss but kept Maggie in his firm embrace. "*Yes?*" His voice came out as strained as he felt.

"Mr. Nash?" a man's voice called from outside. "I have a message for you from Mr. Davenport."

"Leave it," Noah replied then his mouth returned to Maggie's.

The next sound was the man clearing his throat. "I'm sorry to bother you, sir, but I'm instructed to wait for an answer."

Noah took a slow, deep breath. "One moment."

Maggie pushed against Noah's shoulders and gave him a disapproving look that cleared his mind the rest of the way. A heartbeat later he stepped back from her and mouthed that he was sorry. She pantomimed that she was equally responsible.

Noah opened the door wide enough for the bellman to hand him the envelope, then he closed the door again. He took another deep breath, took the message out of the envelope and held it out so he and Maggie could read it together. The personal stationery inside bore the initials RD embossed in gold and contained one scrawled sentence.

I have a free hour at 5 if you would like to come to my suite.

Noah glanced at his pocket watch then Maggie. She nodded. He reached into his pants pocket and dug out a dollar bill. Again opening the door only a few inches, he handed the man the tip and said, "Let Mr. Davenport know we'll be there."

"Yes, sir. Thank you, sir." The man had a big smile as he hurried away.

"I'm pretty sure you're over-tipping," Maggie told Noah as soon as he'd reclosed the door.

Instead of responding to that, he asked, "Do we need to talk about what just happened?"

She gave him a crooked smile. "I don't know what else there is to say. You're the one with…*experience*. This is *all* new to me."

"My *experience* does not include the kind of hunger you stir up in me. I don't remember ever feeling like I couldn't stop myself. If that bellman hadn't knocked…" He shook his head. "Now that I think about it, we came straight here from the manager's office. How did he get a written response from Davenport and have it delivered so fast?"

"Maybe another trick of that supernatural power…like they had to make sure we understood just how vulnerable we are to our human nature." She shrugged. "However it happened, it worked. Now, I barely have an hour to get into something appropriate for meeting the owner and I definitely need to rinse off." She took a step toward him and sniffed. "So do you."

He pretended to look offended. "Just for that I'm taking the first turn in the bath—"

"That's what you think," she said with a laugh as she rushed in front of him.

She only got as far as the bedroom before he grabbed her waist, effortlessly lifted her and dropped her onto the bed. But before he could get into the bathroom, she bolted up and managed to give him a hip shove out of the way. He grasped her wrist at the last second and yanked her back to him. Both laughing heartily, he kissed her forehead then gave her a gentle push to the finish line. "Hurry up," he teased. "You're going to make us late."

CHAPTER 14

In an attempt to give a businesslike impression, Maggie had changed into the dowdy outfit and borrowed a tablet and pencil from the concierge. However, the trip to the Diamond Suite threatened her confident air. Because of old movies, she had seen elevators with grated doors and visible gears and pulleys. The one they were currently in required a skilled operator to work the interior handles and levers. It was interesting from a historical standpoint but being in one of the antiques was a lot scarier than she would have imagined. She clutched Noah's hand the entire, shaky, painfully slow ride up to the fifth floor.

The elevator operator waited as they exited the metal thrill ride and pressed the buzzer for the private suite.

The door was opened a few seconds later by a tall, middle-aged woman with excellent posture and short, finger-waved blond hair. "Mr. and Mrs. Nash. How nice of you to stop by. I'm Patricia Davenport. Please come in." She stood aside and closed the door behind them.

Maggie thought she could see a slight hint of Lillian Davenport in Patricia's posture and confident demeanor but she barely recognized the suite. Instead of the one great room she and Noah had checked into, the area was walled off into several rooms. Mrs. Davenport led them into the one closest to the front door. A tall, thin man with nearly white hair rose from his chair behind the desk as they entered. His height and coloring definitely reminded Maggie of his granddaughter.

Offering a broad smile and his hand to Noah, he said, "Robert Davenport. It's a pleasure to meet you, Mr. Nash."

"Likewise," Noah said, giving the man's hand a firm shake. "Please call me Noah. And this is my wife and publishing assistant, Maggie."

Remembering the manager's reaction to her extending her hand, she simply smiled and nodded.

"Thank you, dear," Davenport said to his wife with a note of dismissal in his tone. "Give us a knock in about forty-five minutes." Patricia gave him *a look*, then nodded and gently closed the office door.

Maggie recognized the polite way Davenport had let them know how much time they were being granted. She also noted that his wife's parting look seemed to contain a message of some sort. Perhaps they were in the midst of an argument when they'd arrived.

Robert Davenport settled into the chair behind the desk and motioned for them to sit in the straight-backed chairs in front of them. It reminded her of how his granddaughter had done the same thing. "I'm afraid I don't have any of your books," he said apologetically as he nodded toward the high bookcases. "But I've heard wonderful things about your writing. I understand you're working on a book to be set in our hotel. While I see how that could be advantageous I would hope that your story would not cast an unsavory shadow over the property."

Maggie suddenly realized they hadn't actually talked about the book Noah was supposed to be writing and she hoped he didn't stick close to the truth for this part.

"A portion of the book would take place in the hotel but I assure you it's my intention to glamorize it and its guests. It's a tale of a young man who lost an arm in the war and is unable to pursue his dream of becoming a boxer. Then his fiancée breaks their engagement and he's thinking of killing himself. But he has a chance meeting with the owner of the hotel and, well, I hope you don't mind if I don't give it all away."

Davenport was obviously intrigued. "I understand, but perhaps you'll at least tell me if the owner helps this poor young man find his way to a good ending."

Noah nodded. "Absolutely. He's a bit of a guardian angel in human form."

Davenport brightened considerably. "That sounds very entertaining. How might I be of assistance?"

Noah began with reasonable questions about owning and running a large hotel for wealthy guests and Maggie scribbled madly on her pad. Only she could tell Noah's questions were all phrased to uncover any possible motive for the owner to be murdered but thus far she hadn't heard a single thing that seemed relevant to their investigation.

She let her mind wander away from the words being exchanged between the men and thought about Mrs. Davenport. The initial impression she gave was of an upper-class woman who was content in her wifely role. But according to hotel history, Patricia and her young son, Chester, managed to keep the hotel going after Robert's tragic death, through the Depression and the Second World War. That had to have taken an incredibly strong, savvy woman. Was she the true power in their relationship or did her husband's death force her to take on a role she'd never chosen to play?

Maggie's intuition told her the Davenport marriage was probably an arrangement rather than a love connection, which led her to an interesting possibility. Rather than being the grieving widow who did what she had to do to support her child, could Patricia have been relieved by Robert's death? Or worse, could she have been involved? What if Lillian wasn't as concerned about her grandfather being called suicidal as she was afraid of someone uncovering a much uglier truth about how he died? Maggie felt something brush her arm and flinched. The contact felt very real yet nothing was there.

"Have I forgotten anything?" Noah asked Maggie, though his look was one of concern for what had made her twitch.

She flipped through the pages of her pad as if checking her notes. "A few things. You had wanted to ask him about whether he would ever consider taking on a partner."

Davenport laughed. "Goodness no. I consider the island to be my family legacy. Patricia and I only have the one son but I've built something here that should stand long after his grandchildren are grown. I would never share this with an outsider."

Noah nodded to her to ask another question so she did. "One of the plots Noah is considering involves the owner's life being in danger and the young man saves him in the end. What sort of threat might you face in your position? If not a greedy partner, what about a competitor?" Something stopped her from suggesting a more intimate motive for murder.

The man furrowed his brow and rubbed his chin. "I can't imagine such a thing. Florida is wide open to developers. It's a gold mine for anyone brave enough to conquer the terrain. It will be a long time before hotel owners have to fight over guests."

"That's very interesting," Noah replied. "I've heard rumors that the Florida land boom is waning."

"Poppycock. Those rumors were undoubtedly started by someone trying to drive the values down for their own investment purposes."

Maggie watched Noah quash the urge to correct Davenport's misconception and came to his rescue. "Can you think of any other enemies a Florida hotel owner might have?"

"Hmmm, you say this is a good man, a guardian angel, so that would seem to eliminate him willingly being involved in any sort of unethical or immoral activity. And quite frankly, under the, uh, current restrictions on alcohol, I have had to establish good working relationships on both sides of the law...not that prohibition is much of a problem this far south." He gave it a bit more thought then shrugged. "Sorry, nothing comes to me that would be life threatening. Unless…"

Both Maggie and Noah stilled in anticipation of a clue. "Unless?" urged Noah.

"Well, I do enjoy a good game of draw poker now and then with a few of our regular guests. I suppose even a very good man could make the mistake of gambling more than he could afford to quickly pay back, and if the debt was to a criminal type…"

"Oh, that's an excellent possibility," Noah said with sincere enthusiasm. "Don't you think so my dear?"

"I believe it would work splendidly in the story." She scribbled a few words on her pad.

"I heard something very curious about this island," Noah said, casually changing the topic. "Is it true you discovered it by accident?"

"A very *lucky* accident. With all the pirate activity that went on around here in the past, it's incredible no one ever recorded its existence. It's as if it suddenly popped up one day just in time for me to sail into it."

"Have you ever considered the possibility that it wasn't an accident?" Noah asked. "That you specifically were meant to find it and build this beautiful resort?"

Maggie noted the way Robert's expression tightened and sensed that Noah's words held more than a bit of truth for the man.

"I don't see how that would be possible," Robert said with a note of finality as he rose from his chair. "Now if I've answered all your questions—"

"Just one more, if you would be so kind," Noah said then waited for Robert to sit again. "Actually, it's not so much a question as a message."

Maggie narrowed her eyes at Noah, wondering where he was going. Robert looked as though he was holding his breath.

Noah patted Maggie's hand. "It's all right, dear. Remember, Sir Arthur said Mr. Davenport could be important to the movement—"

"Are you referring to Sir Arthur Conan *Doyle* and the spiritualist movement?" Robert asked, leaning forward with obvious interest. "I've written to him several times but haven't heard back."

"That's not at all unusual," Noah said. "The only reason we had the pleasure of meeting him was that we just happened to be in New York City when he was there and he allowed us to observe a séance."

Robert's fascinated expression gave him away. "Oh, how I would love to see one of those. Patricia is not at all interested in that sort of thing. Quite opposed actually."

"Oh, that is a shame," Noah agreed. "Sir Arthur was quite generous with his praise of my Maggie's clairvoyant abilities."

It was Maggie's turn to hold her breath. She only knew the name Arthur Conan Doyle in connection with Sherlock Holmes stories. She had no idea what Noah was talking about but she lowered her gaze and tried to look embarrassed by the praise.

"That is most interesting," Robert said in a quiet tone. "But I do hope you will keep that to yourselves while you are here. My wife is not the only one who is suspicious of seers."

"Of course, of course," Noah quickly replied. "It was just that my wife had a dream about you last night and she—"

"You mentioned a message," Robert said, cutting him off.

"Yes, but if you'd prefer not to hear it…"

"I *do* want to hear it, but whatever it is, I must insist you never reveal it to anyone else."

"Actually, that is one of Maggie's personal rules. She never reveals her dreams to anyone but the person involved. Not even to me."

Maggie covered her surprise with a fake sneeze. They hadn't discussed this scenario, but Noah clearly expected her to improvise.

"I can step outside," Noah offered and got to his feet.

"No, no. That would raise Patricia's curiosity."

"My dear," Noah said to Maggie. "Perhaps you could write the message down for him to read."

Robert bobbed his head in agreement and she forced a tight smile as she tore off a sheet of blank paper. She hesitated for a moment then printed the only "message" that could be connected to their mission:

You were lying on the floor in this suite. Blood all around your head. Someone was placing a gun into your hand, to make it look like suicide. I couldn't see the person who shot you but it was not an accident. Then I saw a calendar with the year 1930.

Maggie folded the paper and handed it to Robert. He read the words she'd printed, stared into her eyes and read the message again before folding it and putting it into a desk drawer. His expression gave her no clue to what he was thinking. "I am sorry to give you such a…strange message, Mr. Davenport, but I'm hoping a warning might prevent it."

"That is my hope as well," Robert said. "I might have dismissed this completely, if it weren't for another young woman approaching me a few years ago. In fact, it was at the Grand Opening. She gave me a nearly identical warning. I had forgotten about it until now. Thank you, Mrs. Nash. I will do my best to make good use of your message."

As he said those words, there was a soft tap on the office door.

"Ah, that will be my ever-punctual wife, reminding me that our time is at an end." He stood, walked around the desk and opened the door, outside of which Patricia was waiting with a slight frown.

Noah and Maggie quickly thanked both Robert and Patricia and left the suite.

Maggie remained quiet during the scary downward ride in the ancient elevator, but not a second longer. As soon as they were beyond the operator's hearing, she murmured, "Mrs. Davenport looked annoyed with us."

"I doubt if it was all about us. I'll bet she was listening outside the door."

Maggie nodded. "He said she didn't approve of his interest in—" She stopped talking as they reached the lobby and found themselves surrounded by a large group of jovial men.

"Let's finish this conversation outside," Noah suggested and she tucked her hand under his elbow.

"Would you mind if we headed back to the bungalow? This outfit is really uncomfortably hot."

There were quite a few couples strolling along the beach, enjoying the last of the day's sunshine. Following their example, Noah and Maggie took off their shoes and stockings and he rolled up his pant legs so they could enjoy the squish of the wet sand between their toes and the waves lapping over their bare feet.

Certain the roiling ocean would muffle their conversation, Noah said, "Sorry about throwing you into the fire back there."

She gave his shoulder a playful punch. "That's for not letting me know you were going to go that way."

He rubbed the spot she hit as though it hurt. "Actually, I hadn't thought of it ahead of time. It just came to me, like a hunch, and I played it. And you never skipped a beat."

She made a face at him. "At least not one he could see."

"What made you flinch up there?"

It took her a moment to switch trains of thought. "Oh. It was strange. Like a feather duster ran along my arm."

"Maybe it was a ghost."

She smirked at him. "Thanks a lot. I really needed you to put that thought in my head." She told him where her mind had wandered right before it happened. "I got the sense that

Patricia wasn't entirely happy with being the submissive housewife. I'm not saying she killed Robert but maybe she wasn't all that sad when he died. Maybe she even has an idea of who murdered him—I mean *will*. This time thing is messing me up."

"Considering his answers, it seemed unlikely that he would take a partner. After money got really tight he might have changed his attitude but he was dead before things got hard here. And I don't think he would take the chance of having an affair with another man's wife. The island is too small and he's too well-known to do something that sneaky."

"He admitted to enjoying a game of cards," Maggie added. "Maybe he caught another player cheating or one of them objected to losing to him."

"That sounds feasible. Maybe we're here at this moment because Robert will meet his killer at tomorrow night's reception. We'll just have to see if anyone stands out or gives you a bad feeling."

Maggie cocked her head at him. "You sound pretty sure we'll get invited."

"I don't see the invite being a problem. I'm more concerned about how we'll get close to the engaged couple and their parents."

"Are you kidding? For *the* Noah Nash? Unless the Fitzgeralds happen to be here and agreed to attend, you'll be the most famous author at the party. I'd lay odds on there being a mad scramble to adjust the seating chart tomorrow morning."

He laughed. "Intuition?"

She shook her head. "Common sense. And who knows, it could be as simple as one of the parents being the killer."

"In which case, your warning could have been all that was needed for him to be more careful of who he gets involved with."

"Or plays cards with." Maggie stopped walking and frowned.

"What?" he asked. "I can almost see the gears turning."

Her mouth curved into a smile. "He said he was given the same warning a few years ago but forgot about it. What if someone else was sent from the future with the same task, but he didn't pay attention, and the reason we were sent here now was just to repeat the warning?"

He gave her a hug. "In which case, we've accomplished the mission and get to go home. In fact, look where we are."

She looked in the direction he pointed and saw the geode that Reynard had called a portal. "How is that possible? I thought we were walking in the opposite direction."

"Who cares? Let's just grab the chance while it's being offered."

He took her hand and they jogged the short distance to the rock. The setting sun kept the moon from being visible, and yet, there was a definite glow inside the geode's crack.

Maggie smiled up at Noah and he placed their held hands over the crack. She prepared herself for the shimmery sensation that would take them on a return trip through time but for several seconds nothing unusual happened.

Suddenly a bolt of lightning struck directly overhead and a clap of thunder followed close behind. A few drops of rain instantly turned into a heavy downpour and the wind whipped up a funnel of stinging sand around them. Maggie could still feel Noah's hand pressing hers against the rock but she could no longer see him through the blinding cyclone.

Then, as quickly as the freakish storm had started, it stopped.

CHAPTER 15

"Are you okay?" Noah asked anxiously.

She was drenched and her teeth were chattering but she managed to bob her head. He hugged her tightly against him until the shivering stopped.

"That was…"

"Please don't say cool," Maggie muttered.

He snorted. "I was going to say interesting but that wasn't right either."

Maggie's stomach suddenly felt queasy, which usually preceded something that wasn't right but she was pretty sure it wasn't his choice of words. "Noah?"

"Yes?"

"I lost my shoes and stockings. I know they were in my hand…"

He chuckled and looked around them. "Same here. But I was more worried about holding onto you than a pair of shoes I could replace."

She exhaled heavily and was quiet for a moment before repeating "Noah?"

"Did you lose something else?"

"No. At least I don't think so. But I have a really bad feeling."

He eased her back a few inches and met her gaze. "Yeah. Me, too. But I'm hoping we made it back to our time and there just happened to be a flash storm going through. Do you feel steady enough to walk back to the hotel and find out?"

She took a deep breath and latched onto his hand. "Just don't let go, okay?"

He brought her hand up and kissed her knuckles. "Never."

A few minutes later they were close enough to see a large, structure where the Davenport Resort should have been, but it wasn't the luxury hotel where they had been staying in either time period.

What was in its place was something straight out of a post-apocalypse movie. There were no bungalows or cabanas on the beach. Sections of the building were down to rubble, the domes were gone, only jagged edges of glass were left in the window frames of the section still erect. The carefully attended landscape around the building was wildly overgrown with vines winding their way in and out of every crack and opening.

"Maybe there was a hurricane while we were gone," Maggie offered hopefully.

"This didn't happen in the last twenty-four hours," Noah said with a frown. "Maybe we're in another time period, like after the 1928 hurricane or one of the ones that hit afterward…"

"Or we're in a more distant future when—"

"Stop right there!" a man shouted from somewhere. *"This is private property and you're trespassing."*

Noah drew Maggie's attention to a loudspeaker high up in a tree. They took a step toward it and a shot sounded.

"Turn around and leave the way you came or the next bullet will be into one of you."

Noah raised his hands in surrender and Maggie did the same. "We didn't mean to trespass,'" Noah shouted. "But we're lost. We just need some help."

Several seconds passed before a man came out of the least damaged part of the building and walked toward them. He was carrying a rifle but it was pointed toward the sky rather than them. His only clothing was a pair of tan shorts. The man was quite tall, with the lean body of a runner. Very light blond hair was tied in a bun on top of his head and he had a short beard of the same hue. The skin on his forehead and cheekbones bore lines that seemed to come from too much sun rather than old-age. The closer he got the more familiar he seemed to Maggie.

"How did you get here?" the man asked in a tone that dared them to lie.

"A life preserver," Noah said without hesitation. "Our sailboat capsized about a mile out. The tide brought us in near a giant rock. The preserver's still there if you want to go—"

"Not necessary. I guess that explains why the two of you look like drowned cats. What it doesn't explain is why you were headed for my island."

"*Your* island?" Maggie asked with wide eyes. "Are you a Davenport?"

"You say that like you're surprised. Don't bother pretending. If you're another one of my so-called cousins or step-siblings, you can jump right back in the ocean with your preserver and swim home. I won't stop you. But I won't help you either. I've said this a hundred times and I'll say it again. I am not selling the island, nor am I willing to break it up into shares. I don't care what the offer is or how many attorneys bring suits against me. I am not giving up what is mine. Now get—"

"You're wrong," Noah said bluntly. "We aren't part of your legal problems. My name is Noah Nash and this is my fiancée, Maggie Harrison."

Maggie saw Noah rub the spot on his arm where she had punched him and got ready to improvise again.

The man narrowed his eyes. "Noah Nash? Like the author?"

"Not like," Maggie said lifting her chin a bit. "He *is* the author. And even though we're engaged, I'm still his research assistant."

"Hmmph," the man sounded. "I don't suppose you have any ID on you to prove that. I've read one or two of Nash's books. Not bad, but I prefer stories based in reality. Don't move from this spot. I'll be right back." Without another word, he turned and headed toward the part of the building he had come from.

"Okay," Noah whispered to Maggie. "If he knows who I am, we're at least back to our time."

She made a face. "Or much later, based on the hotel's condition."

At least ten minutes passed before the blond man returned, but they had stayed in place as ordered. At least he had left the rifle behind.

"Okay. You're Noah Nash, or his identical twin."

"Do you have one of his books here?" Maggie asked.

He smirked. "No. I looked him up. There are thousands of photos of him on the net. The fans really love posing with him." He frowned at Maggie. "I didn't see any of you though. Or any sort of engagement announcement. I gather you don't have accounts on any social media sites. You did say Maggie Harrison, right?"

As he began spelling it out she cut him off. "You have internet here?"

He rolled his eyes. "Yes. I have internet and electricity and a sewage disposal system that meets Florida's codes. I also have a very advanced security system, which is how I know you're here alone and didn't arrive by boat or helicopter. And you didn't parachute in. So your capsized sailboat story might be the truth. But I'm still waiting to hear *why* you're here at all."

Noah let out an audible sigh. "I read an article about Crystal Island and the resort that Robert Davenport had built in the nineteen-twenties and it triggered an idea for a new book. When Maggie did a little research, she found some articles about one of the heirs living on the island and I was hoping to interview that person."

"I'm afraid I don't remember your name," Maggie added, hoping he would finally introduce himself.

It took him a moment to lower his guard. "Paul Davenport." He shook each of their hands. "My brother Brad and I are the only true heirs to the island. I have his power of attorney to do whatever I want here and he manages a hotel in Vegas."

"What about—" She reconsidered what she was about to ask. "I thought there was another grandchild…a woman."

Paul shook his head. "No, there are only two direct descendants left alive. And as long as one of us maintains our residence here, no one can force a sale."

"Not even the State of Florida?" Noah asked.

"Good old granddad may have been certifiable but the deed he created has held up in our favor. What did you want to interview me about?"

Noah paused long enough for Maggie to look at his face and notice how the color had faded from his cheeks and how his eyes had shifted from side to side with an awareness of…*something.* "Noah?" she said softly. "Are you all right? Do you need to sit down?"

He squeezed his eyes shut for a moment then rubbed his forehead. "I, uh, just got dizzy for a second. I'm okay now."

"No, I don't think you are. I'm sure you bumped your head when the boat flipped." Maggie nudged him into sitting on the sand then turned to Paul. "Could we possibly bother you for some water…and maybe some aspirin?"

Paul looked skeptical but he nodded and headed back toward the hotel.

"Are you really okay?" Maggie asked as soon as Paul left.

"Yeah, I'm fine," Noah murmured. "Keep your voice down just in case that sound system goes both ways. I was trying to think of what story I could tell him when it suddenly occurred to me that this could all be our fault."

Maggie's jaw dropped but she kept her voice hushed. "How can you think that? If anyone's to blame it's whatever super power is messing with us."

"I don't disagree with that. But what if we made the wrong choice about who we were supposed to save? Maybe we missed an important clue. What if the warning message to Robert Davenport made things worse? What if—"

"Stop," she ordered. "Before we come to any conclusions, we need to find out exactly what happened to this place. The good news is, whatever year this is, you're still a famous author and apparently you still look like your photos. I am confused about why he couldn't find anything on me. I don't do a lot of posting but I do have a Facebook page with a few photos of myself."

"Maybe he misspelled it."

She looked doubtful but let it go. "Have you got a story in mind that might get him to fill in some blanks?"

"I think so, but feel free to jump in if—hey, what was that about a granddaughter?"

"I met with Lillian Davenport in her office yesterday. She's Robert's granddaughter and the current general manager of the hotel. Or rather she was in *our* 2018. Now she never existed."

He was about to say something else when Paul arrived carrying two small bottles of water and a bottle of aspirin. As Noah took the pills and they drank the water, Paul sat down on the sand in front of them.

"You look better," he told Noah. "I'd like an explanation now."

Maggie held up her index finger. "One second," she said to Paul. To Noah, she asked, "What is your name?"

Noah squinted at her.

"Humor me." She gave him a wink that Paul couldn't see.

Noah sighed. "Fine. I'm Noah Nash."

"Where are we?"

"Crystal Island, off the coast of Florida."

"And what's today's date?"

He took a breath before answering. "August 6, no, August 7, 2018."

"Enough," Paul said with obvious annoyance. "His brain is fine. I radioed the Coast Guard to come pick you up. So you'd better get on with whatever you came here to ask me about."

Maggie was relieved by his unspoken confirmation of the date. However, rather than a sense of security, the mention of an imminent Coast Guard rescue filled Maggie with dread. A quick glance at Noah told her he probably had the same thought. They dared not leave the island—or the portal—just yet.

Noah wasted no more time. "Mind you, I have no intention of referring to Crystal Island or the Davenport family by name. In fact, that's why I wanted to interview you—to make sure I don't accidentally use some fact that might suggest *Hotel Hellgate*—that's the name of the new book—is based on any actual events."

"I guess that makes some sense," Paul said with a shrug. "Especially considering everything that happened here. Besides, a big-name horror author suggesting he based his book on Crystal Island might just stir up more attention than we already have, which is definitely not to our advantage at the moment."

Through a series of carefully-worded questions, Noah and Maggie extracted the revised biography of Robert Davenport.

Around the time they delivered their message of doom, Robert became a fanatical believer in all things mystical. Anyone claiming to be a psychic or medium was given free rein on the island. As stories spread about ghostly encounters and mysterious deaths, the regular, wealthy clientele found more pleasant places to vacation.

When the Okeechobee hurricane took a great number of lives and destroyed a portion of the hotel in 1928, Robert's fascination became a debilitating obsession. Rather than repairing the hotel, his savings went into the pockets of charlatans who claimed to have the ability to exorcise the evil spirits that were causing all the problems on the island…in exchange for large amounts of cash.

Even before the stock market crashed, Robert was deeply in debt and virtually without income. In 1930, Patricia and Chester left Crystal Island and moved in with her family in New York. But Robert refused to go with them. Despite his financial downfall, he insisted on remaining in residence on the island in order to maintain what he called his family legacy.

Although Patricia never visited the island again, she used her personal inheritance to make sure Robert was cared for until he died following a bout of pneumonia in 1952.

By the time Maggie and Noah heard Paul's version of what had happened, they had no doubt that their meeting with Robert Davenport was the trigger for his ruined life.

"Paul? The Coast Guard just radioed with a message for you."

Paul looked up at the loudspeaker and called, "I'll be there in a minute."

"And please bring our guests with you. They look harmless enough."

Maggie's gaze shot from the loudspeaker to Noah, who looked just as surprised as she was to hear the woman's voice.

"Apparently, my wife would like to meet you," Paul said as he got to his feet. "I'm afraid she's a fan."

They followed him across the sand, over some broken concrete, and along a nearly invisible path in the thick foliage, until they came to a portion of the exterior wall that appeared to be completely boarded up.

"Turn around," he ordered and they obeyed. A moment later, he said, "Okay. Follow me."

The panel of boards had been moved sideways to reveal a very narrow opening through which they squeezed one at a time. It took Maggie a few minutes of staring at rubble and stacks of broken furniture to realize they were in the speakeasy version of the Amethyst Cave lounge. Noah squeezed her hand and she smiled up at him despite the sad state of the room.

"Step only where I do," Paul ordered.

176 *Marilyn Campbell*

As they continued to follow his zigging and zagging through the room, they passed the amethyst geode where Maggie had originally heard The Weeping Woman. Not only did she hear nothing now, she felt nothing coming from the stone. Its energy was totally depleted.

As they crossed from the lounge to another boarded up wall across the wide hallway, she caught a glimpse of an even greater disaster in the lobby, where shattered glass covered every inch of the large, roof-less area. Paul didn't ask them to turn around this time as he pushed the boarded section along an invisible track to reveal an ancient elevator, similar to the one they had taken to visit the Davenports.

"I don't mean to be rude," Noah said as they stepped into the iron cage. "But why hasn't any of this damage been repaired, or at least cleared away?"

Paul grinned and manipulated the gears and levers to get the old machine rising. "Doesn't look very inviting does it? Well, that's part of it. It's enough to discourage the average trespasser. And if someone's more serious about causing us trouble, there are a lot of booby-traps all over this place. The high-tech security system is more for my wife's peace of mind."

"I would also have some serious concerns about the state of mind of someone living like this on purpose," Maggie noted. "Especially once I found out he had a shotgun."

Paul chuckled. "I only fire warning shots…and those are blanks. But it usually does the trick even before they get close enough to look inside."

Noah had another question ready. "You mentioned some illegitimate claims and law suits. I'd think the condition of the property would be enough to discourage most people."

Paul brought the elevator to a stop on the third floor before responding. "There is that. Unfortunately, until all the claims and suits are dismissed, I can't generate the kind of money needed to rebuild. But I'm patient and, as you'll see in a minute, we're quite comfortable."

Paul hadn't exaggerated when he said they were comfortable. Beyond another false door was a totally renovated, thoroughly modern apartment. The instant they stepped inside, they were exuberantly greeted by a petite redheaded young woman.

"Hello! Welcome to our home. Can I get you a cup of coffee? Or maybe you're ready for a glass of wine. Oh, my. I just realized you're probably starving. Just give me a couple minutes to throw something together."

"Noah Nash, Maggie Harrison, that bundle of energy is my wife, Sheryl."

"Lily?" Paul called toward a hallway. "Would you come here please? I'd like you to meet someone."

The name surprised Maggie but the teenage girl who appeared a few seconds later looked a lot like a young Lillian Davenport. But rather than the pretty girl with the happy smile Maggie had seen in the photograph, this girl looked more like the stern-faced, mature Lillian who had threatened her. This girl was definitely not happy.

"It's nice to meet you, Lily. You have a very pretty name."

Lily smirked. "It's a funeral flower."

Paul's jaw clenched and he glared at his daughter but Sheryl quickly lightened the air. "Mr. Nash is a famous writer," she told her daughter.

"What do you write?" Lily asked him in a flat voice.

"Horror novels," Noah answered. "Do you enjoy that genre? I could send you—"

"No thank you," she said, cutting off his offer in the same disinterested tone. "May I go back to my room now?" she asked her mother but didn't wait for an answer before walking away.

Paul took a slow deep breath.

It was Maggie's turn to try to ease the tension. "I guess teenagers are the same whether they grow up in a crowded city or on a private island."

"She's just like my brother Brad. Can't get away from the island fast enough. We've already agreed to send her to college on the mainland but I can tell, she'll never be content to stay here."

"Now, Paul," Sheryl said in a gently scolding voice. "You don't know that. Once we get the hotel up and running again, everything will change. There will be lots of guests and social events and boats coming and going. Just like it was in the beginning. She'll want to be part of it then."

Paul forced a smile. "My wife, the eternal optimist."

"Please sit," Sheryl told Maggie and Noah. "Which will it be? Coffee or wine?"

"Coffee," they both answered simultaneously.

As she headed toward the kitchen, she said, "And I'll make sandwiches with my home-made bread and special dressing. Do you prefer turkey or ham?"

Noah said turkey and Maggie requested ham, but Sheryl gave no indication that she'd heard them.

"So, where were we?" Paul asked as he motioned for them to sit on the couch while he took one of the chairs on the other side of a rectangular coffee table.

A purposeful glance from Noah told Maggie to take over the "interview" lead. "Robert had just died and it looked like the State of Florida was gearing up to take possession of Crystal Island by eminent domain."

Paul nodded. "Right. From what I was told, grandma Patricia was willing to let the State have it for a substantial payment to my father, Chester, the only heir to Robert's estate. But his wife, Irene, was intrigued by the Beat Generation movement and convinced him to thumb his nose at civilization and make a life for themselves on his island."

"That must have been really hard."

Paul chuckled. "Dad spent his childhood in a luxury hotel filled with staff then moved to Patricia's family mansion filled with servants. You'd think he'd have given up after a couple months. But the opposite happened. He had enough money to get the generator working and make this apartment livable. They learned to fish and harvest their own fruits and vegetables. They always seemed happy to me. And when she had a fatal heart attack, dad wasn't far behind her."

"So you and Brad were both born here and you never left?" Noah asked.

Paul nodded. "Brad and I both went to college in Florida so that we were close enough to come back here on holidays. When Brad finished with a degree in hotel management, he headed straight for the opposite side of the country. But I knew I had to come back here. I learned how to program computers so that I could make a good living without leaving the island."

At that moment, Sheryl set a steaming teapot and a plate of cookies on the table between them and sat down beside Paul.

He squeezed her hand. "I was just lucky to meet my perfect partner."

Maggie smiled at the couple but one glance at Noah told her he noticed what she did—Sheryl had brought a teapot that smelled of a strong herb rather than coffee, and no cups to drink whatever was in the teapot, and instead of sandwiches with either turkey or ham, there were cookies with burned edges. She had also had a change of personality. The perky, thrilled-to-have-some-company woman was now silent, sad-looking and her pupils were obviously dilated.

"Does Brad have children?" Noah asked.

"No. He's never met anyone he wanted to settle down with."

And with that comment, Paul grew quiet as well.

Maggie suddenly remembered what Sheryl had said over the loudspeaker. "Did the Coast Guard say when they might get here?"

Paul's attention immediately returned to her. "Oh, that's right. Sheryl, honey, you said the Coast Guard radioed with a message? Did you write it down like we talked about?"

She turned and stared at him with a sad expression.

"It's okay," he told her, giving her hand a squeeze. He rose, went to the kitchen and returned with a piece of paper in hand. "They should arrive any minute," he announced. "They'll meet you by the rock where you came in. I'll have to lead you out."

Without further discussion, he went to the front door and left.

Not wanting to fall behind and accidently run into one of Paul's booby traps, Noah and Maggie both hurried to catch up.

"It was very nice meeting you, Sheryl," Maggie said before walking out the door, but she got no response.

The moment they were on the beach, Paul pointed them in the direction of the geode and went right back into the hotel. The next instant, Maggie and Noah took off at a trot and didn't talk until they reached their destination.

"Conclusions?" Noah asked after several seconds passed in silence.

"Are you kidding? I don't even know where to start. That was a whole lot of crazy we just saw. We gave a man a hint about his death and it caused everything in his family to change. One person in particular no longer exists. Since I never asked to be sent back in time, I refuse to accept the responsibility for such a mess. At least we're back in 2018 and it doesn't seem to have touched your life, so that's something positive."

"Maybe. Maybe not. Remember what you said about the ripple in the pond theory. We won't know for sure until we go home and check everything out."

"*Home*." Maggie's shoulders slumped. "I never thought I would miss my little apartment so much."

"It hasn't been all bad…has it?" Noah tucked a loose strand of Maggie's hair behind her ear.

She saw the concern in his eyes and wrapped her arms around his waist. "Most of it has been amazing. I'm hoping that part of it doesn't have to be over just because the resort and our belongings are gone with the wind. I'm also hoping you'll come back to my apartment with me. We still have a book to work on."

He kissed her forehead and grinned. "Or we could just stop there for an hour to pick up some of your things, catch the first flight to Maine and work on the book at *my* home."

Maggie rested her head on his chest. "*Mmmm*. That sounds even better." Noah held her close and ran his hands up and down her back, but she couldn't make herself completely relax. "Shouldn't the Coast Guard be here by now?"

"De Coast Guard will not be coming at all," a man's voice informed them in a sympathetic tone…and a distinct Jamaican accent.

Maggie instantly stepped out of Noah's arms and gaped at the man. *"Reynard?"*

"Yes, it be me. Sent on another errand, dough not in secret dis time."

"This is *not* our fault," Maggie said sharply.

Noah's voice was even angrier. "You can go right back and tell your bosses, whoever they are, that we're done playing puppet for them."

"Dey have discussed your situation and agreed dat ya are not to be held responsible," Reynard assured them. "Because I interacted with ya before, I was assigned to explain—"

"Explain what exactly?" Noah demanded. "Nothing that's happened makes any sense. Why us? Why the mystery? Who has the power to send us through time?"

"I do not have permission to answer dose questions. I can only explain dat ya were sent to de past to save someone, but *not* Robert Davenport. It was to be a small event correction, with limited but positive results. Robert was fated to die when he did, de way he did, for de good of Crystal Island and protection of de portal. De method ya chose to change dat fate created a scenario dat had not been foreseen. Dey would have prevented ya from intervening in Robert's fate if it had. But unpredictability is one of de human traits dat fascinates dem."

"You're still talking in riddles," Noah complained. "The bottom line is, we played our parts, the show's over. Now just let us go home and we'll pretend the whole thing never happened."

"But dat is not possible," Reynard said with a shake of his head. "Ya are being given another opportunity to complete your original mission. T'ree full days still remain before your deadline."

"That's totally unfair!" Maggie exclaimed. "Without any specific clues, we prevented a man from killing himself. That should satisfy whatever twisted mind came up with the game. Under the circumstances, we should have the right to refuse."

"Maggie's right," Noah agreed. "You told us *we* had to figure out who we had to save. You never said there might be a red herring or two!"

Reynard looked upward for several seconds before speaking again. "Granted. Ya may refuse, but I am to tell ya de reason ya should not. Ya discovered dat Lillian Davenport was never conceived in dis timeline. But she is not de only one. De Davenport Resort was responsible for many introductions of pairs who would never meet in any other way. At least not in dat lifetime. De destruction ya see here on de island was not limited to de Davenport family. T'ousands of other lives were altered dat should not have been. Just like Lillian Davenport, Maggie Harrison was never born."

"How could that be?" questioned Noah.

"Her grandmother was being courted by a young man from a wealthy family. When he went on a vacation with his family to Crystal Island, she met and fell in love with Maggie's grandfather." To Maggie he said, "Because dere was no Crystal Island vacation, your grandmother never met your grandfather. She married the wealthy young man and although she lived a life of ease, she never had children."

Maggie let that sink in. "So I was never born. That's why Paul couldn't find my Facebook page. But then, how am I standing here?"

"Ya exist only as long as ya are on Crystal Island. If ya tried to leave…"

"She would disappear," Noah finished. "Which is why we can't refuse to continue with our so-called mission." He exhaled heavily. "So what happens now?"

"Ya connect wit' de portal as de moon rises and ya will be taken back to de moment before ya asked for a meeting wit' Robert Davenport. But this time, it would be best to avoid interacting wit' him entirely. However, ya should continue wit' all your other plans of action. Dat is all I am permitted to say. I wish ya success."

"Wait!" Maggie yelled as he began to fade and his image solidified again. "What happens to all of this and all the other people you mentioned?"

"As soon as ya go back, this newly created time line disintegrates." And with those words, Reynard vanished.

A moment later, the moon became visible above the horizon.

Noah grasped Maggie's hand and asked "Ready?"

She frowned. "You could save yourself a lot of trouble and just go home to Maine—"

He brought her hand up and kissed her knuckles. "I promised I'd never let go and if that means another risky trip back to the Roaring Twenties, so be it."

She smiled up at him then pressed their hands on top of the geode's crack. This time was very different from the first two. There was no shimmering sensation. There was no thunder, lightning or drenching. There was only darkness and silence…and waiting.

CHAPTER 16

Maggie had no sense of how long she was in a limbo state but suddenly they were back in the hotel lobby, being ushered to the manager's office by the concierge. She glanced at Noah then down her body. They were once again dressed in the cooler outfits they'd had on for the morning walk-around.

"Excuse me, Mr. Eckhart, Mr. and Mrs. Nash asked to speak to you."

Exactly as the first time, Mr. Eckhart greeted them as though they were honored guests.

Maggie called up her memory of the original conversation in which she boasted of her husband's accomplishments, requested a tour of the service areas of the hotel and wrangled an invitation to the Hampshire-Gaviston engagement reception. She carefully avoided any mention of Robert Davenport.

This time Maggie refrained from offering her hand as they were thanking him for his help.

"Is there anything else I might assist you with today? Perhaps dinner reservations?"

She turned to Noah. "What do you think, dear? Emerald Patio at six thirty?"

Noah shrugged. "Whatever you'd prefer, dear."

Once they were back in the lobby, Noah leaned down and whispered in Maggie's ear. "At the risk of inciting uncontrollable lust, I have to repeat, you were fantastic in there. Maybe even better."

"Having a rehearsal probably helped. I figured you wouldn't mind if I moved dinner up by an hour. It's been a long time since breakfast."

"I got that. But since we didn't ask for an appointment with Davenport, we still have some free time before dinner. Is there anything you'd like to do?"

"Honestly, I'd like to take a nap. A *real* nap. It's been a helluva day and my brain could use a break before we start strategizing again."

"I agree completely."

She tucked her arm into his as they headed out to the planked walkway.

When they got to the bungalow, they opened several windows to let in the ocean breeze then stripped down to their underwear and stretched out on the clean bed sheets.

"I miss air conditioning so much," Maggie muttered.

He leaned over and gave her a light kiss. "Close your eyes. It will be cooler in a couple hours." With a muffled groan, he rolled away from her.

"Noah?"

"Hmmm?"

"I wouldn't mind getting a little hotter—"

"Please don't finish that sentence. I'm having a hard enough time pretending we're back in high school and you're not the least bit interested in anything but friendship."

"I hope you know, I'd change that if I could." When he didn't respond, she turned on her side, facing the wall. Her last thoughts before nodding off were of how different her life might have been if she *had* been interested in something more than friendship with him back then.

When they awoke, they barely had time to wash and dress for dinner and rumbling stomachs demanded they not postpone their reservations.

They were almost at the Emerald Patio when Maggie stopped and looked around as though seeing the area for the first time.

"What is it?" Noah asked.

"The driver who picked me up at the dock said the island was about two miles square. That seems about right from west to east, but from the northern beach where the bungalows and cabana tents are, through the hotel, to the front entrance might be a half mile or so. The golf course is close to the southern beach, and the tennis courts and clubhouse are along the southwest corner. That seems to leave quite a bit of land in between with no designation, which, of course, makes me curious about it."

"Let's find out what's there in this time."

They walked up to the maître d' and Noah gave him their names.

"Hello again," Maggie said brightly as the host confirmed their reservation in his big book. To Noah, she explained, "Connor was the one who brought us all that bubbly champagne last night."

The maître d' smiled politely. "Of course. I remember thinking what an attractive couple you are. I work in a lot of different areas, depending on the need."

"Then you're the perfect person for me to ask a question about the hotel," Noah declared.

As Noah told Connor what they were curious about, Maggie took a closer look at Connor's name tag. This time, she could see that he was from Philadelphia. Again, she had the feeling she'd seen him and the name Connor before last night at the speakeasy, even though that wasn't possible.

Or was it?

A small photo on a wall…a young couple smiling happily at each other…engraving on a silver frame—*Lilli & Connor … 2/14/05.*

"Oh my gawd," Maggie blurted out. "You're Lilli's Connor!"

CHAPTER 17

H umor let out an audible guffaw. *I do love this pair! So bright and so marvelously unpredictable.*

Karma found nothing to be delighted about. *They were not supposed to encounter him. Connor O'Malley chose his fate. Judgment was passed. There should never have been a possibility of her recognizing him.*

Justice sided with neither. *I am beginning to doubt they will ever begin their primary mission let alone complete it. We should terminate this test before they cause more disruptions than we can rectify.*

I still believe in them, Love stated, sending Humor a hug. *Maggie and Noah are obviously more elevated than others we have chosen in the past, more curious, more intuitive, more creative, more—*

Enough, The First declared, ending the debate before more of the Abstracts got involved. *The test will continue without further assistance or intervention from this Council. However, if this pair is a true example of humanity's evolution, it may be time to redesign the guidelines for evaluating their progress. Therefore, I hereby request that all members of The Council begin considering possible alterations. Any and all ideas will be discussed after the current test comes to an end.*

Having given The Council something unexpected to focus on instead of questioning who was to blame for Maggie's recognizing Connor, The First retreated from the collective consciousness. There was merit in Karma's and Justice's concerns about Maggie and Noah, but The First's immediate reaction mirrored Humor's.

Whether the pair completed their primary mission or not, observing them proved quite entertaining, which was one of the reasons The First had purposely arranged for Connor O'Malley to show up in Maggie's path despite the obstacles in place to prevent such an encounter. Another human may not have realized who Connor was and nothing would have come of it. But not Maggie. The First could hardly wait to see what she would do next.

The other reason The First had intervened was to follow through on a private promise made to Mercy. Like Love, Mercy was always given a bit more flexibility than certain other Abstracts. Mercy rarely took advantage of that, but several times it had requested a particular favor for its present human charge and, considering the fact that Mercy's charge was Robert Davenport's granddaughter, The First had agreed to personally grant that favor as soon as an opportunity arose.

And because Maggie and Noah had all the elevated traits Love had credited them with, that opportunity was now at hand.

CHAPTER 18

Lillian crossed her arms and stared at the closed wardrobe doors in her bedroom. It felt as though the concealed mirror was taunting her, daring her to take another trip. Last night had been the first time in a very long while that she had given into the urge and it had been far from satisfying. Tonight was the first time in six years that she felt unable to resist the mirror's lure.

She thought she had overcome the need completely, that taking advantage of what the mirror offered was at her prerogative, but staying in her office today, doing the work she loved, had taken all her strength. Of course, Mercy had noticed something was wrong with her boss and kept asking if there was anything she could do to help. But this was not a weight her efficient executive assistant could take off her shoulders.

Her brain was overwhelmed with thoughts of Connor, memories of the hours they had shared and the years they were apart, years when she spent every day anticipating his return and escaping into the mirror every night when he didn't.

It always came down to time lost.

Once they had given in to the attraction, they had spent every free weekend of the next year and a half together. And between living in two different cities and both having overloaded schedules, when they were together, most of their time was spent having sex.

In her innocence, she had assumed that meant they were in love and headed for marital bliss.

His experience told him it was the perfect part-time, temporary relationship for two very busy people who were strongly attracted to one another.

She had expected an engagement ring when she graduated from Harvard. What she got was her freedom.

Connor had a list of logical reasons for making a clean break: he was taking an offer of a full professorship in Colorado; she had to take her place on Crystal Island; the ten-year difference in their ages would matter even more as the years passed, he wasn't sure he ever wanted to get married and have children; and so on and so forth. There was no good reason to keep trying to hold on to a relationship when they were clearly headed in opposite directions, both geographically and in their lives.

Lilli remembered crying a lot at first, but her father, brother Paul and her Crystal Island "family" quickly put a stop to her self-pitying and she gave herself over to the family business.

One year later, Paul, his wife and their three children moved to Honolulu to turn an old beach motel property into another Davenport resort and Chester turned management of Crystal Island over to Lilli, despite her being only twenty-three years old.

Then, in 2005, five years after she had locked away all the memories of Connor O'Malley, he showed up at her hotel with a list of apologies and promises three times as long as the list of logical excuses he had given for their parting.

The more mature, much more confident Lilli made him wait an entire day before forgiving him for everything.

The mirror beckoned with a promise that she could relive that joyous day or any other if she just quit fighting the inevitable submission. Perhaps last night's full moon was still affecting her emotions but, whatever was making her weak had won. She opened the wardrobe doors, placed her hand on the mirror and whispered, *"Connor."*

"Behave yourself!" Lilli muttered through a fixed smile but a giggle softened the order as she moved Connor's hand from her bottom to her hip.

His fingers tightened and she shifted her gaze from the photographer's lens to Connor's dark eyes. And that quickly, she didn't care where he put his hands or in front of whom, as long as he never stopped looking at her like that.

The flash of light as the souvenir picture was taken broke the spell.

"You're going to love that one, Ms. Davenport," the photographer said. "A real keeper. It will be delivered to your suite tomorrow. Happy Valentine's Day."

It had been Lilli's idea to have a photographer set up outside the Emerald Dome restaurant and from the long line they had waited in, it looked like a success. Thinking of having their picture taken was what had prompted her to wear her red, Mandarin-style dress and have Connor wear his black sports jacket and white dress shirt. He had suggested they have their Valentine's dinner somewhere besides the Davenport but she had not wanted to be off-island in case she was needed. Besides, no one prepared a better meal than Chef Gerard.

"Let's take a walk on the beach," Connor said, giving her hand a tug.

Before heading outside, he stopped at the concierge desk and picked up a stuffed hotel gym bag. Lilli saw a note tied around the handle—*Hold for C. O'Malley.*

"What are you up to now, O'Malley?"

He hugged her close to his side and kissed her temple. "Just a wee bit of Irish romance. Having dinner here felt like you were still working. Do you know how many times we were interrupted?"

She did her best to look apologetic. "Two?"

"*Hmmph.* More like six. And none of them were emergencies or problems only you could deal with." He stopped and turned her toward him. "I know the hotel is your baby. And I know you're the one in charge. But for the rest of tonight, you need to trust all the capable managers under your leadership. I may never understand why you would want so much responsibility, but I am trying to respect your choice. However, this is Valentine's Day *and* your birthday and you deserve some time away with the man who loves you, even if only for a few hours. So for the rest of this night could you try to not be the Davenport's general manager and just be Connor O'Malley's sweetheart?"

She almost told him the two couldn't be separated, that the Davenport had been part of her life long before he came into it. But then she met his adoring gaze and all resistance melted away. She pulled the cell phone out of her bag and let him see her turn it off. "I love you. You know that, don't you?"

He kissed the tip of her nose. "Yep. But sometimes I feel like I have to remind *you* of that fact." He led her over to a golf cart, set the bag in the back and helped her board. Before they got started, he took off his jacket and set it on the back seat then took a pair of her casual sandals out of the gym bag and supported her while she switched shoes. "Trust me," he told her before she could ask again what he was up to.

Connor parked the golf cart at the entrance to one of the nature trails. He positioned it to block the path and hung a *No Trespassing* sign on the back end.

Since Lilli knew every inch of Crystal Island, his surprise was no longer a secret.

"Okay?" he asked, holding his hand out to her.

"Absolutely," she replied and accepted his assistance. As soon as her feet touched the ground, she drew his head closer for a long, deep kiss. She didn't need to kiss an army of men to know that no one else would ever make her feel the way Connor did every time their lips met. And no matter how many times they'd made love, it always felt new and different. She pressed her hips against his and moaned her approval.

Connor broke the kiss and let out a low chuckle. "If you keep that up, you'll be getting one of your presents right here."

She wrinkled her nose at him. "And if you weren't so damn sexy, I wouldn't need to be reminded to behave."

He gave her a quick kiss on the mouth then grabbed the gym bag. It only took a few minutes of quick walking to reach the end of the trail, where the sweet smell of night-blooming jasmine announced their arrival at the lush tropical lagoon, with its splashing waterfall. The fact that it was completely man-made and purposefully landscaped took nothing away from the beauty of the spot.

Lilli sat on a boulder while Connor removed one thing after another from the bag, making her think of a clown car. Within minutes he had set up a self-inflating air mattress, covered it with a sheet and poured her favorite amaretto liqueur into two cordial glasses. She kicked off her sandals, sat down on the mattress and accepted one of the glasses. She smiled as he slipped out of his loafers and settled down beside her.

He touched his glass to hers then dipped his index finger into the liqueur and used it to outline her lips. "Happy birthday to the sweetest, most beautiful, smartest, *horniest* girl in the whole world."

She stuck her tongue out in time to lick his fingertip then imitated his action, outlining his lips with the sweet liquid from her glass as she said, "And happy Valentine's Day to the sexiest, most wonderful, romantic, *patient* man in the world. Thank you for putting up with my workaholism."

He brought their mouths together to share an almond-flavored kiss that slowly deepened as their hands entered the play. He always knew what she wanted and gave her what she needed. He never rushed, no matter how much she begged and, when their bodies finally came together, she was always glad she let him be the boss in this part of

her life. After they were both fully satisfied and the
delicious tremors subsided, they remained together without
talking for some time.

For Lilli, it was because she couldn't find words to
express the intensity of what he made her feel.

For Connor, it was more than just a reaction to mind-
blowing sex. He gently rolled her to his side. "That was…"
Rather than define it with words, he kissed her with a
tenderness only possible when true love is in a man's heart.
"Actually, the plan called for something else before we—
hell, I should've known that wasn't going to be possible."

She smiled. "Well, I believe you were the one who said I
was the horniest girl in the whole world."

"Anyway," he continued, ignoring the opening she gave
him. "I want you to know that what I'm about to say has
nothing to do with how good that was or how good it
always is—"

"Connor!"

He took a deep breath and sat up. "Okay. Here goes."

Not sure whether to be nervous herself, Lilli sat up with a
serious expression.

Connor unzipped a side pocket of the gym bag and pulled
out a small, burgundy velvet box. "Lillian Davenport," he
began then had to clear his throat before continuing.

Lilli held her breath, glanced at the little box and forced
herself to keep her gaze on Connor's dreamy eyes.

"I love you, Lilli. I want nothing more than to be with
you and make you happy for the rest of our lives, whatever
it takes to make that happen. I've been offered a position at
Florida International University. So I'd still be able to teach
but be within boating distance of Crystal Island. So now
there's only one more thing on my wish list." He cleared
his throat again. "Lilli, love of my life, light of my world,
would you do me the honor of becoming Mrs. Connor
O'Malley? Or letting me become Mr. Lillian Davenport?
Or any combination of the two?" He opened the box and
held it out to her.

A shaft of moonlight caught on the solitaire marquis-shaped diamond in the simple setting of the white-gold engagement ring and she didn't waste a moment before putting it on her finger. "Yes, yes, oh my goodness, *yes!*"

Lilli's happiness faded quickly once she returned to reality. This time she achieved the physical satisfaction she had missed last night, but where last night reminded her of the beginning of their relationship, tonight she had relived one of her last, totally happy, carefree hours.

Having gone that far down memory lane and feeling as sad as she possibly could she opened the cabinet door of her nightstand and punched in the code that unlocked the safe inside. Under a stack of folders, envelopes and jewelry pouches was a leather covered cigar box that had belonged to her grandfather. She couldn't even remember the last time she opened it, but tonight she felt compelled to do so.

Taking her time, she looked at each souvenir from her times with Connor and recalled the moment or event connected to it. When the box was empty of everything except a small, burgundy velvet box, she opened it, removed the diamond engagement ring and placed it on her finger. Tears immediately blurred her vision. But before she completely submitted to the ache in her chest, her attention jumped to how warm her finger suddenly felt. A heartbeat later she realized the warmth was emanating from the ring. Thinking she was having some sort of allergic reaction, she tried to remove the ring, but it wouldn't budge. It had slid onto her finger easily enough and it had been cool to the touch. Now it was very warm and getting tighter.

Lilli hurried to the bar in the living room where she had a bucket of ice and dunked her whole left hand into it. The ice closest to her ring finger melted quickly. Only when numbness set in did she remove her hand. The ring was no longer radiating heat but neither was it ice cold. She gave it a tug and, though there was some resistance, she was able to remove it. She put the ring back in its box and hurriedly returned that and everything else to the safe.

By the time the safe was securely locked and Lilli was back in bed, her hand felt almost normal again. There was no lingering heat, redness or rash to suggest she'd had an allergic reaction, but her finger still felt like the ring was on it. If she had never experienced a paranormal event, she might have chalked it up to her imagination, but her experiences told her the incident meant something. *Something to do with Connor.*

Her thoughts automatically plummeted to the worst thing it could mean and she let the held-back tears flow.

CHAPTER 19

"I beg your pardon?" the maître d' asked in a voice that cracked with shock.

"Lillian Davenport," Maggie elaborated with obvious excitement. "You were in the photo with her. *Lilli and Connor, February 14, 2005.* There was a big pink heart behind your heads and she was wearing a red—" Noah's fingers squeezing her elbow stopped her description.

"You must be mistaken, dear," Noah said in a warning tone.

Maggie looked from Connor's dismayed expression to Noah's concerned one and closed her mouth. If she was wrong—

"You're right," Connor muttered quietly as he scanned the area around them. "And I *really* want to know how you know that, but we can't talk here." Returning to his normal speaking voice, he said, "Let me show you to your table and I'll try to answer your questions about the island after you order your meals."

Connor introduced them to their waiter and returned to his post.

"What was that about?" Noah asked in a lowered voice as he pretended to study the menu.

Imitating his tone and action, Maggie said, "Remember I said I'd met Lillian Davenport? The photo was on the wall in her office and the date and their names were etched into the frame. I'm sorry I blurted it out like that but I actually forgot what time we're in now. I thought he and the name on his tag seemed familiar last night in the speakeasy. It was pretty dark in there though and I forgot about it until I saw him again just now."

"Well, apparently it's true so no harm done. But if he and the current Davenport owner were a couple in the future and she's there and he's here—"

The waiter's reappearance cut off Noah's conclusion. Rather than have him leave and return a few minutes later, they hurriedly selected the chef-recommended dinner for two along with an appropriate bottle of wine. As soon as the waiter left, Connor came to their table.

In a tone audible to any passing staff, Connor said, "In answer to your question, along the southern beach, parallel to the golf course, are the long-term rental cottages. There are also some shorter-term ones along the eastern end. They're usually fully booked year-round but, sometimes there are openings for the summer months. If you're interested, the concierge can tell you more about them. It would be much appreciated if you'd tell him I told you about them. I wrote my name down for you." He set a piece of folded paper on the table in front of Noah.

"And in between the hotel and the cottages?" Maggie asked to stop Connor from leaving while Noah glanced at what was written on the paper and put it in his pocket. "Besides the golf course & tennis courts."

He glanced casually around before answering. "We're not supposed to say, but I heard you two are here doing research for a book, so you might find this interesting. But you've got to promise not to tell anyone who told you."

Maggie made a cross over her heart. "We promise." She nudged Noah's foot with her own.

He immediately nodded. "We're very good at keeping secrets. At least as good as you must be."

"I've had no choice. The area you're talking about is where the help lives. Not upper management of course. They're put up inside the hotel."

Maggie asked, "Why would that be something you're not supposed to talk about?"

He made a face. "I guess it would be a little like looking behind the wizard's curtain. Most guests wouldn't want to know how we have to live in order to have full-time jobs here."

Maggie frowned. "Aren't there any jobs in nice hotels on the mainland?"

He nodded. "And workers come and go from here to there and back all the time, which is one of the reasons I get shifted around."

She felt her chest tighten, but it was coming from his heart not hers. "But you can't leave," she said sympathetically.

He shook his head. "I have to stay, at least—" He stopped and met Maggie's gaze. "How is she?"

She took a moment to consider what he would want to hear. "Not nearly as happy as she was in that photo."

For a heartbeat Connor looked sad but the waiter's reappearance with a bottle of red wine had him force a polite smile. "Do be sure to ask the concierge about those cottages and I hope to see you both again before you check out."

They smiled appropriately during the waiter's bottle-opening and pouring ritual and toasted to each other's continued good health and fortune before reverting to hushed conversation.

"What's on the paper?" Maggie asked.

"He asked us to meet him by the big rock on the eastern beach at nine."

"That's the portal, and if he picked that as a meeting spot with us, he probably knows how we got here. So if he knows that, why can't he leave?"

Noah shrugged. "Didn't Reynard say something about having to remain in this time period if we don't complete our mission?"

"Yes, but he talked about pairs, not an individual."

"Maybe their circumstances were different. I mean, this is *her* island after all. I guess we'll have to wait 'til nine o'clock to get the answers. That's when he gets an hour off between his duties here and his shift in the speakeasy. So we have time to enjoy our meal and pretend we aren't both dying to find out what he knows."

Maggie sighed. "I guess I can manage that. I'm still curious about the other side of this island. Just not as curious as I am about him."

Dining on the Emerald Patio was a treat for all the senses, the sound of the gently rolling ocean lapping the beach, the feel of the warm evening breeze wafting through their hair, subtly fragrant yellow and pink azaleas and flickering hurricane candles on every table. The meal itself was a gastronomic delight adapted from the newly discovered flavors of Havana, Cuba. And accompanying all of it was a very talented harpist.

By the time the waiter served their dessert of flan with warm caramel sauce, Maggie wondered if there was such a thing as sensual overload. But of all those delights, nothing was more sensually arousing than the man across the table from her. She moved her foot until she found Noah's and tapped his shoe with hers.

His mouth curved into a sly grin and she watched his eyes darken with desire. In an instant she felt her body demanding pleasure from his. Like the sweet sauce on her tongue, his heated look was warm and tantalizing and made her anxious for another taste. Silently she mouthed the words, *I want you*, and his sharp intake of breath assured her he liked the admission and was more than willing to accommodate, but the look he gave her immediately afterward reminded her that they had a job to do first.

For so many years she had believed she lacked the ability to enjoy sex like the heroines in her favorite romance novels. Passion and desire were abstract concepts, completely alien to her outside those books. And yet, since Noah had come back into her life, desire had become a driving force. He had called it an obsession.

Even though an obsession may sound less harmful than an addiction, it still wasn't a good thing and she truly believed everything about her and Noah being together was good. Her wanting to be as close to him as possible, all the time, could be because the feeling was so new. Or it could be the awareness that their situation was so outrageous that the intensity of their feelings could fizzle once they'd returned to the lives they had before it all began…unless they failed their mission and couldn't return at all.

She scolded herself for *obsessing* over any of it when there was so much around her to appreciate in the moment, including Noah.

Two hours later, they'd finished their leisurely meal and Noah signed the tab. Again, they removed their shoes and stockings to walk through the sand. They only had a short wait before Connor joined them at the geode.

"Is this where you were when you jumped?" he asked without preliminaries.

"Jumped?" Maggie repeated.

"From a future time to now. What year was it?"

"2018," Noah replied.

Connor grimaced. "And I'm not there. Damn, something must have gone wrong with the plan."

"You had a plan?" Noah asked with surprise. "We could use one of those. Maybe if we exchange stories it might help figure some things out."

"They'll have to be short stories. I can't afford to be late."

"Why don't you start. And if we run out of time, we can meet up again tomorrow."

Connor launched his tale without hesitation, as though he had gone over it many times before. Noah thought his story poured out like the synopsis of a novel.

"It happened on Valentine's Day, 2005, which was also Lilli's birthday and the night I asked her to marry me."

"Oh, that's so romantic." Maggie said sincerely but Noah's glance stopped her from saying more. "Sorry. Please go on."

"The moon and stars were so bright that night, we took a long walk on the beach before returning to her suite. We were talking about what the resort must have been like when her grandfather had his grand opening in 1924. Maybe I should mention I was an economics professor with a focus on the Roaring Twenties."

It was Noah's turn to interrupt. "And you're waiting tables?"

Connor shrugged. "Not much choice about that. But at least knowing the ways of the time period helped me blend in immediately."

"Did Reynard help you also?" Maggie asked.

He frowned. "I don't know anyone named Reynard."

"So you were walking along the beach…" prompted Noah.

"When we got to this rock, Lilli saw a falling star and made a wish about our always being as much in love as we were that night. My wish was a fantasy of my own. I wished we could actually attend her grandfather's big celebration."

"Oh no," muttered Maggie.

Noah made a groaning sound. They hadn't even made a wish when they got sent back.

"Anyway, the moonlight made something glow inside the rock, the ground quaked for several seconds and, the next thing we knew, we heard a band playing down the beach. It didn't take long to realize we weren't having a joint dream and that I had somehow gotten my wish. And from what you said about Lilli, it sounds like her wish came true too. Unfortunately, being in love with someone you can't be with isn't as romantic as the poets make it out to be."

Connor paused for a moment before changing topics. "We thought about making another wish to go right home, but neither of us could resist taking a look around first.

Luckily, the clothes we had on were appropriate enough to keep us from standing out. You mentioned having help?"

Maggie nodded and told him a short version of how the bellman from their time showed up to help them when they got to 1927.

"Obviously, he was no ordinary bellman," Noah added. "His real bosses are apparently responsible for our time traveling."

Connor shook his head. "At least you had help. We were on our own. Well, that's not entirely true. We told a friendly waiter a story about being stranded. He took pity on us and pointed us in the direction of the workers' barracks so we'd have a place to sleep that night if we needed one."

Noah decided not to tell him about the advantages he and Maggie had been given. "Did that waiter say anything about your having some sort of task to complete, like saving someone, in order to get back home?"

"A task?" Connor asked with a confused expression. "No. Are you saying you were told you had to do something specific?"

"Something, yes. Specific, not in the least." Noah gave him an overview of the minimal information they'd been given by Reynard.

"That sounds crazy," Connor said. "And not at all believable."

"We thought that too," Maggie replied. "But I never believed time travel was possible either. We still don't know why we were chosen to complete a mysterious task, but they seem very serious about it...whoever *they* are."

"Well, maybe no one had to tell us we had someone to save because it was already fixed in Lilli's head to save her grandfather. Lilli's family never believed it was suicide but she was very intent on erasing what she considered a stain on her family's history. She was convinced my wish was granted so she could warn Robert about what would happen to him if he didn't take steps to prevent it."

Connor checked his watch then continued speaking a little faster. "It wasn't hard to find him and his wife, Patricia, and, without explaining who we were or how we got there, Lilli told him a story about having a dream the night before about his being murdered in 1930. He listened to her politely, but Lilli's grandmother was furious and made sure we were immediately escorted away from the party.

"That's when we came up with the plan I mentioned. Well, to be perfectly honest, I came up with a plan and she reluctantly went along with it. I told her I wanted to give her the one thing she couldn't buy for herself—a change in the historic record. She would go back and I would stay as long as it took for me to prevent her grandfather's death, whether by his own hand or someone else's. I promised to return to her in six years, which would be 1930 here, after I spared her grandfather. I assumed that meant I would return to her by 2011, at the very latest."

Connor paused a moment then asked, "What do you know about her grandfather?"

Maggie answered before Noah could speak. "History says he committed suicide in 1930. There are statements that the family never accepted that as truth but it still stands."

Connor's shoulders slumped. "In that case, along with you saying I hadn't returned to Lilli by 2018, something must happen to *me* before I'm able to save Robert."

"A lot of things could have gone wrong," Noah said. "But we were shown firsthand how catastrophic interfering in Robert's fate would be."

Connor's expression went from confusion to shock. "*Catastrophic?*"

Noah did his best to summarize how history had changed after they warned Robert Davenport of his impending murder.

"And Lilli?" Connor asked quietly, as though he'd already guessed the answer.

"Never born," answered Maggie. "And neither was I. We were told a lot of people never came to exist because of one conversation we had with Robert Davenport in 1927. It reminded him of the warning he'd received from a young woman—who we now know was Lilli—and the two warnings together made him change his life...in a bad way."

"Wait. You spoke to him in 1927? But that's *this* year. Where...*when* did a catastrophe take place?" Connor shook his head. "I'm confused."

Noah snorted. "Welcome to the club. Apparently, after we triggered the catastrophe, the mysterious *they* rewound time to before we spoke with Robert. Then they gave us another chance to save the person we were sent here for."

"Maybe it's me," Connor said with hope in his voice. "If Robert's death is not supposed to be prevented, I don't need to stay here."

Maggie gave Noah a questioning look.

He frowned. "That doesn't make sense. Remember, Reynard said the pair usually has an idea of what the task is, based on something they were already discussing."

"*We* may not have been discussing it," Maggie countered. "But I had seen the photo and wondered about him earlier that day. That's not as strong as our discussing Robert Davenport or the pregnant maid's suicide, but we have more information about him than we did about The Weeping Woman or the male suicide."

"The Weeping Woman?" Connor asked.

She realized they had cut Connor out of their conversation and turned back to him. "One of our potential people to be saved or helped. What do you know about her?"

Connor shrugged. "Nothing. I never heard of her."

Noah nudged her foot and she understood that she shouldn't say more on that subject, so she quickly switched. "One thing I'm not clear on. You said the plan was for you to stay here for *six years*, but you had just gotten engaged. I don't understand how that plan sounded reasonable to either of you."

Connor threw his hands up in frustration. "It wasn't! But somehow, at that moment it made sense to both of us. Or maybe I was just so intellectually excited by the idea of doing historical research in the actual time period, she pretended it made sense. She said the hotel would keep her busy and the years would go by in a blink, and if the reward was having her grandfather be part of her life, the wait would be worth it.

"She may have meant that then, but as time passed, I came to realize that was her way of giving me something she couldn't buy for me. Maybe that's why she got to go back. Her wish was completely about us as a couple and she was willing to sacrifice her happiness for mine, while I was selfishly thinking of the fantastic career opportunity I was being handed."

He exhaled heavily. "All I know is, a month later, I realized what a mistake I'd made...*again*. So I went back to the rock and made the wish to return. I waited, put my hand on the rock and finally hugged the thing. But nothing happened. I did that every day and night for months before I gave up and focused on how to make this life as bearable as possible until it came time to save Robert Davenport."

When Connor didn't immediately continue, Noah had a question. "Earlier you told us you *couldn't* leave the island to get better work or living conditions as others had done. Why did you say that?"

"*Hmmph.* Believe me I tried to leave, at least a dozen different times and ways, but something always happened to keep me here on the island. I finally quit trying when I came to the conclusion that, since I didn't leave with Lilli, I wasn't *allowed* to leave this location until I lived up to the promise I'd made to make sure Robert Davenport did not die in 1930. Now I don't even have that to look forward to."

The man looked so dejected, Maggie said the only thing she could think of to get him to smile. "Well, if we don't figure out who we're supposed to save, and succeed in doing it in the next three days, you won't be the only time traveler sentenced to remain on the island. At least that's what Reynard told us."

Connor narrowed his eyes in thought. "Maybe I could earn a few points with the powers that be if I help you." He pulled his watch out of his pocket again and groaned. "I've got to go. But if you'd like to continue this tomorrow, just ask one of the staff where I can be found." He took a step then stopped and spoke to Noah, "I'm curious. What made you choose being an author as your cover?"

Maggie smiled. "Not a cover. He really is one. A very famous one in fact."

He made a face. "Then I must apologize for not knowing your name. But at least if you get stuck here, you might not have to wait tables to get by."

Before they could respond, he jogged off at a brisk pace.

"Thoughts?" Noah asked as they headed back to the bungalow.

It took Maggie a moment to pick one of the dozens in her mind. "I don't think he's the one we were sent to save. He's been stranded here for three years. We didn't need to come to this precise time to help him get back. Plus, it just doesn't feel like he's the answer. But he did tell us something relevant. He said he never heard of The Weeping Woman, which would seem to mean whatever happened to her hasn't happened yet. That's enough to keep her on the possible victims list...if we had a single tidbit of information about her, but we don't."

Noah shook his head. "In other words, no new thoughts."

"Well, I liked what he said about you not having to wait tables if we don't get to go back."

Noah put his arm around her and brought her closer as they walked. "And you could be my agent as well as promoter, assistant and wife."

She made an effort to keep the light mood going. "Sounds like I'll be pretty busy. But that reminds me. We'll probably be socializing tomorrow night. Do we have a back story?"

He glanced down at her with one brow arched. "Very good question, Mrs. Nash. It could come up and we'd want our stories to match. But it would have to be pretty good, just in case we have to live with it for the rest of our lives. Why don't you pick one?"

Her mind honed in on the phrase, *for the rest of our lives*. She understood he simply meant, in case they don't get to return to the future, but, with each passing hour, she was thinking about it becoming a reality in either time. "I think we should follow what you said before, that the best lie sticks close to the truth."

"Okay. So we met in school when we were kids. I was head-over-heels in love with you, but you just wanted to be friends. Many years later, I ran an ad to hire an assistant and you applied." He furrowed his brow. "Where did those two things happen? How long before we got married? Was it a big wedding?"

They had reached the bungalow, but rather than go inside, she sat in one of the yellow rockers on the porch. He moved the other one so they could sit side-by-side, and when he held out his open hand, she accepted it without thinking. She also ordered herself not to think about his saying he was once head-over-heels in love with her as she answered his questions. "I don't think women moved around much in this time period and Florida wasn't very populated. So maybe, we met *and* got back together in Tennessee. Clarksville then Nashville."

"Got it. And the marriage?"

She swallowed hard. "Um, I don't know. You choose."

"Sticking close to the truth, I'd say, once we got together again, we were in a big hurry for the honeymoon. So-o-o, I'd say I asked you for your hand two weeks later and we eloped."

She made a face. "Okay, as long as we did something very romantic for our honeymoon…like a trip to Paris."

That prompted him to make a face right back. "I'm not a fan." Then he grinned. "But I guess a slow trans-Atlantic cruise would make it worthwhile." He gently squeezed her hand.

The squeeze along with the steamy suggestion in his tone made her blush. "I wouldn't mind that…as long as it's not on the Titanic."

That made him laugh. "No worries. That happened a few years before we reconnected."

They continued to embellish their back story, adding in some actual incidents from their school days, until the waning moon had traveled past its mid-point in the heavens.

CHAPTER 20

"Ready to go inside yet?" Noah asked without taking his gaze off the rolling waves.

She sighed. "Not really."

He shifted to face her. "What's wrong?"

That made her exhale more audibly.

"Would it help if I slept out here tonight?"

It took her more than a moment to reply. "Don't be ridiculous."

"But it *is* about our sleeping together."

She met his gaze. "Sort of."

"Let me rephrase. Is it about our literally sleeping together without doing what we both want to do?"

Not comfortable with the words she wanted to say, she just nodded.

"Would you say our *not* doing those things might be getting in the way of our thinking clearly about the mission?"

Her eyes widened and she bobbed her head.

He fought back a grin. "I don't know about you, but I think we put in as much time on our mission as humanly possible today. In fact, considering the time rewind, you could say we put in overtime."

She couldn't resist smiling at that and she relaxed enough to contribute to his analysis. "It would seem to me that we've earned a little...*down time*." He stood and brought her up with him. Wrapping her arms around his neck, she drew his head down for a long kiss that spoke of everything they hadn't said aloud.

They were about to go inside when she had a very practical thought. "We're going to track in sand."

He laughed aloud and gave her a quick kiss. "We're on the beach. I think the maid expects to clean up sand in the room. But I'm not too keen on getting it onto the bed sheets."

He led her straight into the bathroom and turned on the water in the tub. As it got warm, he pulled down the shoulder straps of her lightweight shift and sent it to the floor. She chuckled at how swiftly he managed to get both of them out of their clothes. But when she leaned into him, he held her away.

"Don't distract me," he said firmly. He stepped into the tub then held her arm to make sure she didn't slip as she got in. "Now just stand still and let me give you a shower, old-style."

She was skeptical but obeyed.

Using the large pitcher by the basin, he poured lukewarm water over her until all the loose sand and dust was washed down the drain.

She continued to stand very still as he quickly soaped her body without stalling over her breasts or between her legs. Only her feet got a little extra TLC. It didn't matter how fast he did it, however. It still counted as effective foreplay to her. Several more pitchers of water followed the soaping.

"My turn," he said, handing her the pitcher.

With considerable effort, she managed to imitate his speed and efficiency, though his response to her attentions was more visible than hers had been.

Towel-drying each other took a bit longer due to several kissing breaks that progressed to stroking and holding until they finally dropped the towels and tumbled onto the bed.

Every cell in Maggie's body felt as though it were vibrating in anticipation, but she felt him slowing down and again followed his lead.

By both of them exercising control, the urgent groping, ravenous kisses and driving thrusts were held at bay, and soft caresses, silky touches and a slow melding of their bodies took the lead. The result was an exquisitely sensual, completely satisfying hour.

They silently enjoyed the peaceful afterglow for several minutes before Maggie murmured, "That was lovely."

"Mm-hmm."

"We should do that again." She sighed softly. "Maybe in a month or so."

When her words sank in, Noah laughed out loud and propped himself up on his elbow to look at her. "I can't tell if you mean it was so good you won't need sex again for a while or it wasn't worth repeating anytime soon."

She tweaked his nose. "Neither. It was *lovely*. It's just that, well…I wouldn't mind mixing in a little *less*-bridled passion from time to time."

He pulled her close for a hard kiss. "That's fine with me, just so we don't go back to pretending that we don't need to do it at all."

"We just have to make sure the mission remains our top priority." She sighed. "Unfortunately, our mission is still a mystery, with or without distractions. In fact, now we have to add the slight possibility that our mission might be to save Connor from whatever terrible thing is in his immediate future and help him get back to Lilli where he belongs."

He gave her another kiss and drew her into a snug embrace. "To quote another brave woman, 'tomorrow is another day'."

Maggie tried to think of an appropriate Rhett Butler reply but she was suddenly too tired to keep her eyes open. Totally sated and happier than she ever thought possible, she gave in to the cozy cocoon of slumber where a dream was waiting to take her away.

"*Watch your step now. It can get mighty slippery down here.*" Reynard lowered the torch so that it illuminated the narrow stone path in front of her.

The descent into the cave had not been very steep at first but it suddenly changed to a severe downward slope with only an occasional outcropping of crystals to stop her from sliding. The rock walls on each side seemed to be closer now as well. She hoped her curiosity hadn't led her into a situation that had no exit.

When the path leveled out and they stepped into a cavern, she asked her guide, "*How much farther?*" Reynard turned toward her and she noticed his head was that of a red fox with eyes that flashed with golden flames but his voice confirmed it was still him.

"*Dat depends on which path ya choose next. Your first choice led to disaster and it would be unwise to go dat way again. Another of de remaining choices requires a map which ya do not have and if ya choose that one, ya could find yourself in a cave much like this one but ya would not have my help to find a way out. Dere is only one path dat will get ya back home.*"

He waved the torch and she could see three openings in the cave wall. They looked identical but reminded her of the three nature trails.

"*But how will I know which is—*" Reynard was gone and the torch was in her own hand. Why would he bring her this far and not show her which was the safe one? "*At least you could have given me some sort of clue!*" she shouted in frustration.

Though the fox did not reappear, she heard his voice. "*De clue is knocking at your door...*"

CHAPTER 21

K *nock. Knock. Knock. Knock.*

It took Maggie several seconds to realize she was hearing actual knocking at the bungalow door. "Just a moment," she yelled and scrambled for her cover-up. The dream continued to cloud her mind as she made her way to the door. Reynard had said *the clue was knocking at her door.*

She shook the cobwebs from her brain and opened the door to find a bellman and Moira, the Irish maid, standing behind her housekeeping cart. The bellman handed her a square, ivory linen envelope addressed in elegant script to Mr. and Mrs. Noah Nash. On the back was a palm tree logo embossed in gold above the name of the hotel. It was similar to the embroidery on the plush robes they'd left behind.

"One moment please," she said to the bellman then asked Moira to follow her inside while she found a quarter to give to the man. His forced smile suggested he was appreciative but disappointed that she had figured out the appropriate tip amount.

She quickly opened the envelope to confirm that it was the expected invitation to the evening's affair. Then she turned her attention to the maid, who was once again holding a stack of linens in front of her stomach. "I'm sorry about the sand everywhere. If you wouldn't mind starting in here, I'll be dressed and out of your way in a few minutes."

Moira bobbed her head. "As you wish, ma'am."

Maggie's mind raced. Wherever Noah was she hoped he stayed away a bit longer. This was the perfect opportunity for some girl-talk with Moira and his appearance could put a quick end to it. As she quickly washed, brushed her teeth and dressed, Maggie thought about the strange dream and what it could mean. After all, they had been transported to the Roaring Twenties, saw the hotel in ruins in the future and were part of a time rewind. Why shouldn't she receive a message in a dream about the helpful bellman with a fox's head?

Noah kept telling her anything's possible.

There were three, and only three, paths in the dream, and she felt certain that the paths represented the original three victims she and Noah had settled on. Davenport was definitely the disaster. The one for which a map was needed had to be The Weeping Woman. And if a clue had been knocking at her door when she awoke, she had just been clearly informed that the maid was the one they were sent to save. And since they were almost out of time, the hour of her death had to be soon.

But did the bellman delivering the invitation represent something also? A heartbeat later, she realized the invitation itself was the clue. As she had sensed when she saw the article in the hotel's promo piece, tonight's party was an important piece to their mystery puzzle. She remembered her strong reaction to the photos of the engaged couple and was again filled with the certainty that they, or their parents, were involved in whatever was about to happen. But there were still far too many possibilities. She needed to talk it out with Noah.

When she came out of the bathroom, Moira was hurriedly changing the bed linens. "You work so hard," Maggie said in an attempt to open a conversation.

"Thank ye, ma'am, 'tis a good job I have."

"When are you due?" The question was out of her mouth before she realized how shocking it would be to the girl.

The poor maid's face turned white then flushed hot pink. "I...I don't know what ye mean." She looked like she was about to run.

"Oh, I'm sorry. I didn't mean to be rude. It's hardly noticeable but I, uh, I have a sense about these things. Maybe it's because I just found out I'm expecting." She stuck out her stomach and rubbed it. And hoped she wouldn't be struck down, or immediately impregnated, for lying. It was apparently the right thing to say because Moira relaxed a little.

"Please, ma'am. Ye mustn't say anything ta anyone. I would be sent away for sure. And I have no place to go for some months."

Maggie frowned and walked over to the maid. "That's terrible. You shouldn't be fired for getting pregnant. And why would you have no place to go? Where's the baby's father?"

Moira's freckled cheeks flushed again. "'Tis my shame ta say I haven't seen him for more than a month. Since I told him about the babe. And if I were ta be let go, I would have ta leave the island." She went back to her task without looking at Maggie again.

Maggie's heart went out to the maid. She was just a girl. With the troubles of a grown woman. And it sounded like she had no one to turn to. Maggie sensed she had learned all she could for the moment. "I'm sorry, Moira. I promise I won't reveal your secret."

"Thank ye, ma'am," the maid mumbled without turning around.

Maggie sighed and headed out to find Noah, invitation in hand. As luck would have it, no sooner did she step on the wooden walkway than she saw him rising to his feet in the shallower part of the ocean. He looked like a beautiful Greek god crowned by the morning sun. As he shook his head from side to side, droplets of sparkling water flew off his hair.

She loved his hair.

As he pushed his way to shore, his firm, near-naked body was revealed inch by sexy inch.

She really loved his body.

The first thing he did when he reached dry sand was bend down and pick up a seashell.

She really, really loved the way he appreciated little things.

Rather than wave or call to him she decided to simply enjoy the view. He went over to a water faucet with a bucket under it, filled it and rinsed the salt off himself then accepted a towel from a beach boy. She couldn't help but think about how they'd towel-dried each other's bodies last night. She sighed. There was no help for her.

She was totally, irrevocably in love with Noah Nash.

Suddenly he stopped toweling his legs, turned toward her and grinned. *As though he had heard her thoughts.* She waited on the porch until he donned a cover-up, also provided by the boy, then walked toward him. His grin broadened the closer they got to each other.

She loved that grin.

He gave her a quick hug and kiss then tucked her arm under his as they started strolling. "If I'd known you were getting up so soon I would have waited."

"I had visitors."

He raised an eyebrow. "Oh? Did any of them bring you your coffee?"

She laughed. "No, but one of them did come bearing a gift." She handed him the invitation.

He smiled. "Told ya so. Now we just have to hope *you* were right about the seating arrangements." Without further discussion he guided her to an umbrella-covered table at the Quartz Café Poolside.

He waited until a waiter had taken their breakfast orders before getting back to her comment. "You said visitors, plural."

Maggie quickly related her talk with Moira. "I couldn't help but remember the piece you copied from the book on the hotel's history. It said she was 'despondent' over her illegitimate pregnancy. There's no question she's sad and frightened about the future but I didn't get the feeling she would take her own life, let alone her baby's."

Noah nodded his agreement. "And I remember you saying she wore a crucifix. An Irish Catholic committing suicide really goes completely against the grain. Her being pregnant out of wedlock is bad but I'm pretty sure killing the baby gets her a ticket straight to hell. Plus, we can't forget about the doctor's report that was ignored. Bruises around her neck definitely suggest foul play." He combed his fingers through his hair. "If the baby's father is out of the picture and she's accepted the fate of a single mother, why would someone kill her?"

Maggie noticed the waiter's curious look as he served their coffee and pressed her finger to her lips to remind Noah to lower his voice. She leaned forward and spoke quietly. "Maybe it has nothing to do with her pregnancy. Maybe she witnesses something or overhears a plot to do something illegal. If I remember correctly, a few gangsters spent time here."

"I like your thinking so far. Go on."

"A lot of important people will be in the ballroom tonight. With the father of the groom being a politician in prohibition times, the odds of a shady deal going on in a back room seem pretty high."

He winked at her. "You're thinking of the wedding scene in *The Godfather*."

She chuckled. "Not intentionally but it fits. Especially adding in that the bride's father is wealthy and they're from Chicago, home to some pretty famous gangsters. The problem is how can the two of us eavesdrop on the engaged couple and their parents and look for secret meetings behind the scenes? It's not like either one of us is a trained detective."

He started to contradict her but she had more to tell. "I had a weird dream right before I woke up. It could mean something." The slight raise of one of his eyebrows was enough for her to relate every detail she could remember.

Noah hung on every word she said. Though he recognized the importance of her dream information, he would have been just as enthralled if she was reading from a phone book page. He couldn't explain it. He didn't even want to try. She had described his caresses as *bewitching*. But the truth was, he was the one completely bewitched by the magical creature in front of him.

He'd had a major crush on her when they were just kids. As adults, she had instantly become the partner he'd never even known he wanted. She matched his imagination, supported his work, and complemented him in bed. Discovering she naturally possessed the enhanced mental abilities he found so fascinating was like the whipped cream design on top of a perfectly brewed cappuccino. He could never go back to a life without her in it. He wanted to tell her that, but the surreal situation they were caught in demanded that their personal desires be shoved aside.

Besides, she hadn't uttered a single word suggesting she wanted a long-term relationship with him. Or had she?

...maybe in a month or so. She had said those words last night. Although she was kidding about gentle sex at the time, it let him know she was giving thought of some kind to a time beyond the present. It wasn't the long-term, settling-down sort of commitment he was hoping for but it was better than nothing.

"Honestly, I've been going over this from so many directions, I'm no longer sure about anything. What do you think we should do next?" she asked, yanking him out of his personal thoughts.

Noah made a face then sat forward, taking both her hands in his. "Okay. Close your eyes." Maggie obeyed without hesitation. "Take a deep breath and imagine that all the thoughts and suppositions bouncing around your head are on a big whiteboard. Now, as you exhale, imagine pushing all the people we've been discussing off to the side and erase everything else on the board." He gave her a moment to follow his instructions. "Next, without forcing anything, ask your spirit guide who we should watch most closely to complete our mission."

She saw the fox's flashing eyes, thought of the clues he'd given in her dream then followed Noah's directions. One name popped onto her blank screen. She opened her eyes and said, "Moira."

He looked at her curiously. "The maid? She's clearly the one we have to save, but I planted the suggestion that you ask about who we should *watch* for the solution. I expected you to name someone who would be at tonight's party. The maid shouldn't be anywhere near there."

"Hey, I just did what you told me. I never claimed to have any special gift."

He stroked her cheek. "You *are* the gift, Maggie. And whether or not you believe your intuition is a gift, I trust it. So if you say we need to watch the maid, that's who we focus on. And the only way to do that is to walk in her shoes."

"Are you saying I need to be a maid for a day?"

He laughed aloud then leaned close enough to whisper. "I'm saying we should spy on her. Surreptitiously follow her around. See what she sees, hear what she hears." He loved the way her eyes brightened when her interest was piqued. "Unless you have a better idea of how to spend the day?" Her flushed cheeks told him exactly what she would want to be doing…if they didn't have a mystery to solve. Before he could tease her about it, the waiter arrived with their breakfasts, so he just gave her a knowing wink.

A half hour later they were officially in stealth mode. Following Moira turned out to be a simple matter because the bungalows seemed to be her assigned area and they could simply sit outside or stroll back and forth and watch the girl go in and out of each building. Even at the end of her shift they were able to follow her into the working areas of the hotel because of the pass Mr. Eckhart had provided for Noah.

Nothing of interest happened until the end of her shift. As employees were signing in and out, another maid slipped Moira a piece of paper and whatever was written on it completely changed Moira's demeanor from sad to glowing. She was in such a great hurry to leave, she accidentally walked right into Maggie in the staff hallway.

"Oh goodness," the maid gushed with a quick head bob. "Apologies."

"It was our fault," Maggie said quickly and looked up at Noah. "Darling, this is the very helpful maid I told you about. Moira, this is Mr. Nash."

"'tis a pleasure ta be sure. I was told of yer generosity, sir. Thank ye kindly. And congratulations to ye." She made a partial curtsy and hustled past them.

Noah noted the girl's flushed cheeks but she seemed to be more excited than embarrassed. "Something important was in that note."

"Agreed," Maggie said. "Let's see where she's rushing off to."

As they followed Moira at a discreet distance through a maze of hallways, Noah asked, "What was she congratulating me for? Did she hear about my big movie deal?"

Maggie chuckled. "No. She thinks you're going to be a daddy."

He stopped in his tracks and gaped at her.

She tugged on his hand to keep him moving. "It was all I could think of to get her talking."

Maggie abruptly blocked him from taking another step and put her finger to her lips. Only then did he realize Moira had turned a corner and her footsteps could no longer be heard. The sound he now heard made him think of...*two people kissing*.

"I'm so sorry," a man's voice gushed in between kisses and soft moans. "I was a fool. A complete idiot. Please say you forgive me. I'll die if you don't."

"'tis no matter now," Moira replied in a tone filled with unconditional love.

"Oh!" the man exclaimed after another few seconds of making-up sounds. "What was that?"

She giggled. "'twas just yer babe sayin' hello."

He sighed aloud then there was more kissing before he spoke again. "I can't wait to see him."

"It might not be a boy ye know."

He snorted. "If it's not, we'll just have to try again."

The next sounds Noah heard assured him they were sufficiently distracted and he took the opportunity to peek around the corner and get a look at the guy. He couldn't see all of his face yet there was something familiar about him.

"I can walk you to your barracks," the man said after a moment. "But I must come right back. There's something I need to take care of before it's too late. Tomorrow we can start making our plans. By next week, I'm going to make everything up to you, including making sure our baby is born with the last name of Hampshire."

CHAPTER 22

"Oh...my...*gawd*," Maggie gushed as soon as she was certain the couple had left through the exit door near their rendezvous. "Should we try to follow them?"

Noah shook his head. "They're headed to the workers' barracks. Too many witnesses for anything to happen while she's there. Plus, we'd have no good excuse for being in that area."

"Right. Boy, I thought my head was spinning with possibilities before! Any chance he was *not* the Hampshire announcing his engagement tonight?"

Noah grimaced. "I guess it could be a coincidence or another family member but I think the article mentioned Broderick was an only child and this guy bore a resemblance to the photo in the newspaper. Obviously, the message you got about following Moira was right on. The interesting part to me is that he sounded truly sorry about screwing things up with Moira. I'm thinking he's really in love and wants to make an honest woman of her. Either that or he's a world-class actor. What feeling did you get?"

She wrinkled her nose. "I don't think he was acting. From what I heard, that guy was ready to do whatever he had to for Moira and their baby. He hurt her by running away but I don't think he'd ever hurt her physically."

"Well, there's still a chance her death has nothing to do with their relationship but if I heard correctly, he may be planning on spilling the beans to the family when he gets back here. The announcement sounded like that match had more to it than two young people falling in love. No matter how much or how little he actually tells them, if he says he's backing out, somebody could be pissed off enough to do something drastic."

"Too bad we can't just transport ourselves to wherever that conversation is going to be held. Oh dear. Tonight's party might be canceled," Maggie said, frowning. "I'm not sure what we could try next."

He squeezed her hand. "Have faith. We have an ambitious politician, a wealthy family and a guest list of prominent people, many of whom would have come a long way just for this event. They may have to switch gears but there should still be a party."

"Then we'd better get moving," she said, giving him a push back the way they'd come. "We need to put on our party clothes and get there early. We definitely won't want to miss any important preannouncement announcements."

As soon as they reached the hotel lobby they knew the affair had not been canceled. Elegantly attired and bejeweled women and tuxedoed men were conversing in small groups. Outside, a line of carriages were depositing more, resplendently dressed guests who must have just arrived on the Davenport King.

Maggie was glad they had opted for the finest ensembles their wardrobe had to offer. Noah looked absolutely dashing in his long tails and white silk cummerbund and tie. Maggie had chosen a full-length, sleeveless, satin, black sheath with an overlay of extremely sheer silvery gauze. She felt like a fairy—albeit a very wealthy one. She was pretty sure the gemstones in the white-gold choker necklace and matching teardrop earrings were real diamonds.

A number of people glanced their way, obviously making guesses as to who they were. Not having any idea who they should or shouldn't be seen talking to, they made their way toward the ballroom where a line of guests had formed. The final confirmation was on a large sign set on an easel that read *Gaviston–Hampshire Engagement Party*. In much smaller print busy-bodies were notified this was an invitation-only affair.

"Curiouser and curiouser," Noah whispered. "Makes me wonder if sweet Broderick chickened out after all."

She frowned. "That doesn't feel right. Something else must be going on."

When they reached the front of the line, Noah handed their invitation to the man at the door and they were directed toward a table behind him.

"Ah, the moment of truth," Noah murmured in her ear. "Now we see just how good you were at promoting me." Because the tent cards were arranged alphabetically, it was easy enough to find one for *Noah Nash* and another for *Mrs. Noah Nash*. Inside each was the table number four and Maggie winked at Noah.

Once the question of seating was settled, she was able to appreciate the fabulous, old-world-style décor of the ballroom. If she didn't know better, she might have thought they had just time-traveled again. Renaissance-aged murals covered the walls and everything seemed to be gilded. Ornately sculptured, marble columns were spaced along the outside walls and divided the room into three areas. To one side was a dance floor and platform with an orchestra that was playing quietly enough to allow conversation. The reception area they were in had a long bar set up— obviously no one expected this party to be raided. A squadron of white-jacketed young men was offering hors d'oeuvres from gold platters. Golden stanchions topped with marble lion heads and brown velvet ropes prevented guests from entering the dining area but Maggie could see the gold lamé tablecloths and white orchid centerpieces.

Hundreds of little mirrors cut in the shape of stars hung down from the glass-domed ceiling, imitating the real starry night sky above. Maggie caught sight of the waning moon and felt a strong shiver. It seemed to be telling her that their time was slipping away.

"We have to figure this out tonight," she abruptly told Noah. "We're not going to have another chance."

"That sounds ominous. A feeling?"

"Yeah. A really strong one." No sooner had Maggie finished her sentence than Connor approached them with one of the gold platters.

"May I offer you a canapé?" he asked in a clear voice then quickly murmured, "I don't know if you tried to find me today but I couldn't have gotten away. I'll be on the nature trail at nine tomorrow morning." He moved on before they had a chance to take one of his canapés.

As more guests entered it was impossible not to be pulled into conversations. They had their back story polished, but they soon discovered most of these people were more interested in boasting about who they were and how they knew the hosts than learning anything about Mr. and Mrs. Nash.

If Mr. and Mrs. Davenport had been invited as guests, they had chosen not to attend. They stayed alert for any sign of gangsters—as if they would recognize one on sight—or any conversations that appeared to be unusually secretive. Absolutely nothing seemed out of the ordinary for the occasion.

Connor only managed one more, brief pass by them but it was enough for Noah to let him know they would be walking the nature trail in the morning.

Neither the engaged couple nor their parents made an appearance during the cocktail hour, but the four parents arrived in time to greet guests as they entered the dining room.

The receiving line moved too quickly for Maggie and Noah to do more than introduce themselves. The Gavistons appeared to be in their late fifties and had an air of royalty about them. They smiled politely but did not seem impressed by anyone they were meeting. The Hampshires, however, were hand-shakers. They looked younger than the other couple and seemed happy about their son's choice of bride.

On the way to their table, Noah said, "Not too hard to tell which man is the politician and which one has money. Makes me wonder what Gaviston will get out of this match."

"Maybe he's just giving his daughter what she wants," Maggie offered.

"Or maybe he thinks he's buying himself a future president."

As they had hoped, they were assigned to a large round table right in front of the head table. They quickly took seats that gave them a chance to observe all six of the key players without being conspicuous.

Amelia and Broderick were not brought in until everyone was seated and their entrance was accompanied by a romantic violin and piano duet.

Amelia was a rather tall, very thin woman with brown hair, pale skin and unusually large, somewhat bulging eyes. Her facial expression seemed to be one of personal discomfort, or distaste, but it changed to obvious adoration when she looked at her fiancé. She definitely did not look like a woman who had just been dumped.

Broderick was definitely the young man they had seen kissing Moira a short while ago. Either he looked very young for his age or Amelia was quite a bit older. Plus, he was very good-looking, with dark hair parted in the middle, a thin moustache and a sexy smile that probably had a number of females besides Moira willing to go beyond what was considered proper.

As Maggie watched the couple take their seats at the head table, she thought the smile Broderick gave Amelia looked strained. Instead of giving his fiancée a loving kiss on her lips he gave her a brotherly peck on her temple then cast a quick yet meaningful look at the woman on the other side of him—his mother.

"Did you see that?" she murmured to Noah.

"I see a couple who look more like they're entering a business partnership than a happily-ever-after. And I'd bet my next royalty check that girl does not know what he's been up to."

"I agree with you about it being a business arrangement, but I was talking about the way he looked at his mother when his attention should have been on his fiancée. *I'll* bet your next royalty check he told Mama and she convinced him to go through with things as planned."

Noah grimaced. "You mean this party or the wedding?"

"Does it matter? At least one other person now knows there's somewhere else he'd rather be."

Speeches were given in between meal courses and French champagne flowed freely the whole time. Dessert and coffee were being served before anyone at their table attempted to engage them in conversation. A plump, white-haired man on the opposite side had to repeat Noah's name twice before he could be heard.

"I heard we had a famous author at our table," he said loudly enough to get everyone else to stop their conversations. "I've been thinking of doing a little writing myself now that I've retired. Got any suggestions?"

Maggie turned her to Noah and gave him an encouraging smile.

"Write what you know," Noah replied. "And if you don't know anything about what you want to write, research it. That's what I'm doing now. I'm working on a murder mystery with some high-society people and politicians. I thought this party would be the perfect place to pick up some gossip. Got any for me?"

Everyone laughed then one woman ventured a tidbit. "Well, I heard the Gavistons aren't as high society as they want everyone to believe."

"I heard their money came from blockade-running in the Civil War," her husband added.

"I heard they sold secrets to the Germans during the big one." This from the man on Maggie's other side.

"Close, but no cigar," said the aspiring writer firmly. "I know for a fact that the old man is related to the boss of one of Chicago's well-known *Italian* families. Vincent Gaviston isn't his birth name. I also know he's made his current fortune running hooch across the Canadian border. We're probably drinking some of it tonight. He likes coming down here because he and the wife get to pretend they're aristocracy and everyone here pretends they believe them."

"Now *that's* the truth," the man beside Maggie interjected. "And a matchup like this could give the family an inside man where they make the laws…if you know what I mean."

From the looks passed around the table, *everyone* knew what he meant and decided it was time to change the subject.

The band started playing and put an end to any further group conversation, gossipy or otherwise.

Maggie watched Mrs. Hampshire give her son a silent reminder to take his fiancée out onto the floor for the first dance. As he rose he touched his mother's arm. They were definitely close but did his loyalty go so far as to walk away from the woman he loved and their baby? The parents followed the engaged couple onto the dance floor then most of the guests rose and made their way to the outer edges.

"Shouldn't we join them?" Maggie asked Noah.

"Naw. As soon as the guests crowd onto the floor, the parents will probably come back. And they're the ones we need to keep an eye on now. If they think no one is watching, they might take their masks off for a moment. Just pretend we're wrapped up in a private conversation of our own."

As he predicted, the four parents soon made their way back to the head table, though the Hampshires made several stops along the way to exchange comments with possible supporters. Maggie leaned closer to Noah and let her peripheral vision take care of spying. It didn't take long to see something of interest.

Mr. Gaviston was very annoyed about something. Mrs. Gaviston seemed to be reminding him to behave like a gentleman. When the Hampshires drew close, however, the older man shot the politician a distinct warning and the politician nodded. Then there was a very quick exchange between Mr. and Mrs. Hampshire as they took their seats. The only difference was their words took place behind frozen smiles.

"If I'm not mistaken," Maggie said close to Noah's ear, "the only one who *doesn't* know about Broderick's wanting to defect is the bride-to-be."

"This would actually make an interesting murder mystery plot," Noah replied as he brushed an imaginary crumb off her shoulder. "Which would you make the killer?"

She gave his chest a poke. "This isn't fiction. A *real* girl and her baby are going to die if we don't figure out how to stop it. And I have a terrible feeling that it's going to happen tonight."

He sobered immediately. "But Broderick was walking her to the barracks. Unless…"

She waited several seconds before poking him again. "Unless, what?"

"Unless he changed his mind and told her to wait for him on the beach. Or maybe she came back after he left her, just to see what the important thing was he said he had to do before they could be together."

Maggie gave that a doubtful look. "*Or…*one of them followed Broderick and saw where Moira lives and they're planning to kill her there and take her body to the beach to make it look like a suicidal drowning."

Noah nodded slowly. "You could have something there. I remember the medical report mentioning the throat bruising but not whether there was water in her lungs, or which side of the island she was found on. They wouldn't have bothered to do an autopsy. You know, you've got a damn good imagination."

"I read a lot of imaginative books," she answered with a smirk.

"Only one problem with that scenario. Moira wouldn't be the only one there. If there was a struggle in or around the barracks, wouldn't there have been a witness?"

Maggie frowned. "Maybe any witnesses were threatened...or paid off." Noah nodded in agreement. "So, what now?"

He shrugged. "Guess we just keep watching and hope to catch a break. But as long as we're stuck here..." Noah stood and held out his hand. "How about a dance? I think they're playing our song."

CHAPTER 23

L ove's glow brightened with hope. *They are getting very close.*

Karma ignored her and directed his thoughts to Time and Justice. *Status?*

They have forty-eight hours, replied Time.

Justice reported next. *A new trap has been set for the fox. Because we had to use him in connection with the time line rewind, he took advantage of an opening to escape again. This time he left the island as we had feared he might. However, he will not be able to resist observing how the humans cope with such a hotbed of lies and deception. And the moment he steps back onto the island the magnetic field will be activated. He will be back in his cage very soon.*

Love could only hope the fox was not captured before he had a chance to do one last favor for her. With only two days left, his assistance could be the defining factor in whether Maggie and Noah got to experience eternal happiness or suffer the everlasting heartache Lilli and Connor knew.

CHAPTER 24

The party remained in full swing until well after midnight when the hosts and honored guests said good night. Those who were not ready for bed were invited to go to the Amethyst Cave. Although the hotel's speakeasy was supposed to be secret, no one needed to ask what it was or where the Cave was hidden.

It was easy enough to follow the two families to the lobby and watch the three Gavistons head to their rooms upstairs. It took a while longer for Mr. Hampshire to do a bit more back-patting and hand-pumping before he, Mrs. Hampshire and Broderick headed home together.

"I feel like we missed something," Noah said. "We've been alert all evening and although we came up with a lot of guesses, I didn't expect it to end like this."

"I felt so sure tonight was *the* night. Maybe my intuition isn't as good as you think."

"Maybe this was the night when someone *decided* to take action. About the only thing we can do is follow Moira around again tomorrow. Based on what Reynard said, we do still have one more day."

Neither of them liked that plan but with no other ideas they headed out the rear door of the lobby. As soon as they were outside Noah pulled Maggie into an embrace and pressed his lips to hers. "It feels like years since I got to do that."

Maggie smiled. "You really are quite the romantic." She drew his head down for another kiss. "Even though we didn't solve anything tonight, I had a very enjoyable evening. There were whole minutes at a time when I felt like I was on a date rather than a mission."

He chuckled and kissed her nose. "I promise to take you on lots of real dates when we get back."

She gazed up into his eyes and saw the promise of a future filled with love and laughter. "I'd like that," she whispered and gave him a deeper, sexier kiss. Within seconds she felt his body changing against hers and there was no question of what her body wanted from him. "Take me home, Mr. Nash."

"With pleasure, Mrs. Nash."

They had reached the first of the bungalows when a four-legged creature tore across the boardwalk in front of them.

Noah froze. "What the hell was that?"

"A cat?"

"Too big. But it didn't look like a dog either." Before he could make another guess, the animal raced back over the walkway toward the ocean, whirled around, leapt over the walkway in front of them again and dodged between the last two bungalows.

Maggie stared into the darkness without feeling brave enough to keep walking until two golden eyes flashed at her from the corner of one of the buildings. "It's the fox! From my dream. We have to follow it." She grabbed Noah's hand and pulled him as fast as she could in her heels. When they reached the spot where she had seen the eyes, she stopped until she could see the animal in the moonlight. It was quite a ways ahead but had paused again for them to catch up.

Maggie took one look at the sand between them and the fox and got rid of her shoes. But she and Noah had only gone a few steps when she suddenly felt a wave of electrical energy. It was accompanied by a loud yelp from the fox and he vanished in a crackle of light. She and Noah glanced at each other but said nothing as they found themselves next to the area that later became the golf cart parking lot. At this time it was used to stable the horses and park the carriages.

Maggie opened her mouth to say something but Noah clapped his hand over it and pulled her down to the ground. He pointed at a moving figure ahead of them. There was just enough moonlight for her to recognize Amelia Gaviston's gown and see her heading straight toward the tall hedge of foliage. Ruffling branches along one section, she seemed to be looking for something and a few seconds later she disappeared into a thick bush.

Maggie turned to Noah and arched one eyebrow. He nodded to let her know he was as surprised as she was.

"I'm guessing that's the passage to the workers' barracks," Noah whispered.

"Shouldn't we follow her?"

"In a sec. I want to make sure she doesn't come right back out and run into us."

"What do you think she's doing?" Maggie asked, still keeping her voice quiet.

"She could be sneaking off to meet a working-class lover of her own but odds are we were wrong about her not knowing about Broderick's change of heart. She just might be a better actress than the rest of them. Maybe she even knows about Moira and is taking matters into her own hands. C'mon," he said, abruptly pulling her to her feet.

Behind the bush where Amelia had vanished, they discovered a fair-sized passage that led to a well-worn path in the sand. From there it looked like they were walking into a maze of tall hedges. Apparently the Davenport's were *very* serious about keeping this part of the island obscured from the guests' view. Fortunately, Amelia's direction was revealed by the one set of heeled shoe impressions.

Several hundred feet along, they caught sight of Amelia, struggling along in her inappropriate footwear. She didn't seem concerned about the possibility of someone following her but Noah and Maggie stayed to the path's edges just in case she should turn around.

The hedge maze ended and the path widened a few steps later. On each side were two long, one-story, flat-roofed, wooden buildings. Signs designated that the left was for "Men" and the right was for "Women". There were doorways and window openings but no doors, glass or screens.

Keeping an eye on Amelia from the corner of the first men's building, Maggie could see forty or fifty narrow cots inside. A trunk and a metal pot sat at the foot of each. Half the cots were occupied by snoring men. The horse's stables had smelled better…and appeared to be in much better condition.

Amelia entered the first women's barracks, came out a minute later and marched into the second one. When she didn't reappear quickly, Noah and Maggie crept closer to that building. As they neared a window, they heard a woman's hushed voice.

"Wake up, Moira. But be very quiet. We don't want to wake the others. You need to come with me. Quickly now. Broderick is waiting. No, no. There's no time to dress. He has clothes for you. Pretty, pretty clothes for his pretty Irish lass."

Maggie looked to Noah for guidance and he signaled that they should wait, watch and listen before making their presence known. So when Amelia led Moira out of the barracks and back through the maze, they followed, but not too closely.

"We can't be sure what she's up to," Noah whispered. "But I doubt she's taking Moira to meet Broderick. What's your intuition say?"

"I agree but I feel like we have to wait for her to show her intention before we intervene."

They continued to follow at a distance until Amelia and Moira passed the stables and continued along the carriage path all the way to the dock. Because they couldn't stay hidden and get closer, they couldn't hear the beginning of the conversation. But it looked like Moira was asking where Broderick was.

Abruptly, Amelia slapped Moira's face and rage had her raising her voice.

"You stupid little Irish whore! Of course he's not here. He will never be meeting you here or anywhere else. I saw you together, your hands all over him until he couldn't think straight. Do you really think he believes that bastard inside of you is his? He told me he's just one of many men who crawled between your fat thighs."

Moira tried to leave but Amelia grabbed her arm and held tight. Maggie wanted to rush to Moira's rescue but Noah held her back. *Not yet*, he mouthed.

"You're probably too empty-headed to realize he was lying to you, just to get what he needed after you seduced him," Amelia continued.

"*No,*" Moira refuted. "He would not lie ta me."

"Oh? Did he tell you we were engaged to be married? That we had the big announcement party at the Davenport this evening?"

"He...he said he had ta take care of something and tomorrow—"

Amelia shook Moira. "You silly, silly girl. Tomorrow morning Broderick and his parents are leaving for Chicago. To meet *my* family's friends at our *second* engagement party. I don't know what he said to *you* to keep you from making a scene, but he told *me* you'd make a good kitchen maid and said we should move you to Chicago with us tomorrow. That must have been what he meant about taking care of something. But I can assure you I will *never* have one of his sluts living under our roof no matter how good a maid she is."

"No. *No!*" Moira futilely strained to get away. "Yer wrong. Rick loves me."

Amelia straightened her spine and lifted her chin. "Perhaps he does. Men are fools when they're being diddled by a girl with experience and my dear fiancé is a bigger fool than most. He's also completely dominated by his mother who has *millions* of reasons to force him into going through with our betrothal. So regardless of who *Rick* loves, *Broderick* will be marrying me. So you may as well start forgetting about him right now."

"Twill be a might hard ta forget about him when I be carryin' his son." She proudly smoothed the loose nightgown over her swollen belly. A bit too proudly.

Amelia let out a growl and tackled Moira to the sand. In a blink, her fingers wrapped around the girl's throat. "He's mine. Mine! *Mine!*" she screeched, slamming Moira's head against the ground with each word.

With lightning speed, Noah bolted out of hiding and across the beach. He yanked Amelia off Moira and easily tossed her several feet away. As he prevented her from rising merely by looming over her, Maggie hurried to help Moira. The girl was gasping for air but seemed more shocked than anything else.

Amelia rose to her feet but kept some distance between her and Noah. "How dare you touch me? My father will hear about this. He's had men killed for less. Whoever you are, you will wish you were never born."

Noah looked down his nose at her. "I met your father this evening and I know how important it is for his family to keep up appearances here. I think he would be very interested in hearing about the trouble you were stirring up when he thought you were safely tucked in bed."

Amelia was spitting mad but no further threats came out of her mouth.

"Now get the hell away from here and never come near Moira again or, I assure you, I will make sure everyone knows what phonies your parents really are."

In her rush to escape Noah's wrath, Amelia tripped over her gown's hem then stumbled in the sand several times before actually getting away from the scene of her attempted crime.

"I do not understand," Moira said a bit hoarsely, glancing from Maggie to Noah and back to Maggie. "Mind ye, I am most grateful but what are ye doin' here at such an hour?"

Maggie gave Noah a look to let her explain. "Do you believe in angels?"

"Of course," she said and quickly made the sign of the cross.

"Well, an angel came and told me you were in trouble and where to find you. Are you sure you're okay now? You got knocked down pretty hard."

Moira smiled. "'tis a good thing I'm already so close ta the ground." She rubbed her bottom. "And there be plenty of paddin' too."

Maggie wasn't convinced. She looked at Noah. "I don't think she should stay alone tonight. Or go to work tomorrow either. She should rest with her feet up until we're sure the baby wasn't injured." *And that no one else planned to do her harm,* she added as though he could hear her thoughts. He nodded as though he had.

The girl's eyes opened wide as she shook her head. "I can see ye mean well but I mustn't miss work. I'm not a silly girl. In my heart I know what that woman said be true. Rick loves me but he…" She shook her head and wiped at the corner of her eye. "He is not so strong ta be standin' up against his kin. Even when he kissed me today and said he would be back, I knew he mightn't be after keepin' his promise. I cannot take the chance of losin' me job too."

Noah ran his fingers through his hair. "I'll tell you what. Stay with us tonight. Bring your uniform and whatever else you might need. At least that way we can see how you're feeling in the morning." He pulled out his pocket watch and amended his statement. "In a couple hours. If Amelia told the truth, she and her parents, and maybe the Hampshires as well, will all be on their way back north tomorrow and you'll be safe."

It took a few more minutes to convince the girl but soon they were heading to her barracks to get a few of her belongings.

Maggie could not begin to imagine herself in this girl's position. She wasn't sure she would be nearly so strong…or so wise. There was no question in her mind that Moira Flanagan deserved a second chance to live, even if it meant changing history.

For some reason she and Noah had been chosen to make that change and, if they had actually done what they were sent here to do, by this time tomorrow they should be back in their own time.

Instantly, her stomach soured. As much as she wanted to ignore it, she knew what it meant. Their task was not yet finished. Had they rescued the wrong person again? Had they missed something important? Something that would prevent them from ever going back to their own time?

Her thoughts followed that train, imagining a future right when and where they presently were. Noah's earlier question came back to her.

Would that really be so bad?

She remembered Noah's sweet words and her logical response. She had no doubt that, as long as they were together, they'd figure out everything else. It probably wouldn't take long to get accustomed to not having twenty-first century advantages.

Abruptly, a thought she'd had before came back. *But what if one of the restrictions Reynard had mentioned was that she and Noah were separated?*

Just in case, she reinforced her intention to keep her thoughts focused on returning to their own time.

Luck stayed with them as they sneaked Moira into their bungalow without anyone seeing them. Maggie had to use the angel card again to get Moira to lie down on the couch with her feet propped up. And after Moira felt an uncomfortable twinge in her lower belly, she grudgingly told Maggie how to find another maid who would explain to their supervisor that she was too ill and feverish to work in the morning.

As soon as they were alone behind the closed bedroom door, Maggie whispered to Noah. "I'm worried that she's still in danger. Amelia's attack was enough to trigger a miscarriage. Moira wouldn't be able to go to a hospital and she's far enough along that she could bleed to death. Or maybe Amelia won't leave in the morning and she could come after her again or maybe she'll convince her father to—"

"*Sh-sh*," Noah sounded then touched his lips to hers. Whispering into her ear, he said, "We don't have anything better to do tomorrow than keep a close eye on her. Reynard said after we fulfill our mission, we had to be at the exact same spot on the beach when the moon is at its zenith. Assuming saving Moira was our assignment, tomorrow night's the magic time and we'll be ready."

Maggie sighed. Even if her feeling about there being something more to do was accurate, nothing more could be done that night. Moira was safe. They hadn't been seen in an off-limits area and Amelia had no idea who they were or where Moira might be hiding.

By this time tomorrow they should be in the Diamond Suite…with air-conditioning and hot showers, television and the internet.

The fancy dress clothes and accessories were set aside, but underthings stayed on, just in case Moira suddenly needed their help. But that didn't stop them from spooning after they got into bed.

Noah kissed her neck and murmured, "You truly are the most amazing woman I've ever known. I would give up everything to have your face be the last thing I see every night and the first thing I see every morning." He was quiet for a moment before adding, "For the rest of my life…whatever time period we end up in."

Maggie's heart swelled with emotion. She wanted to say something just as eloquent, something that would make his heart soar like hers but only three words came to mind and she was afraid to say them aloud.

He made her feel worshipped. Adored. Loved in the way that lasts forever. In this moment, with this man, she had absolutely nothing to fear and there was absolutely no other place she wished to be.

"I love you," he whispered into her ear. "Always have. Always will. No matter where. No matter when."

She felt his heart beating steadily against her back and knew she didn't need to wait for the adventure to end. Her feelings were real and they weren't going to change. Turning in his arms, she gave him a soft kiss, and whispered, "I love you too. And I want to be with you, wherever, whenever, however. I finally understand what you meant about fate bringing us back together. It was always meant to be you."

A confirming shiver ran through her body and she embraced it without question. The eerie sensations were now familiar. It was how she knew the connection between her and Noah was far from ordinary. It was extraordinary.

CHAPTER 25

M aggie opened her eyes to find herself alone in a room filled with sunlight. She was getting used to Noah not being in bed when she awakened but she had thought this morning would be different. That thought barely registered before the bedroom door opened and her darling man entered carrying a large tray. The smell of coffee had her sitting up in an instant, wondering what culinary delights were on today's menu.

Noah set the tray on the dresser then greeted her with a brief kiss. She instantly wanted more but excused herself to take care of her morning needs. By the time she came out of the bathroom, her head was clear and she remembered they had a guest. She grabbed her cover-up and whispered, "Moira?"

Noah motioned her back to bed and handed her a cup of coffee. "She's on the couch, with her feet up. She's eaten and swears she feels fine but I convinced her to let us keep an eye on her anyway. And before you ask, I already took care of explaining her absence and turning down maid service for today. So you can relax and enjoy breakfast." He presented her with two dishes. One offered scrambled eggs, sausage links and a buttered muffin. The other held a big golden waffle topped with bright red strawberries and whipped cream. Her stomach gurgled and she took the waffle.

Noah kept the other dish for himself and settled down beside her. "Since this could be our last day here, what would you like to do?"

Maggie didn't need to think about it. "Maybe I'm being overly cautious but I still have a bad feeling."

"Bad, like Moira's still in danger or bad like we haven't done what we're supposed to do yet?"

She shrugged. "I'm not sure. But I still have the feeling that it's not over. Maybe we need to split up today. Take turns staying with Moira, or at least watching the bungalow, while the other one keeps roaming around the island. Maybe try to find out whether the Gavistons checked out."

"Okay," Noah agreed without hesitation. "Moira is going to be more comfortable with you so I'll take the first roaming-around shift. Maybe I'll be able to confirm what Amelia said about both families heading up north today."

Maggie abruptly straightened her back. "What time is it?"

He pulled out his watch and said, "A little after ten, but we never got to sleep 'til—"

"We forgot about Connor! Remember? Nine o'clock on the nature trail. Oh my, he must think we're horrible people to ignore him like that."

Noah chuckled. "I'm sure he realizes we slept in, but I'll track him down and explain while I'm roaming."

Noah headed out right after breakfast and Maggie offered Moira the use of the bathroom. Considering what the girl was used to she thought it would be a real treat but when she was taking longer than Maggie thought she should, she checked on her. Moira had gotten cleaned up and dressed and was on her knees cleaning the floor.

"What are you doing?" Maggie asked unnecessarily. She grasped the girl's elbow and made her rise. "You need to rest today."

"I really am quite perfect," Moira insisted. "Me head is fine, just a bit of an ache and sore neck. And me babe is moving and not causin' any pains."

"Good. But today I'm your boss and I say you're going to rest." She walked her back to the couch, fluffed up the pillows and stood with hands on her hips until Moira settled back down. "Now stay right there while I bathe and get dressed. I mean it," she added in a very stern voice that was negated by a soft smile.

Maggie guessed Moira was probably as fine as she claimed. After all, the girl walked several miles a day and worked at a physically demanding job with a baby growing inside her. Yet Maggie felt compelled to do something worthwhile and hovering over the expectant mother was better than doing nothing. When she came out of the bathroom, however, Moira was sound asleep. Not wanting to do anything to awaken her, Maggie tiptoed out onto the front porch and sat in one of the yellow rockers.

Considering their active evening and minimal sleep, Maggie should have been tired. Rocking in the shade, watching the waves and being fanned by the salty breeze should have been relaxing. Instead she felt as though electric current was zipping through her body. If she hadn't agreed to stand guard over Moira, she would have taken a swim or run in the sand. Something was about to happen and she was confined to the front porch.

As soon as she heard Moira stir, she hurried inside to make sure she was still feeling okay. Other than not being accustomed to lying around, the girl was fine and after a few minutes Maggie got her talking about how she got from Ireland to Crystal Island, Florida. Her story was similar to others Maggie had read about European immigrants who fled one desperate situation only to be caught in another on the other side of the Atlantic.

Moira's Catholic upbringing helped her through the death of her grandparents, who had both succumbed to influenza shortly after they had brought her to New York City. Her emotional and physical strength helped her survive a nearly lethal stint in a workhouse. And, according to Moira, a bit of Irish luck created a chance meeting that got her a menial position in an upper-class Boston home.

The children there became so attached to Moira, the parents took her along on their holiday to Palm Beach, Florida. Unfortunately, that was the season Moira's body blossomed into womanhood and the father took such a fancy to her, the wife insisted "the little whore" be left behind. Being a generally good man, before he boarded the train with his family, the husband arranged for Moira to be employed as a maid at the new hotel on Crystal Island.

A year later, while scrubbing the bathroom floor of a suite, "Rick" Hampshire walked into Moira's life and captured her heart. That season, they'd done no more than meet secretly to talk, but, when the Hampshire family returned the following year, conversation gave way to love…in all its forms.

Maggie wished she had a tape recorder so that Noah could hear Moira's tale himself. Maybe one day, when he decided to write something other than horror, he could write about this incredible young woman…and give her a romantic, happy ending.

Noah returned with lunch for everyone before Maggie had to think of another subject that would keep Moira from dwelling on the virtues and weaknesses of Broderick Hampshire. However, Noah's news involved him.

"I'm sorry to have to tell you this, Moira, but it looks like he's gone. The concierge confirmed the Gavistons left for Chicago this morning. I told him I had a gift for the engaged couple and he told me which cottage the Hampshires had rented on the other side of the island. But when I got there, the maid said the family had left for an extended trip north. I wish I had happier news but at least you don't have to worry about Amelia or anybody else in either family bothering you."

He flashed a look at Maggie and she understood. His news meant they had saved Moira. She would be alive to see her baby born.

"'Tis fine," Moira said, though her eyes brimmed with tears. "'Twas only in a moment of foolishness I thought 'twould be any other way."

Noah handed her a linen napkin as Maggie patted her hand. She wanted to say something encouraging but the truth was she had no idea what could help under the circumstances. She certainly couldn't tell her not to worry, that everything was going to turn out nicely. All she knew was Moira had already been through hell and survived. She would undoubtedly figure this out as well. At least they had given her the chance to try.

"Me sister and her husband are after leavin' Dublin next week. When they get settled in New York I'm sure they'd be willin' ta take me in. They have a wee boy and a new babe is on the way so I can be useful."

Maggie patted her hand again. "Family is good. But are you sure you want to go back north? New York is a very hard place for—" Noah nudged her before she revealed anything about the future. "The weather. It's very cold there."

Moira laughed. "'Ta be sure. But 'twas not exactly paradise in Boston nor Dublin neither."

Noah and Maggie both smiled in agreement then Noah smoothly changed the conversational direction. "By the way," he said to Maggie. "I ran into that fellow we met last night. You know, the one from back home. He said his wife will be arriving at two this afternoon and thought you might like to greet her with him at the boat dock. I already told him I had another appointment but I accepted for you."

Maggie nodded her agreement though she wasn't sure what she and Connor would have to discuss now that it seemed certain Moira was the one they were to save.

After lunch, Noah pulled a deck of cards out of his pocket and introduced Moira to gin rummy while Maggie got ready for her appointment.

Connor was already at the boat dock when Maggie arrived. His warm hug was unexpected but it allowed

Maggie to sense how much he missed being his true self. She really did wish she could help him, but she had no idea how.

He drew her back onto the path just in case someone happened to stroll by that section of the beach. "How's the mystery coming?"

"Solved. At least we're ninety-nine percent sure it is." As she gave him a rundown of the events of the previous evening, his expression changed a dozen times but he didn't comment until she was finished.

"I'd say that was unbelievable but I've been here long enough to know how the privileged see themselves above everyone else *and* the law. I guess this means you'll be going home tonight."

"After what happened the first time we saved someone, I sure hope so."

"Would you do me a favor?"

Maggie was fairly sure she knew what he would ask for. "If it's within my power, absolutely."

"Please tell Lilli you saw me and that I'm okay and my not getting back to her wasn't because I didn't want to. If for any reason she doesn't believe you, tell her I said I forgive her for being so rude to me that first day. Tell her I'm sorry. And tell her what happened when you saved her grandfather. She won't like it, but she needs to know why her warning to him didn't help. Tell her…"

Maggie waited for him to say the one thing Lilli probably wanted to hear the most.

Finally his shoulders slumped with resignation and he murmured, "Just tell her I love her."

Maggie couldn't resist giving him a comforting hug. "I wish you could tell her that yourself." A strong shiver ran through her and she stepped back from him. "Maybe you *can*! Maybe, when Noah and I go back, we can take you with us! Reynard had told us clothing and whatever we were *holding* could travel with us through the portal. Maybe the reason he said that was so we would bring you back by holding on to you." The idea seemed so logical she couldn't understand the doubtful look on Connor's face. "What?"

"I can't even get off the island in *this* time period. Why would you think they'd let me piggyback on your success?"

She shrugged. "Maybe whoever's in charge of all this will see that you've paid the price for whatever you did or didn't do. If nothing else, they might *want* to make sure you leave so there's no chance of your saving Robert Davenport in 1930 and causing another disaster like we did. At least it's worth a try."

He almost appeared to be convinced then shook his head. "It could boomerang. My being with you could prevent you from going back. I really don't want to be responsible for anyone else's misery."

She shrugged again. "For all we know, part of our assignment *was* to bring you back. Or maybe none of us will go back because our mission was to save someone else entirely."

Connor continued to frown. "I don't know—"

"That's okay. Neither do I...at least not with absolute certainty. But I have a really strong feeling about this. If it doesn't work, you're no worse off. If we get stuck here, you'll help us figure things out. And just in case *you* were the one we were sent here for, we've covered that possibility. We have to be at the rock when the moon reaches its zenith tonight. Since we don't know how to figure that timewise, we'll be ready once the moon rises and cross our fingers. Just be there and trust that everything will work out for the best."

"Maybe you should discuss this with Noah—"

"Already did...well, sort of. Believe me, he would want to help you if at all possible and we both made our peace with the possibility that we could end up living the rest of our days in this time."

* * *

Maggie heard the laughter even before she reached the bungalow's porch. She wasn't the least bit surprised that Noah had not only distracted Moira but had her smiling.

"I think I've been conned," Noah said with phony pout. "She swore she never played gin rummy but she's beaten me three games in a row."

Moira giggled lightly. "I think your mister may be playing poorly on purpose."

"Oh, I doubt that," Maggie said seriously. "We used to play this game when we were younger and I beat him all the time. Deal me in!"

The card game helped the rest of the afternoon pass quickly and when hunger set in, Noah had a selection of sandwiches and fruit delivered to the bungalow. By the time the sun began to set however, Moira was clearly getting antsy.

"You have been more kind ta me than anyone has ever been and 'tis not right for me to intrude on your privacy any longer."

Although Maggie and Noah both felt confident Moira was not despondent enough to take her own life, they still felt more comfortable knowing she was safe and protected until the time came for them to be transported home.

Noah slowed Moira's departure by reminding her that she'd been too sick to work that day. "It wouldn't be good if someone saw you looking perfectly healthy this evening. You'd be better off staying here again tonight and going right to work in the morning. Besides, Maggie and I will be meeting friends on the mainland tonight and won't be back until morning. And then we'll be checking out. So you can just make yourself at home."

"The extra rest will be good for the baby," Maggie added and Moira relented.

Since a card game had kept her distracted all afternoon, Noah taught her how to play solitaire for her evening's entertainment.

Once they were certain Moira would not be leaving, they went into the bedroom and Maggie told Noah about her conversation with Connor. "I assured him that you would want to help him but I'm not sure I convinced him that he should try to come with us."

"But you had the feeling you were supposed to offer him the chance, right?"

"Yes. Definite shiver confirmation."

"Good. Then I'll hope his chivalry doesn't get in the way of his good sense."

They dressed as though they were actually going out on the town. Noah pocketed a little cash and left the remainder in an envelope with a note for Moira to use it for her new life. They recalled Reynard telling them the only things that could travel through time with them were what they were wearing or holding. After a brief debate as to whether they had the right to take a souvenir back with them, they decided to each choose one item that could be easily worn.

Noah decided the pocket watch was the most relevant souvenir he could think of, then insisted Maggie put on the diamond earrings because they were the only items in the bungalow that came close to matching her brilliance.

As the three-quarter moon began to inch above the horizon, they strolled arm-in-arm to the spot on the beach where they hoped to soon be transported back to the future.

"I have a confession to make," Maggie said once they'd reached the portal.

"Isn't that one of those scary conversation openers?"

She smiled. "Not this time. I just wanted to tell you that I've had a wonderful time. Here, in this completely unreal situation, with you."

Noah angled his head toward her. "Doesn't sound like much of a confession. I've had a blast too."

"The confession part is that I was beginning to hope we would fail and be forced to stay here. In spite of all the conveniences we'd miss, this time has some things I'll miss in the future. It just seems…quieter, less…complicated."

Noah leaned down and kissed her mouth. "I love you, Maggie. I love you enough to stay here, knowing exactly how difficult our lives would get, if that really was what you wanted to do. I'm yours to command, Sugarlips. State your desire."

In spite of the importance of the moment, Noah's words delivered a trill of sexual desire and she closed her eyes to savor the feeling. His chuckle brought her part of the way back.

"If *that's* what you want, we should probably find somewhere more private."

She drew his head down for a long, slow kiss before giving him her conclusion. "As tempting as staying here seems in theory, the reality could be very, *very* complicated. We have to go home for all the time-travel-paradox reasons we've ever seen in movies and because we might not resist the temptation to take advantage of future knowledge if our circumstances became desperate."

"Okay, the noisy, complicated future it is." He looked up at the moon then along the beach. "I don't see any sign of Connor."

Maggie looked up at the darkening sky. "There's still time…I hope. But he seemed truly concerned that his trying to travel back with us could prevent any of us from returning. I got the impression he would sacrifice the possibility of his getting back rather than put our opportunity at risk. I think he's *that* good of a man."

Noah drew her close and leaned back against the geode. "And if that's your impression of him, I have no doubt he deserves a second chance. Since he and Lilli seem to have been brought here by his wish, maybe a wish by a gifted woman is all that's needed to get him home."

It took Maggie a moment to understand he meant *her*. She smiled and said, "I *wish* for Connor to be able to travel into the future with us and be with Lilli again."

They both stared down the beach in hopes of seeing Connor coming their way but there was no one in sight. There was nothing more to do but wait.

And wait they did. Five minutes passed, then ten, then sixty as the moon traveled amongst the stars, yet there was still no sign of Connor.

Maggie remembered the tingling sensation that had crawled up her legs before they were transported the first time but so far she hadn't felt anything unusual at all. What she did feel was the same uneasiness that she'd had off and on since they'd saved Moira. "Something's wrong."

Noah frowned. "Something like our timing's off or wrong in a big way?"

"Big, I think. I don't know. I just feel…off-kilter, as though I should be doing something other than standing here."

Noah scanned the area around them for the umpteenth time. "Speaking of being off-kilter…"

She followed his gaze and saw a figure in the distance. The person seemed to be weaving in and out of the tide, falling down, getting up and staggering a bit forward before falling again. With nothing better to do while they waited for transport, they found themselves watching the awkward calisthenics. When the person was about a hundred feet away they could tell it was a man in a tuxedo, taking drinks out of a large bottle, which he managed to keep upright even during multiple stumbles and recoveries.

The man finally stopped trying to walk when he had drained the bottle. With a disgusted growl he tossed it into the ocean. For a moment he stood staring out at the water then he removed his tie, jacket and shoes.

"What's he doing?" Maggie murmured to Noah.

"It looks like he's about to take a swim but he looked too drunk to be doing that. Maybe I better—"

"*No.*" Maggie grabbed his arm as he started away. "We can't move from here. We could miss our chance to get back. He might just want to wet his feet."

Noah returned to her side. "Okay. Let's give him a minute."

The full minute wasn't needed however. Without removing any more clothing, the man walked straight into the ocean and disappeared from their sight in seconds.

"Stay here," Noah ordered Maggie as he dashed off.

"Not without you!" she replied, running right behind him.

He managed to shed his shoes and jacket before jumping into the waves. Maggie stared in horror as Noah ducked below the surface, came up for air and dove down in another direction. Was this the cause of her edginess? Was this the *something wrong* she'd been sensing? Would this man die because she stopped Noah from going to him immediately? Or was it her fate to lose Noah after admitting she loved him?

Dear God, please help them both.

The next few seconds felt like an eternity but Noah reappeared and walked out of the water, hauling the man along with him.

As soon as Noah released his hold, the man dropped to his knees on the sand and began to cough and gag and throw up a disgusting amount of the liquid he had recently swallowed. However, the instant he got control of his stomach he got to his feet and swung at Noah. "Damn you! Damn you!"

Noah grasped the man's flailing arms. "Damn yourself. I just saved your drunken ass."

"Did I ask you to save me?" the man yelled hoarsely then started to cry. "I wanted to die." He plopped down onto the sand, sobbing, gasping and sputtering before adding a pitiful, "I don't deserve to live."

Noah glanced at Maggie. "Should I throw him back in?"

Her mouth dropped open in shock before noticing his smirk.

Grasping a handful of wet hair, he forced the man's head toward Maggie and said, "Recognize him?"

She stared and blinked at the sad, soggy drunk and suddenly realized who it was. "Broderick?"

He squinted up at her. "Do I know you? Never mind. I don't care. I hate you both." He bowed his head and sobbed like a wounded animal.

Maggie murmured to Noah. "Could *he* have been the one we were supposed to save? Could it be that everything else was only leading us up to your saving *him*?"

He shook his head. "That seems overly convoluted. But we can't eliminate the possibility since I had told you about a man committing suicide by drowning in 1927."

"Well, I'm sure the Hampshires could have kept his identity a secret. Especially since it was obvious they knew about his wanting to get out of the formal engagement."

Broderick appeared to have dozed off where he sat so Noah gave him a nudge with his foot that knocked him sideways. "Hey. No sleeping. What are you doing here? I was told you were on your way north."

The young man turned his head slowly from side to side but his eyes remained closed. "Uh-uh. Nope. I tricked 'em. It was the only way. I told 'em I wanted to take the train an' I told the broomstick I was drivin' and they won't know until they all get there." His words were slurred but he seemed somewhat proud of what he'd done. When he didn't receive any praise he gave his excuses. "I tried to tell 'em. I did. They wouldn't listen. They all wanted to stick me with that bug-eyed old broomstick. They didn't care what I wanted. They didn't care about what was right." He sniffed and blew his nose in his hand only to be confused about what to do with his hand.

"Stay with me, Hampshire. Why were you trying to drown yourself?"

"I had to get drunk first, you know. I'm not even man enough to do it sober. She deserves so much better than me."

"She, who?" Maggie interjected.

"My sweet Irish rose. The mother of my child. She's gone an' it's my fault. I'd rather die than live without her." His head dropped to his chest again with another wounded-animal cry.

Maggie poked him to make him look at her. "If you're talking about Moira Flanagan, she hasn't gone anywhere."

"Oh yes she has. I found out the broomstick went to see her. I don't know what she said or did but when I went to her barracks, Moira was gone, with some of her things. Then I looked for her inside the hotel an' they said she didn't come to work. I had no idea where she would go. I didn't know what else to do."

"So you got stinking drunk and walked into the ocean," Noah finished for him. "Tell me the truth now. What were you planning to do if you found Moira last night?"

He did his best to straighten up and look dignified. "I was gonna take her away from all this," he said with a royal wave of his hand. "I wanted to make her my wife. She's gonna have my baby, y'know."

"As a matter of fact we do know," Noah said. "We also know where Moira is. And although I think you might be right about not deserving her, I'll let her decide what to do with you." He gripped the man's arm and jerked him to his feet. "Come on. I'd wait until you were less disgusting but I think enough time has been wasted already."

Broderick was clearly bewildered and very inebriated but Noah didn't give him much choice about what to do next. Maggie quickly gathered up both men's shoes and jackets and caught up with them. By the time they neared the bungalow, Broderick seemed to be walking a little steadier.

Before stepping onto the porch, Noah grasped the man's shoulders and gave him a rough shake. "Listen to me now. You got lucky tonight. In fact, you are one lucky son-of-a-bitch to have somebody like Moira love you. If I ever find out you mistreat her in any way, I will come after you and finish what you tried to do tonight, only you'll be stone sober when it happens. Got that?"

Broderick straightened his back and lifted his chin. "Yes, sir. I'll take care of her, I swear. I love her more than life itself."

"Then go on inside and tell her what an idiot you are."

Maggie handed the man his jacket and shoes and wished him good luck. Noah took his own things and waited to make sure Moira accepted her man's apology. Of course she did. The fool was as alluring as a drenched, lost puppy.

Noah took another several minutes to go inside, change into dry clothes and transfer the watch from the jacket to his pants pocket. As he and Maggie headed back to the geode, he said, "Well, that was certainly an interesting turn of events."

She hugged his waist as they walked. "I'm pretty sure *interesting* is an understatement. Now it looks like our mission might have been to save *two* people and put them on the road to a happily-ever-after."

"After the first wrong guess, I'm not assuming anything. We won't know for sure unless we get sent forward again. And if we missed the zenith, we'll have to wait until tomorrow night, which will take us right down to the deadline."

Maggie sighed. "If that's the case, I think you should talk to Connor tomorrow and convince him—" She went rigid as a tingling sensation tickled the bottoms of her feet. Uncertain if that meant they were about to be zapped where they were or if it was a warning, she grabbed Noah's hand and pulled him into a run. "It's time! Hurry up."

As they neared the portal, a figure could be seen leaning against the rock. But their concern gave way to pleasure when the potential witness to their departure turned out to be Connor.

CHAPTER 26

"It's time!" Maggie repeated as she grasped Connor's hand and pressed it to the rock. Noah took hold of his other hand and did the same.

"I wasn't going to come," Connor said quickly. "Then all of a sudden, I felt someone give me a hard shove and—" He gasped and squeezed his eyes shut against whatever he was feeling.

The tingling had traveled up Maggie's body, inching higher and growing stronger by the second. By the time the sensation filled her completely, she could barely breathe. Rather than a shimmering peak and a slow fading, the finale was more like a brief but painful electric shock along her entire spine followed by a sense of wellbeing. "Did either of you feel that?"

"Are you kidding?" Noah replied. "It was like holding on to a live wire."

"Same here," said Connor. "I don't remember anything like that the first time."

It took them another moment to release each other's hands and take some deep breaths.

Noah lifted Maggie's chin with his finger and stared into her eyes. "Are you okay?"

She did a quick mental check. "Not just okay. I actually feel really good. Like I had a great massage and received exciting news at the same time. It's hard to explain."

He gave her a quick kiss then turned her head with his finger. "Look."

She dragged her gaze away from his face and grinned when she realized what he wanted her to see. The moon and stars offered just enough light for her to see the row of colorful cabanas in the distance. "We made it," she exclaimed and threw her arms around his neck. His arms closed around her waist and he swung her around several times before setting her down again.

The mini-celebration ended with a kiss that said everything about how happy they were to have made it back to their own present, to have saved two people and their baby, to be together, in love in the perfect time and place.

"I love you, Sugarlips," Noah murmured.

"Really?" she asked, tilting her head at him. "After *all* this time? Things have changed, you know."

"*Ahem,*" Connor sounded, reminding them of his presence as politely as possible. "I certainly don't want to take anything away from your happiness, but I'm not quite sure what to do next."

Maggie's cheeks warmed with embarrassment but Noah chuckled. "Sorry about that," he said, giving Connor's shoulder a pat. "I think the first order of business is to figure out what *year* we landed in." He reached into his pocket and took out the gold watch. Flipping it open, he turned to let the moon illuminate the inside.

Maggie felt a flutter of happiness when she saw the wedding photo was still in place but got confused by the placement of the timepiece's hands. "Nine-thirty? Wasn't it going on midnight a few minutes ago?"

Noah studied the watch then looked up at the sky. "And the moon was definitely in a different position a few minutes ago. I'm sure of it." Suddenly his eyes lit up with awareness. "The moon looks *full*. Like it was when we left.

But I also remember looking at the time when I first opened the watch…when we were getting ready to go out that first night in the bungalow."

The memory came back to her in a flash. "Yes. I remember you saying something about it being around nine-thirty when we were transported. Is it possible that we've been brought back at the same time we left?"

He chuckled. "Anything's possible. But there's one easy way to find out for sure." He took her hand and Connor followed them to the cabana where they had dined in such exotic luxury. Aware of the possibility of intruding on another guest, he cautiously poked his head into the opening and laughed aloud.

He threw back the flap so they could see what he found so humorous. Their dinner remnants were exactly as they were when they decided to take a walk. The empty bottle of German ice wine was upside-down in the bucket of only *slightly* melted ice. Even their robes were on the lounge where they'd tossed them.

"It's exactly as we left everything," Maggie explained to Connor as she took their suite key card out of her robe pocket. "Which makes today August 7, 2018."

"Which also makes it thirteen years since Lilli has seen me," Connor returned with a tense expression. "What if she doesn't recognize me?" He sighed. "What if she doesn't want to see me?"

Maggie made a face at him. "Remember, I told you she has the picture of the two of you in her office. If she didn't want to see you, she wouldn't keep that photo in a place where she'd have to look at it every day. And by the way, you've only aged three years so you don't look any different. Lilli doesn't look much different, except for the happiness factor, but it has been thirteen years for her and she is a woman—"

"What Maggie is trying to say," Noah cut in, "is be aware that Lilli might be worried about how she looks to *you*."

Connor chuckled. "That's ironic. Our relationship started off with me thinking she was too young because she was only twenty and I was thirty. Now, through the miracle of time travel, we're the same age. But I'll keep your words in mind."

Noah nodded then asked, "Any idea how we should handle the big reveal? I haven't met her but she doesn't sound like the type to faint from a shock."

"It's impossible to guess how she might react, but I'm positive it needs to be in private," Connor replied. "And I'm guessing by this hour she might be in her apartment...but that doesn't mean she's alone." His expression fell as he gave that possibility some thought.

"I know what to do," Maggie said confidently and both men raised their brows with attention. "I'm not going to explain now, but she's waiting for...some information from me. I think if I have the front desk call her and say I have something of urgent importance to discuss with her, she might invite me to her rooms."

Noah quickly countered. "Or she may come to the lobby, which would definitely not be the best place for this reunion."

Maggie shook her head. "No, this matter is very personal to her. I think she'll bite."

"Okay," agreed Noah. "But I expect to hear about this important information, personal or not, before we go to sleep tonight."

"I promise to tell you all about it, but for this to work, the two of you have to stay out of sight while I go to the front desk."

Without knowing why, Noah and Connor took a side entrance into the hotel and waited for Maggie in the alcove by the tree house elevator. Mere minutes later, she joined them.

"She instructed me to come right up," she said with a grin as she used the key card to open the elevator door. "Her suite is on the second floor."

"She always said she liked that apartment better than the penthouse," Connor noted. "Should I come up with you or—"

"Come." Maggie motioned for him to step inside quickly. "I don't think we should give her a chance to think about what your return means. Ripping the bandage off abruptly is usually best."

A range of emotions crossed Connor's face as he obeyed. "Maybe I should take a shower first and get the goop out of my hair, maybe put something on besides this waiter's tux—"

Noah cut him off this time. "In sixty seconds, none of that is going to matter."

When they stepped out of the elevator and into the garden foyer outside Lilli's apartment, the men stood to the side as Maggie knocked lightly on the door.

"Ms. Harrison," Lilli stated without any expression of welcome or invitation to enter. "I was not expecting company this evening but I was told you have something important to relate."

Maggie forced herself not to react to the sight of the barefooted woman in the plush white robe, long blond hair brushed out over her shoulders, makeup removed...and slightly red, puffy eyes, as though she'd been crying. "May I come in please?"

Lilli frowned. "Right here is good enough. I'd prefer you give me the bad news quickly and leave me to figure out how best to deal with it."

Maggie's gaze darted to Noah, who pretended to rip a bandage off his arm and she got the message. "Okay. I know Crystal Island and this hotel has all sorts of paranormal secrets."

Lilli rolled her eyes. "I've heard that before and it's all nonsense. I thought you had something to tell me about Mr. Nash's book. Now I would like you to leave...or I will buzz for security." She started to close the door but Maggie blocked it with her body and sped up her delivery as Lilli glared at her.

"I know it's not nonsense because I've seen scenes from the past in mirrors and heard voices when no one was around. I know the big rock on the beach is a portal to travel through time."

That statement was rewarded with an audible snort from Lilli.

"And I know that's true because Noah Nash and I just returned from a visit to 1927!" She held out her hand and drew him to her side.

Noah gave Lilli a lopsided grin and simply said, "Hello."

Before Lilli could decide what to say in return, Maggie continued. "I also know that thirteen years ago *you* traveled back to 1924. And the reason I know that for a fact is because we brought someone back with us."

Maggie and Noah took several steps back.

Connor moved into the doorway.

And Lilli dropped to her knees.

In an instant, Connor lifted her into his arms and, looking toward Noah and Maggie, said, "Thanks guys. I'll take it from here." Then he kicked the door closed.

Noah and Maggie stared at the door for a second then smiled at each other. "So much for Lilli not being the type of woman who would faint from a shock," Noah said with a chuckle.

"Well now, she didn't completely faint, but that wasn't exactly your everyday sort of shock." She turned her ear to the door. "I don't hear anything. Should we wait to make sure she's all right?"

Noah hugged her to his side as he pressed the elevator button. "I'm quite sure we can trust Connor to take care of her. I'm also very sure that I'm more than ready to go back to our suite upstairs…our *air-conditioned* suite with the king-sized bed."

"And our huge shower stall with the two massaging heads and *really* hot water."

The elevator door opened and Maggie dashed inside. "Hurry up slowpoke," she teased. "It's not like we have all the time in the world."

* * *

For the first time, Noah was still in bed next to Maggie when she opened her eyes in the morning. She smiled and yawned and stretched with a satisfied groan. "I feel like I slept for a week," she said.

He leaned over and kissed her navel. "You almost did. It's nearly noon. But I'm not one to talk. I just woke a few minutes ago. Must be time-travel's version of jet lag."

Everything came back to her in a rush and her fingers flew to her earlobe. No earrings. *Was it all a dream?* A moment later he dangled an antique diamond earring in front of her.

"I took them off you before I closed my eyes. Didn't want to risk choking on one of our souvenirs."

She relaxed a little but not completely. "I don't know about you but I'm feeling…disoriented. We just had this amazing, totally weird week and then, *bam*, we're back where we were before it happened. I know we fixed what we were sent there to do, and maybe even more, but I feel like I was reading this exciting book and then got left hanging at the end. I want to know what happened to everyone."

"Me too," Noah said. "And since we're back in our high-tech world, it should be easy to find out. I have a great program that allows me to search all sorts of reference materials about people, including genealogies."

Maggie abruptly rose and headed for the door.

"Hey! Where are you going?"

She flashed him a smile. "I just realized I'm late for work."

"But your boss wants to cuddle."

She came back and gave him a firm closed-mouth kiss. "And your assistant would enjoy that too but then it would be another couple hours before we got to work and my curiosity is killing me."

He crossed his arms and pouted. "Fine. But you'll owe me."

She smirked at him and hustled to her bathroom before she gave into the temptation to ask about what he might demand of her.

Maggie felt refreshed and appropriately dressed when she returned to the living room. Noah was already working at the computer on the dining room table and brunch had been ordered.

He motioned for her to sit beside him, but when she got close he pulled her onto his lap and into a slow, tongue-stroking kiss. Despite her intention to stay in work mode, it took him less than ten seconds to melt her resistance. "You win," she murmured against his mouth.

"You agree I'm the boss?" He rubbed his nose against hers.

She sighed and relaxed into his embrace. "Yes, sir. You are the boss."

"And you agree you're supposed to do whatever I ask of you?" He nipped her ear lobe.

"Yes, sir, if it is in my skill set, it will please me to please you." She purposely wriggled her bottom more firmly into his lap.

He groaned. "And you will never ever leave my bed again without my permission."

She straightened her back and made a face at him.

"Too far?" he asked with a crooked grin.

"Just a tad." She shifted on his lap so she could see the computer screen. "Anything yet?"

"I just logged onto—" A knock on the door interrupted him. "That should be Room Service."

"I'll take care of it," Maggie said cheerfully as she hopped off his lap. "You keep going."

Maggie opened the door and exclaimed, "Oh my goodness. What is all this?"

Noah was at her side in an instant.

A waiter with the expected room service cart was indeed one of the people at the door and he entered the suite first. Behind him was a housekeeper with two folded, freshly laundered hotel robes, and bringing up the rear of the staff parade was an attendant with a cart bearing two large vases of very different, exquisite bouquets of tropical and traditional flowers. A gold-edged envelope poked out from the most ostentatious bouquet. After they all left, Maggie extracted the card and read it aloud.

"There are no words or gifts that could adequately express our appreciation for what you did for us. We cannot imagine either of you needing a return favor of equal magnitude, but if you did, we would do our best to grant it. At the very least, we hope you will join us for dinner in our suite this evening. The conversation should prove quite illuminating.

Meanwhile, do know you have our promise of everlasting kinship. From this day on, you will be considered a member of the Davenport family and, as such, there will always be a complimentary room for you at a Davenport hotel…wherever and whenever you arrive."

The card wasn't signed but it left no question as to who sent it.

"Wow," Maggie said with a shake of her head. "Talk about someone having a total personality change overnight. I guess it took something as supernatural as Connor's reappearance to get the wicked witch's heart beating again."

Noah arched one brow. "The wicked witch? Maybe now would be a good time for you to explain what you meant about her waiting for information from you."

Maggie sighed. "I doubt if it matters any more, but I would have told you about it eventually."

"I'm listening." His mouth tightened and he crossed his arms.

She took a breath. "First, understand the only reason I didn't say anything before was because I didn't want to do anything that might affect your creative flow."

"Okay. You were being thoughtful. Got it. Go on."

"Second, the afternoon I told you I was filling out paperwork in Human Resources, I had actually been ordered to report to the General Manager's office and not tell you anything about it. I would have ignored that order except Ms. Davenport threatened me and my friend Tanya, who owns the agency I work for."

Noah's jaw clenched and his eyes narrowed. "She *threatened* you? You should have told me anyway. I'm sure I could have helped."

She bit her lower lip. "Please don't be angry."

He looked angry anyway. "Just explain."

"She told me I had to report to her every week. Tell her what you were planning to write about. And if it looked like you were going to say anything about her grandfather, directly or indirectly, I had to give her advance notice so she could stop you."

Noah's expression relaxed. "And that is the direction I was going in. I see. And you didn't want to warn me because…"

"If I told you, it could have made you go in a different direction just to help me."

He mulled it all over. "You're right. That's what I would have done. But after everything that's happened, I've been thinking of going a different way with my next book anyway. I may not use the Davenport at all."

Her eyes widened. "Really? Tell me more."

His stomach rumbled and his gaze shifted to the room service cart. "That'll take more than a few minutes and our food's getting cold. Besides, I thought you were anxious to find out what happened to the people in our personal *Magical Mystery Tour*."

Noah hadn't exaggerated about how easy it would be to trace what had happened to Moira, the Hampshires and the Gavistons. Easiest to find were the two fathers.

George Hampshire served two terms as a Florida State Representative then retired from politics…possibly because Vincent Gaviston, aka Vincenzo Vespucci, would have withdrawn his financial support when the marriage of their children was called off.

Vespucci was investigated by the FBI on several occasions, mainly for racketeering and illegally importing and distributing alcohol, but was never convicted of a crime, possibly due to the fact that a marriage was consummated between Amelia and the troubled son of a U.S. Senator within a year of her broken engagement to Broderick.

Moira and Broderick were married in 1927 and had one son and three daughters between 1927 and 1932. Noah couldn't find anything on Broderick's early work history, but during the Depression, when others were suffering, he moved the family to California and ended up having a decent career as a movie actor, using the name Morey Flanagan.

Their four children grew up, the girls got married to men in various lines of work and the boy became involved in California politics after a short stint as a child actor. None of them were still alive. However, there were ten grandchildren, eight of whom were still alive, twenty-one great-grandchildren and eighteen great-great-grandchildren currently living in various parts of the country.

"Amazing" summed up Maggie's overall impression. "We didn't just save Moira, Broderick and their first child. Fifty-two more lives took place because she wasn't murdered and he didn't commit suicide in 1927."

Noah nodded slowly. "I'd bet that if Broderick wasn't the unidentified male suicide, and if we hadn't been there, and he had gone ahead with marrying Amelia, he may have never done anything on his own. And the records show that Amelia never had any children with her husband."

"Well, we'll never know what might have happened without our butting in, but I'm satisfied with how things turned out for Moira and Broderick. Just look at the career choices of the great-grandchildren—an environmentalist, a medical research scientist, a college professor, a computer programmer; there's even one who's gotten into politics.

Their names practically jumped off the computer screen for me. It's like I *know* they will be doing important things. Who knows, the research scientist could discover the cures for all kinds of diseases, or the politician could be a future governor or even the president. I realize that sounds crazy—"

"Whoa. If you'll recall, I'm the one who insisted you have special talents. If you have a feeling, that's all I need to know. And the coolest part is we'll be around to see it as it happens."

His enthusiasm was so contagious, she couldn't help but chuckle. "Very cool indeed. And look, there's even a great-great-grandchild named Moira. I can't wait to see what she'll end up doing with her life. Who would have thought a poor Irish maid and a doomed mama's boy could have planted such a strong tree?"

Noah pulled her close for a long kiss. "Have I told you lately how much I love the way your brain works?"

She kissed him softly. "You may have said something along those lines once or twice, but I will be sure to remind you if you ever forget."

"Even when we're ninety-four and forget why we sleep in the same bed?"

A hint of desire twinkled in her eyes. "We may forget a lot of things in our old age, but I'll bet your next royalty check that *why* we sleep together *won't* be one of them."

He gave her a quick kiss and stood up. "I'm tired of staring at the screen...and sitting. Let's take a walk and see if anything's changed since our last walk-around."

"Maybe we could stop in the Executive Office and accept the dinner invitation...and say thank you for the flowers."

Noah laughed. "Do you seriously believe that after waiting all this time for Connor to return, Lilli is going to be at her desk today?"

Maggie's cheeks warmed with the thought of what that couple would undoubtedly be doing this morning. "No. At least I hope not. I was thinking of leaving a message with her assistant."

As they ambled through the hotel lobby, Maggie couldn't help but think about the day she first arrived at the Davenport. So much had happened since then. Her world and her view of it had been completely altered.

Suddenly she felt a small shiver and someone very familiar came into view. Pushing a fully loaded baggage cart was their time-traveling bellman. She gave Noah a nudge and they both strode directly into Reynard's path.

"Excuse me," he said politely.

"Reynard, it's *us*," Maggie said with exaggerated meaning.

He smiled and nodded. "Ah, yes. Ms. Harrison. And de most famous author, Noah Nash. I hope ya are having a pleasant stay. Was dere somet'ing I might do for ya?"

She frowned. He looked the same and sounded the same but he didn't seem to be aware of any of the supernatural encounters they had shared.

Noah squeezed Maggie's elbow and replied for them. "Oh no, thank you. She told me how helpful you've been and I wanted to say thank you."

Reynard smiled. "Ya are most welcome but I was just doing my job." He waited for them to move and then continued on his way.

"Too weird," Maggie said with a shake of her head. She stared at the bellman's back hard enough for him to glance over his shoulder at her. In that instant, she saw a glint of gold flash in his eyes, then he winked at her before looking ahead again. "Just doing his job, my ass."

Noah laughed out loud. "I'm sure he has his reasons."

A few minutes later they were passing by the shops and Noah said, "I want to buy you a present. What would you like?"

"Don't be silly. You already gave me antique diamond earrings. I don't need anything else."

"I'm not being silly. I missed your last birthday and the one before that and the one—"

"All right," she cut in. "You can buy me something but only if you're going to enjoy it too."

He arched one eyebrow. "I don't think they have *that* sort of shop here."

She chuckled. "You might be surprised. I know exactly what I want that I'm pretty sure you'll enjoy and they *do* have it here."

Without another word she led him directly into a boutique shoe store and stopped amidst the Jimmy Choo, Manolo Blahnik and Christian Louboutin displays. In under five seconds his expression morphed from curiosity to awareness to desire to amusement. She waited for his gaze to land on a particularly sexy stiletto-heeled, platform sandal with a network of skinny snakeskin straps and a crystal-studded anklet before pointing it out to a very solicitous saleslady.

For the next hour, Maggie tried on every pair of shoes Noah gave a nod to and paraded up and down the aisle to *see how they felt*.

He *really* liked eight pairs.

Two of them hurt her feet, but she let him buy the other six.

They were on their way back through the lobby with their purchases when another familiar face appeared in front of her.

"Hello, Ms. Harrison."

"Hello," Maggie said with a bright smile. "I don't believe you've met my...employer. Noah Nash, this is Lillian Davenport's assistant."

The dark-eyed woman instantly held out her hand to him. "Esmeralda Mercedes Martinez, but you can call me Mercy. It is truly a pleasure to meet you Mr. Nash. I'm a big fan."

Noah shook her hand and grinned. "Thank you, Mercy, and please call me Noah."

"We were just heading to your office," Maggie said. Then, as though she didn't know the answer, she asked, "Any chance Ms. Davenport has a minute to spare for us?"

Mercy giggled. "Boss won't be in the office today or for the next week. She's going away on holiday...for the first time in thirteen years. I gather the two of you had something to do with that."

Maggie was more than a little surprised and phrased her question carefully. "She told you what happened?"

Mercy giggled again. "Oh, no, we're not that close. She asked me to go by her suite to pick up a file and I just happened to see the card she'd written to the two of you. I also got to meet the reason she's suddenly willing to take some time off." She stepped closer, took one of each of their hands into hers and whispered, "You did a great job. Thank you from all of us." She stepped back and, in a normal tone, asked, "Will you be able to join them for dinner at six this evening?"

"Yes, that was why we were headed to your office," Maggie replied.

"We're looking forward to it," Noah added.

"Excellent. I'll let her know." As she walked away, she added, "Don't you just love happily-ever-afters?" Then she winked at Maggie, just like Reynard had.

"How odd," Noah said with a thoughtful expression, as Mercy walked away.

"You mean 'odd' like not appropriate, or *odd* like creepy?"

That made him chuckle. "Odd like Reynard pretending not to know what we were talking about. She didn't admit to knowing how we helped and she could have been thanking us on behalf of the hotel staff, but I'd bet my next royalty check Mercy is in on all the big secrets around here."

Maggie shrugged. "That's the feeling I got too. Maybe Reynard isn't the only hotel employee who reports to a supernatural entity." Her eyes widened as she considered that. "Maybe the entire staff is—"

Noah squeezed her hand. "*Sh-sh*. Let's keep that conversation for somewhere more private."

Maggie nodded her understanding then asked, "So, where shall we go next?" She watched his expression quickly change to one she now knew very well.

"I think we should go back upstairs and take another look at our purchases…just to make sure you don't want to exchange the gray boots for the red ones."

Fortunately, they had the treehouse elevator all to themselves.

They were watching the moon inch its way across the sky through the dome in the master bedroom before Maggie remembered something Noah had said earlier. "Are you ready to tell me about the new book idea yet?"

"Well, I can tell you it's not a horror."

She perked up immediately. "I like it already. What else?"

He grinned. "I'm not saying I'm done writing horror, I'm just going to add a different genre to my bibliography. I was thinking about a time-travel suspense…with a hot romance to spice things up."

In response, she planted kisses all over his face. "I love it! And wait until I tell you about Moira's life story *before* we met her. I'll bet you can use it somehow. I was absolutely amazed and I even thought about how you should write it someday."

He held her face still to get one good kiss. "I take it you're happy with my decision…which is good because I'm going to need help from someone familiar with that type of story."

"I'm definitely your girl."

Noah gave Maggie a longer, deeper kiss. "You certainly are, Sugarlips."

The First called The Council of Abstracts to order. *I believe the event correction regarding Moira Flanagan was concluded in a positive way. Are there any objections to recording Maggie Harrison's and Noah Nash's mission as a success and instituting the human upgrade?* When no one spoke The First addressed the three Abstracts most involved in the case. *Justice?*

Satisfied.

Karma?

Satisfied.

Love?

Very satisfied. And thank you, Justice, for getting the fox back in his cage.

You are welcome. Just be more careful next time.

The First recorded the success as confirmed and closed The Book with a dramatic thud. *According to the established rules, The Human Experiment will continue. However, this session is now open to a discussion of the adjustments that should be made to those rules for future tests.* The First withdrew its thoughts so as not to influence the debate that arose.

With the fate of humanity out of jeopardy for another century, The First turned its attention to an issue unrelated to The Human Experiment. This particular matter fell under The First's supreme jurisdiction and thus did not require unanimous approval by The Council.

Because Maggie and Noah had focused so much of their attention on the spirit known as The Weeping Woman, that entity had grown stronger. The First saw the future clearly. It would not be long before other, less intuitive, humans would hear her pleas as Maggie had. Credible testimonials would then demand investigation. The result would not only draw undesirable elements to the Davenport resort, it could be cataclysmic for the Crystal Island portal.

In this circumstance, a time rewind would create more problems than it might resolve. The only solution was to permanently silence The Weeping Woman before it was too late. To accomplish such a drastic measure required the exceptional opening of the portal and the involvement of one particular, independent Abstract.

Unfortunately, *Death* could not be controlled and seldom played well with others.

THE
LOVERS IN TIME
SERIES

OUT OF TIME
JUST IN TIME
SOME TIME AWAY
IT'S ABOUT TIME

Turn the page for an
excerpt from

IT'S
ABOUT TIME

Lovers In Time

Book Four

Marilyn Campbell

In all his years of partying, Sam never remembered feeling *this* bad. His eyes burned like hell and felt glued shut; his head seemed to have been split down the middle by a hatchet that was left in place; his arms and legs felt weighted down, and the nausea and dizziness were far worse than he'd ever experienced with the flu.

What the hell happened last night? His mind strained to remember against the physical pain. The first image that came through involved a beautiful blonde with a body that made him not care how young she might be. He bought her a drink, maybe a few, still not enough to be this hung over. Could she have dropped a little something extra in his glass?

What was her name? Brittany? Tiffany? Emily? He was fairly sure it ended with an "e" sound, just like a lot of the others he'd hooked up with in the last two years.

Where was that? It took him a moment to remember being at the LIV Nightclub in the Fontainebleau Hotel, but that made no sense. He never partied where he worked…but he didn't work there any more; he'd given his notice that afternoon.

Why would he do such a stupid thing? He gave himself a mental forehead slap as the reason came back to him—after eight years of climbing the kitchen staff ladder on Miami Beach, he'd just been hired to replace the retiring executive chef at the Davenport Resort on Crystal Island! *That* was why he'd been celebrating so hard.

Before he could congratulate himself again on his achievement however, he recalled driving north on I-95. His Porsche's top was down, an intense full moon illuminated the clear night sky, and the blonde in the passenger seat kept urging him to go faster. Then her hand slipped between his thighs and his foot pressed harder on the gas pedal.

The last image that flickered in his mind was the back of a semi that seemed to appear out of nowhere...

His recollection was cut off as a hand gently touched his and a woman with a very soft voice—definitely not the "e" girl—spoke close to his ear.

"It's okay, soldier. You're safe now. My name is Milly and I'll be one of the nurses taking care of you. The doctor needs to examine your injuries, so I'm going to give you a nice dose of morphine to help you get through that. When you wake up again, we can talk if you'd like."

Sam felt a needle prick his forearm and a few seconds later the pain and all his questions went away.

"Where's this patient's file?" Captain Norwich called out to no one in particular.

When Milly saw the other two nurses hustle away from the doctor's line of sight, she had no choice but to respond, but she would not abandon the soldier whose wound dressing she was changing. "I'll be right with you," she said as she continued her task. Hopefully Norwich was as tired as he appeared and would forego his usual round of dirty jokes and crude invitations. On the other hand, if he thought she wasn't giving him his due respect, he would likely make her life uncomfortable in some other way. That thought made her pick up her pace.

As she crossed the long ballroom that had been converted into a hospital ward lined with beds, she reminded herself to slouch. There were plenty of men who found her height and full figure attractive qualities, but Doctor Norwich wasn't one of them. At five-foot-ten, she could look down on his bald spot, which he tried to hide with brown strands of hair from the side of his head. Added to his short stature, his very large waistline always made Milly think of the Humpty-Dumpty nursery rhyme. His less than ideal appearance was possibly the cause of a personality that ranged from unpleasant to rude.

But he was a decent doctor and her superior, so she slouched.

He made her wait for a full minute, while he studied another patient's chart, before giving her his attention. "What's the story with that one?" he asked with a nod toward the patient whose entire head and a good portion of his body was wrapped in bandages.

"He was brought in on a transport yesterday morning with three others who were wounded in Normandy two weeks ago. They were patched up at a field hospital before being shipped here for rehab, but only one of them seems healthy enough to be released any time soon. That one's been unconscious the whole time."

The doctor shook his head. "Damn shame it cost our boys so much, but at least it's looking like they helped turn the tide in France. So where's this one's file?"

"There wasn't one," Milly replied. "And no dog tags either. I've already requested a search for both, but nothing's come in yet."

"Did you change any of his dressings?"

"No. They all looked clean, as if they had been changed right before he was brought in."

"Well, clean or not, without any notes, they've got to come off before I can suggest treatment."

Milly took the small scissors out of her uniform pocket and began carefully snipping away the bandages as Captain Norwich stood by. The moment she began revealing the patient's wounds, she felt the doctor's lecherous gaze undressing *her*. She wished she could slap his face or at least walk away, but that wouldn't help the injured man. The only choice she had was to pretend she didn't notice. A few minutes later, she no longer had to pretend because every bit of the doctor's attention was focused on the man's battered body.

This soldier was taller and more muscular than most of the men she tended, but he was in bad shape. Lacerations of varying sizes and shapes, as well as raw patches of flesh, were all over the man's face, shaved head and body, front and back. The largest cuts had been closed with thin pieces of metal, medium ones had been stitched with such a fine thread that it was barely visible and the smaller ones had been covered by an unusual sort of textured tape. The face was puffy and purplish, especially the area around the eyes, and the lids had been sealed closed with the strange tape.

"This wasn't caused by shrapnel," Norwich stated firmly. "I've only seen one patient with this kind of damage, but it was a man who'd been thrown through a window, not a soldier."

"Maybe he was in or near a building with lots of glass windows when it got bombed," Milly offered.

He frowned at her. "Or maybe those sons-of-bitches have a new kind of weapon. I heard both sides are working on something big. Anyway, I've definitely never seen anything like how this man was pieced back together. Makes me think of Frankenstein's monster, but I sure would like to talk to the doctor who did this work."

Milly had the same thoughts, but she knew better than to give her opinion, even if it agreed with his.

The doctor continued to study the body on the bed. "The other odd thing is how fresh the wounds and bruising look. Like it only happened a few days ago…not nearly enough time for him to be fixed up in a field hospital *and* cross the Atlantic. The missing file and dog tags could just be a mishap, but when all the pieces are combined, I'd say we are dealing with something highly irregular." Under his breath he murmured, "Curious. *Very* curious."

Since he had yet to give her any instructions, she asked, "How do you want me to proceed?"

Norwich had to drag his gaze off the patient before answering. "Based on the head injury, we can assume some brain trauma and a helluva headache. When he's able to swallow, give him a couple aspirin tablets every few hours. I don't see any sign of infection but a few doses of penicillin won't hurt. As to the scraped areas, apply that burn salve we got in last week, then just replace the bandages. They were unusually clean, so reuse whatever you can." He started to walk away then added, "Hopefully, the patient will be able to fill in some blanks when he wakes up. Meanwhile, do not say *anything* to *anyone* about him or what you've seen. Consider that an order, Fitch."

The fact that the doctor left without giving her his traditional pat on her behind let Milly know just how disturbed he was by what he'd seen.

Desert-like thirst and a feminine scent of soap and roses finally lured Sam out of the darkness to semi-consciousness.

"Come on, soldier, open your mouth a little."

Soldier? He was a soldier once, but that was years ago. He tried to part his dry lips to speak but only managed a croaking sound before something was eased between his teeth and a bit of water dripped onto his tongue. After a few repetitions, his throat remembered how to swallow.

"Very good," she said. "Now I need to prop you up so you can have a proper drink, but you have a lot of wounds on your back so this might hurt."

Her voice was soft and soothing and made him think of warm béarnaise sauce, which immediately brought to mind the salmon Florentine omelet he'd prepared that morning. His stomach couldn't seem to decide if it wanted food or needed to toss up the bit of water he'd just gotten down. While he tried to figure that out, the woman got his upper body raised with only a little more pain than he felt lying still. He tried to thank her but consonants were beyond his tongue's ability.

"You haven't had anything to eat or drink since you were brought in, which was almost three days ago, so we're going to take this very slow, okay?"

He tried to nod but the movement made the pounding in his head magnify. His hand automatically moved to the source of the new pain but what he felt was not recognizable. Using both hands, he deduced that his whole head was wrapped in gauze, except for nose and mouth holes. That answered the question of why he couldn't open his eyes. Slowly he found his way out of the blurry half-world to relative consciousness. He made some sounds he hoped she could understand.

"One thing at a time, soldier. I'm going to put a straw in your mouth. Try to take a tiny sip."

He took one, then another, but after the third, she withdrew the straw.

"I know you're thirsty but if you force too much too fast, you could throw up and, believe me, your head is not going to be happy about that. I have some pills for the headache once I'm sure you can get them down. The doctor was here yesterday and checked all your wounds. Some of them are pretty bad but there's no sign of infection, which is very good. Okay, let's try a little more water."

This time, she let him have as much as he wanted.

"Thank you," he whispered. "Where am I?"

"The Davenport Rehabilitation Facility."

"Like the hotel?" He heard her let out a soft sound as though she were smiling.

"It *is* the hotel. The owners were kind enough to allow us to use part of it to help the wounded get back on their feet."

He was pretty sure he heard all her words but they made no sense. "Crystal Island?"

"Yes, that's right. It's off the southeast coast of Florida."

I know that, but why aren't I at Jackson or Mt. Sinai Hospital? And why are my eyes bandaged? His thoughts seemed clear in his head but the only thing that came out aloud was the most important question. "Am I...blind?"

She covered his hand with hers. "You suffered some serious head injuries, but until your wounds heal more, the doctor wants to keep them all covered, including your eyes. Until then, try not to think about what may or may not be. Just be happy you're alive."

He felt her hand slip away. "Please don't leave," he said in a shaky voice.

"I wasn't leaving."

"Could you...would you mind..." He wasn't sure what he wanted to ask for. He just knew he was suddenly more afraid than he'd ever been in his life.

She took his hand in hers. "Would it help if I hold your hand when I'm here?"

He nodded then instantly regretted it. "Please." She stroked the back of his hand and he felt a little calmer. "Thank you...did you tell me your name?"

"It's Milly. What's yours?"

"Sam."

"I've always liked the name Sam. And your last name?"

He parted his lips to answer but the name didn't come out. Worse than that, no name came to mind. He felt his heart start to race with anxiety. "I...I can't remember."

She squeezed his hand. "That's okay. Nothing to worry about. The pain medicine sometimes makes us forget things. It'll come to you later."

"Is it making me hot too? I feel like the AC's broken."

"Nothing's broken that I know of, but your hand is a little clammy. Of course, you are wrapped in bandages like a mummy. I have some cold Jello, if you feel up to a spoonful or two. That might help, but I'd have to let go of your hand."

"Stomach's queasy, but I think I'm hungry." A moment later he felt a spoon touch his lips and he opened his mouth as far as the bandages allowed. He couldn't tell what flavor it was, only that it was disgustingly sweet, but it did feel cool in his mouth. "More, please."

She fed him another spoonful of the gelatin then asked, "How's the pain today?"

He swallowed a sugary glob. "It only hurts when I breathe." He thought she might laugh at the corny one-liner, but she didn't. "I think I'm too stoned to tell."

"Stoned? *Oh.* I suggested that you may have been near a building with lots of glass windows when it was bombed but I hadn't considered that the explosion would also cause you to be hit with flying chunks of rock."

She managed to sound completely serious so he played along. "Yeah, I was definitely bombed when it happened." The image of the blonde in the Porsche flashed in his mind and his chest tightened. "The girl...how is she?"

"What girl would that be?"

The question caused his heart to start racing again. "The one I was with...in the car. Is she okay?"

She fed him the last of the Jello then paused for several more seconds before answering. "I'm not sure, but I promise to ask around. What's her name?"

Sam had no idea. The gelatin churned in his stomach as he realized he could be responsible for killing someone and he didn't even know her name.

"Sam, you're hurting my hand."

He immediately relaxed his grip. The last thing in the world he wanted to do was hurt this woman. She was his lifeline at the moment. "Sorry, I..." Whatever he'd been thinking about had disintegrated. "I...forget what we were talking about."

"Nothing important. But I was wondering, which branch of the service were you with?"

He thought that was a peculiar question, but at least an answer came to mind. "Army."

"Division?"

He hadn't thought about that time in years and now he couldn't remember. "I...I'm not sure—"

"How about where you were stationed?"

"Stationed?" The word was wrong. Did she mean where did he work? He hadn't detected an accent but perhaps she wasn't as American as she sounded. "I was at the Fontainebleau but—"

"*Oh!* I know that area. It's right outside Paris. You were brought in with some soldiers who were injured in Normandy, so we just assumed you were involved in Operation Overlord."

"Operation, what?" The pounding in his head got louder with each of her words. "I...don't...understand..." The building sense of anxiety amped up to panic, which triggered head and neck pain so unbearable, he moaned aloud.

"I think I've pushed you a little too hard for the moment, but you'll feel better in a few seconds. Just try to relax."

Sam was still trying to figure out why Milly's words weren't making sense when he felt the needle enter his arm.

Milly continued to hold Sam's hand until she was sure the morphine had put him back to sleep. She hadn't had a chance to ask all the questions she was supposed to but at least she could tell Norwich this man's first name, that he was in the army, and the area where he'd been wounded. She figured the girl in the car was probably a separate memory that had nothing to do with the bombing. As though thinking the doctor's name held power, he entered the ward accompanied by two armed military police officers and two brawny men, dressed as orderlies, pushing a cot on wheels. She didn't recognize any of them.

"Nurse Fitch," Captain Norwich said, gesturing for her to join him at the far end of the ward.

She hurried only to get out of the way of the other four men heading toward the bed she was standing beside.

"Did you get anything out of him?" Norwich asked in a hushed voice.

She saw the two orderlies carelessly lift Sam and turned to scold them but Norwich grabbed her upper arm and held her close. "Don't interfere. They know what they're doing."

She took one more glance in Sam's direction and saw him being pushed out of the ward on the cot. "What's going on? Why are MPs here?"

His gaze darted toward another nurse talking to a patient a few beds away. "Come with me," he murmured to Milly. Tightening his hold on her arm, he pulled her out of the ward with him. Only when they were a good distance down the hall did he release her.

She didn't expect an apology and he didn't offer one. Because of how oddly he was acting, she not only slouched, she bent her knees a little.

"Did you talk to him?"

"Briefly, yes. He had some water and—"

"What did you learn?"

"His first name is Sam, but he couldn't remember his last. He also couldn't remember his division but he's Army, stationed outside of Paris. He became very agitated with my questions and was still in a lot of pain, so I gave him more morphine. Where are they taking him?"

"Was he at ease with you?" When she didn't answer he asked, "Does he trust you?"

"I believe so. But we only exchanged a few words before the pain got to be more than he could handle."

"You remember how he was stitched up?"

"Of course."

He looked from side to side before murmuring, "There were only three men brought in on the transport the other night, and *Sam*, if that's really his name, wasn't one of them. Apparently he only turned up with the others after they arrived here, which could explain the lack of a file and dog tags."

Milly frowned and shook her head. "That doesn't seem possible. You saw how badly he was wounded."

"I certainly did. And that means someone else—not one of *us*—placed him with those soldiers. And you saw how he was patched up. That work wasn't done by any American medic. But there are reports that Hitler has scientists and doctors working on building an army of superior men. It looks like they tried to slip one of them in through a side door."

Her eyes widened. "Are you saying he's a *spy*?" She watched his gaze move to something behind her and turned to see the two orderlies approaching.

"That's *exactly* what we think he is, and his *supposedly* not remembering his last name or which division he was with, goes along with that. At any rate, it's been decided. You're going to help make sure he doesn't get to do whatever he came here to do. These gentlemen will escort you to the private rooms you will be sharing with your patient while you sweetly nurse him back to health so he can stand trial. Of course, if you can entice him into giving away his secrets, including who helped him get in here, there may not be a need for a trial at all."

Milly looked at the two large men and back to the doctor. "This is crazy. I'm a nurse, not a spy."

"As a member of the Army Nurse Corps, you have sworn to save the lives of our boys whenever possible, and at this moment, your patient poses a threat to those lives."

"Captain Norwich, I love my country and I always said I would help however I could, but I have no experience with—"

"Regardless of your experience or interpretation of your duties, I'm afraid you already know too much to refuse this assignment. The only choice you have now is whether to allow these men to quietly escort you to the secure rooms or be taken to another, less hospitable place...by force."

Milly straightened her knees and spine, pushed back her shoulders and lifted her chin. If *this* man was going to force her to do something so objectionable, she would do it without slouching.

IT'S ABOUT TIME

available in print and ebook

MARILYN CAMPBELL has been published in the genres of suspense, futuristic, time-travel, paranormal, erotic and lighthearted contemporary romances, non-fiction metaphysical works and has had a screenplay produced. A true thrill-junkie, she has jumped out of an airplane, raced around the Indy 500 track, driven solo throughout the United States and believes a labyrinth walk under the full moon can have magical results. Unfortunately, Marilyn has not yet figured out how to time-travel…except in her stories. She currently resides in western Massachusetts.